Rebecca L. Marsh

This is a work of fiction. All places, characters, and events in this novel are a product of the author's imagination or are used fictitiously.

Visit the author's website: rebeccalmarsh.com

Cover design by Trim Ventures

www.TrimVentures.com

ISBN: 978-1-949498-03-5

Philippians 4:13
"I can do all things through Christ who strengthens me."

This one is for my mother

Julie,

May every rift
be mended

[illegible signature]

Praise for *The Rift Between Us*

“This might just be one of the best stories I’ve read all year” – Jillian (For the Love of Dewey book blog)

“Marsh’s exceptional writing brings depth to each woman, as we experience their anger, fears, and passions. Don’t be surprised if you find yourself with tears in your eyes searching for a box of tissues. These characters are sure to touch your heart.” – Author Kameo Monson

“I was so drawn to the women and the storyline that once I started the book, I didn't want to put it down. A wonderful read!” – Rae’s Reading Lounge

“*The Rift Between Us* is a very lovely story with resilience and strength at the core of its characters. Mending old hurts and overcoming fears seems to be something that Rebecca Marsh does with aplomb for her characters. I loved *The Rift Between Us* for its theme, characters and it’s writing.” – Frost at Midnite book blog

“This book was meaningful.” – Reading Renee book blog

Other books by Rebecca L. Marsh

When the Storm Ends
Where Hope is Found

Chapter 1

December

Maria

A cigarette burned slowly between Maria's fingers as she stood behind a bush on the side of her father's house. She glanced around, making sure she was alone. No one knew she was smoking again and she wanted to keep it that way, especially when it came to her children.

Once the cigarette had burned down to a nub, Maria knelt down and crushed the ember into the cold, hard dirt. Then, she held the butt in her hand while she continued to stand outside letting the frigid December breeze blow through her red, cable-knit sweater. She hadn't worn a coat. The smoky smell would have gotten trapped in the heavy fabric, and besides that, she sort of liked the chill of the air. Not because it was invigorating—not exactly, but because it made her feel alive in a way that was neither good nor bad. As often as possible, Maria chose to feel nothing. Lately, most of what existed in her life was bad, and she let the good stuff float by her, as if in bubbles, afraid to feel it. She knew all too well that when the good went sour, it was worse than bad. Numbness was easier. She only wished she knew how to stay numb, but the feelings crept in on her far too often.

After a few minutes, Maria headed back into the house with a sigh. She entered through the back door, stepping into a kitchen that was clean and organized, but very stark, lacking a woman's touch. She moved to the trash can, and carefully slipped the cigarette butt under a can that once held cranberry sauce.

Maria glanced at the dining room door, where her family waited, then she looked at the back door. Some strange voice inside urged her to run back out into the cold.

She ignored it, took a deep breath, and headed through the door to the dining room.

"Oh, there she is," said Maria's father, Arthur, who sat at the head of the table. "We were about to send out a search party. Did you find any more juice for the kids?"

"No," Maria replied, pushing her curly hair back from her face. The truth was, she hadn't looked.

Her husband, Hank, glanced up at her from the far side of the table, not bothering with a smile. She sat down next to him. Maria's children, Jonathan and Melanie were at the table. And sitting across from Maria was her youngest sister, Avery. A handsome, Latin man sat next to Avery, holding her hand. Maria hadn't bothered to learn his name because she'd never see him again. Avery never brought the same man to a family dinner more than once, nor did she ever come alone.

Idle chitchat prevailed for a few minutes, consisting mostly of the adults talking to the kids. Maria and her sisters hadn't talked to each other about anything meaningful in a long time. Too much resentment had built up between them.

After a few minutes, Maria's other sister, Lauren, spoke up from her seat at the other end of the table. "I don't know if this is really the right time, but I need to ask both of you a favor." She glanced at Maria, then Avery, making it clear to whom she was speaking.

Avery, a hand to her forehead, sighed heavily, and Maria knew they were thinking the same thing.

"You need money again, don't you?" Avery's caramel brown eyes gave Lauren a steely glare.

Lauren's eyes dropped to the table, and she fiddled with the tablecloth. "A little. My electricity was turned off two days ago."

Maria shook her head. She was tired of dealing with Lauren's irresponsibility. "We're supposed to pick up the pieces every time you lose a job, right?" Maria asked with very little emotion in her voice. She didn't want to argue. She just wished Lauren would grow up.

"Yeah, put a watch on when you're painting, Lauren. Or set an alarm. You can't always expect us to help you out," Avery jumped in.

"I didn't lose my job." Lauren's voice was a defeated whisper.

"Oh, really? Then what did you blow all your money on this time?" Avery asked.

Lauren looked at her sisters, her face pale and regretful. Her blue eyes were watery, and, for a moment Maria felt sorry for her. "Forget I asked," Lauren said.

That didn't deter Avery. She was fired up. "No! Let's talk about it. If you didn't lose your job, why do you need money from us?"

"I said forget it, Avery." Lauren's voice rose, causing both children to look up with alarmed faces. "I don't owe you an explanation."

"I think you do. You're always asking for money. I want to know what you spend all *your* money on."

"That's not your business."

"If you're asking for *my* money, then it is my business."

"Girls, please," Arthur said, but no one really heard him.

"I'm not asking anymore, so back off!" Lauren shot up from her seat, very agitated.

"Let it go, Avery," Maria said, hoping to end this topic of discussion.

"No," Avery said. "I want her to answer."

Fed up, Maria turned on Avery. "Why? Because you're so responsible?"

Avery jumped up from her seat, shaking the Mario Lopez look-alike's hand away as if it were something detestable stuck to her fingers. "I pay my bills, damn it! You don't see me asking for anyone else's money."

Maria didn't leave her seat. She didn't have the energy to be that angry. "Yeah, you pay your bills, but you live like you're still a sorority girl."

"What's that supposed to mean?"

"I think you know what it means." Maria glared at the man by Avery's side.

Arthur stood up, a furious expression on his face. He slammed his fists on the table, rattling the fine china that had been treasured by Maria's mother. "That's enough! Stop this now!"

"Fine!" Avery threw her napkin down. "I'll make it easy. Next time there's a family gathering, don't bother to invite me."

"You sit back down, Avery," Arthur bellowed. "We are a family. Families spend time together."

Avery looked at him with a gentle expression. "Don't worry, Dad, I'll still come visit you … but just you."

"That goes for me, too, Dad," Lauren said. "I can't take this anymore, but I'll always be there for you."

"You think *that's* what I'm worried about?" Arthur asked. "You girls are each other's family too. You must put aside your differences once in a while. Someday you'll need each other."

"Maybe … but not today," Avery said, walking away and leaving her date behind. He hopped up and hurried behind her.

Lauren shrugged. "I'm sorry, Dad." Then she walked toward the door.

Maria remained seated. She really wasn't sure how she felt about this. She loved her sisters, but they were no longer friends, nor did they enjoy each other's company. In recent years, being with them had become increasingly uncomfortable.

She glanced at her children's stricken faces. At ages ten and seven, they probably had no idea what to think. Then Maria looked at Hank who was still eating—as if nothing had happened.

Chapter 2

Avery

Avery waited by her car, tapping her foot with impatience when she realized she'd walked out without her date. When he joined her mere seconds later, she snapped, "Come on! Get in the car and let's go."

With a neutral expression, he slid into the passenger seat. Just as his door shut, Avery sped off.

Several times during the ride, Avery's date tried to start a conversation, but she only responded to him with simple, closed answers. She had no interest in talking to this man.

A few minutes later, Avery pulled up to a plain, brick apartment building in downtown Atlanta. "This is where we part ways," she said.

"Why so soon? I could come up for a while," he said in an alluring voice, caressing her arm.

She brushed his hand away in disgust and pushed farther back from him. "No, thank you."

"But you paid for the whole day."

"Yeah, and it's my dime." She pulled some bills from her purse and shoved them into his hand. "Now, get out!"

He looked at the money, shrugged, and got out of the car. Avery watched him get into his vehicle and drive away. She turned her key, bringing the engine back to life, and drove to the apartment building where she really lived, which wasn't even in downtown Atlanta. No way was she ever going to let that man—or any of the others— know where she *really* lived.

When Avery got home, she went straight upstairs to her apartment. Once inside, she locked the door, staring for a moment at the two extra deadbolts she'd installed. She lived in a safe, quiet part of town, but you could never be too safe.

She headed to the bedroom and stripped off her clothes. After showering, Avery put on a pair of sweatpants, an old sweatshirt, and slippers, then padded out to the kitchen. Her cat, Rocket, meowed and she responded by filling his bowl before fixing herself a cup of tea.

On the counter, near the phone, was a card that read: *Exotic Escort Service, male and female escorts available.* Avery picked up and studied the card, then threw it into the trash can. Since she wasn't going to any more family events, she wouldn't need it anymore.

As she carried her tea into the living room, she realized that the sun was setting. Alarm bells ringing in her head, Avery set the cup down on the coffee table so quickly that tea sloshed out, burning her finger. Not even feeling it, she rushed to the window and closed the curtains up tight.

When she could breathe again, knowing that no one outside could see her, she picked up her cup and sat down on the sofa. After a quick glance at the locks on her door, she clicked on the TV and settled in to watch a movie. Rocket joined her, curling up on her lap. Avery patted the cat's furry, gray head, thinking that maybe she should have gotten a dog instead.

Five minutes later the doorbell rang. Frowning, Avery moved Rocket aside, got up, and walked to the door. She peered through the peephole and saw it was Mike from across the hall.

Avery turned all the locks, opened the door barely a crack, and blocked the opening. She was not quite out of her apartment, and he was certainly not able to come in. "Hey, Mike, what's up?"

"Oh, nothing much. I just wanted to ask you something."

"Sure, what is it?" Avery kept her voice even, but Mike only ever asked her for one thing, a date. And that wasn't going to happen. She wasn't sure how many more excuses she could come up with, yet, for some reason that was inexplicable to her, she could never say the words to send him packing permanently. She didn't know what held her back because she certainly couldn't accept a date with him.

It wasn't that Mike wasn't a desirable man. He was very good-looking; six foot two, wavy dark hair, ice blue eyes, and a good build. Avery was often tempted to say yes to his invitations, but she couldn't. Sure, he seemed nice, but he was a man, and they couldn't be trusted. If there was one thing she was sure of, it was that.

"See, I have this wedding to go to this weekend, and, well, I was wondering if you would go with me," Mike said.

Avery thought for a moment, searching her mind for a plausible excuse. "Oh … uh, sorry, Mike, I can't. I have to help my sister with her kids this weekend." Avery hated herself for the lie, and even more for the way Mike's face fell at the rejection.

"Oh, okay. Well, would you like to come over for a little while? I have a bottle of wine that I would rather not drink alone."

"I can't. I have to work tomorrow and I should get some sleep." Another lie.

"Sure, okay. See you later then." He turned with a sad expression and went back into his own apartment.

Avery stepped back and pushed the door shut. Then she turned all the locks and breathed a sigh of relief.

Chapter 3

Sixteen months later—April
Lauren

Lauren dragged herself into the kitchen/living room of her studio apartment for breakfast after yet another night of terrible sleep. She felt as if she had spent more time awake than asleep, but that was to be expected—at least that's what the doctor kept telling her. She didn't know if he thought telling her that was reassuring, but it certainly wasn't. A good night's sleep was rare for her, and she knew it always would be.

Spooning cereal into her mouth with a shaky hand, she stared at the "almost finished" painting on her easel by the window. The seascape included a picturesque beach, unlike any Lauren had seen before. Her art came from a big imagination, full of exotic landscapes, but she hadn't painted for six months.

A stab of white-hot fury went through Lauren as she stared at the seascape. She took a deep breath and pushed the anger away. She had to accept that painting was a thing of the past. It just wasn't possible anymore. With a sigh, Lauren finished her Wheaties, drank her coffee, and dressed for work.

Minutes later, she hurried to her morning shift at the grocery store where she worked every day except Tuesday. Most days, she had about three hours to go home, eat, and catch a short nap before tending bar in a local Irish pub. She wasn't sure how much longer that job would last—as dropping glasses was becoming a more regular thing.

As she arrived at work, her closest friend, Alice greeted her. "Hey, Lauren. Have you seen Len yet?"

"No, I just walked in," Lauren said. "Is there a problem?"

"He's not happy about you asking for another morning off next week."

"It's for an appointment."

"It always is." Alice shrugged. "I don't think he cares anymore."

Glancing at the floor, Lauren said, "Okay, I'll talk to him." She hoped she could smooth things over with the boss and make him understand. She couldn't afford to lose this job.

Lauren clocked in, put on her smock, and started toward Len's office. She knocked on his door and waited for his gruff voice to answer.

Len sat behind a cheap metal desk in his cramped office. He was a large man, which only made the room feel smaller. "You wanted to see me?" Lauren asked.

"Yes. I got your request for another day off next week. You've already taken more days off—by far—than anyone else here. I can't keep approving them."

"It's for a doctor's appointment, Len. What do you want me to do?"

"I'd like for you to schedule your many appointments on the day you have off, that's what."

"I would, Len, but this doctor doesn't take appointments on Tuesdays."

Lauren considered telling Len about her condition, but she knew she couldn't. If she did, he would know that she was only going to get worse and need more days off.

Len tapped his pen on the desk. "Maybe we can work something out that will help both of us."

"I'm all ears."

"I'm thinking you could switch your off days with Martin. Then you'd have Thursdays off instead of Tuesdays. Your appointment is on a Thursday, so that means your doctor is open that day. How will that work for you?"

Lauren was surprised. She honestly hadn't expected Len to be so accommodating. "Sure. That will help."

"Good. I'll tell Martin. You get your butt out to a register."

Lauren nodded, squeezing her lips together so she wouldn't tell Len that her therapist didn't take appointments on Thursdays. She would cross that bridge when she came to it.

By six o' clock that evening, Lauren was clocking in at the pub, putting on an apron, and taking orders. Her feet hurt, her back ached, and she was tired. She wanted nothing more than to go home and get into bed, but instead, she pasted a smile on her face and began mixing the drinks. She worked slowly, struggling not to drop anything.

Two hours later, a waiter came over to the bar and said, "Lauren, you have a phone call. I'll take over here for a few minutes."

"Thanks." Lauren started off toward the office, where the phone was, wondering who in the world was calling her at work.

She stumbled into the empty office, tripping over her own feet for the umpteenth time that day, and picked up the phone. "Hello?"

"Is this Lauren Anderson?"

"Yes."

"Ms. Anderson, I'm afraid I have bad news for you."

Lauren gritted her teeth and listened to the man on the other end of the line. When he was done, she hung up the phone and wandered out of the office in shock.

Chapter 4

Maria

Maria returned home from a long day at the hospital to find her husband staring blankly at the TV, while her children ran around playing. It was after six o' clock, but Hank hadn't bothered to make dinner or help the kids with their homework, even though he'd been home since four-thirty. A year ago, Maria would have screamed at him for sitting around and doing nothing when there was so much that needed doing. She didn't bother with that anymore. What good had it ever done?

She remembered the last time she'd tried, on a day much like this one.

"Hank! The kids have homework to do and they need to have dinner. You've been home for three hours. Why aren't you doing anything?" She yelled.

"I've had a long day. I need to wind down and have some time to relax," he responded without looking away from the television.

"And you don't think I've had a long day? I've been working for twelve hours, just like I did yesterday and the day before."

"And tomorrow you'll have the day off. *You* can relax then while I'm at work again."

"I work at a hospital. I'm on call tomorrow. I'm always on call. I need your help around here." Still, he didn't look at her. "Hank! They're your kids too."

In response, he turned up the volume on the TV and ignored her.

So today, instead of screaming at him, she went to the kids and kissed each of their heads. "Jon, Melly, bring your homework into the kitchen and I'll help you while I'm making dinner."

Jonathan's smile faded and his whole body seemed to droop. "Okay, Mom," he said.

A few minutes later, Maria stood at the stove, still in her nurse's scrubs, while her children sat at the table with their homework. She did her best to help them. Melanie was pretty easy with her first-grade work, but by the time dinner was ready, Jon was less than half done, and almost in tears.

Maria looked at her son, frustration on his face, and remembered the conversation she'd had with his teacher a year ago when she was informed that Jonathan had a learning disability. The school had promised to do all they could to help him, but it wasn't enough, and neither was the tutor he studied with twice a week. Hank, of course, wasn't any help at all.

When dinner was over, Maria sat at the table with Jon and helped him finish his homework. Once in a while, she would look to see what Melanie was doing. Each time Maria looked, Melanie was playing quietly with her toys. She was good at self-entertainment. Watching her, Maria felt a deep sadness in her heart. Melanie deserved far more time and attention, but there was never any more time to give.

When the phone rang, Maria answered it.

"Hello?"

"Is this Maria Clark?" asked an unfamiliar male voice.

"Yes."

"I'm afraid I have some bad news for you, Mrs. Clark."

After she put the phone down, Maria called to her family and told them she was taking the dog out.

Once outside, she began to pace, trying to take in the news she'd received. She hadn't seen it coming. How could she? Her father hadn't even been sick.

Maria moved to the back of the yard between the fence and a tall bush. She lit a cigarette with the lighter she kept in her pocket and watched the dog, a golden retriever, run around the yard. Sadie was supposed to be for the kids, but Maria had grown to dearly love the dog. Not only did she provide a perfect excuse for Maria to come outside, but she was also a wonderful companion. When Hank "went out" after the kids were in bed, Sadie cuddled with her. When Maria felt like she couldn't go on, Sadie's warm eyes seemed to understand her pain and loneliness.

Maria took the last drag from her cigarette, smashed the ember on the ground, and concealed the butt between her fingers like she always did. But this time, as she looked at it, she remembered what her father said to her two years ago when he'd caught her coming into his house during a family function and putting a butt in the trash.

"Think you're being sneaky, don't you?" he asked.

"How'd you know?"

"Do you really think I raised three daughters, mostly on my own, without knowing when someone is sneaking around?"

"I guess not," Maria said, looking at her feet and feeling like a little girl again.

Maria waited a moment, expecting her father to scold her for returning to such a nasty habit. When he stayed quiet, she started to move past him, back into the living room where the rest of her family was waiting.

Just as she got to the door, he spoke up, "Who are you really trying to hide it from, Maria? Them?" He pointed to the door, behind which her family waited. "Or yourself?"

Maria realized that she hadn't given her father's question much thought when he'd asked it. Now she pondered it and she wasn't sure what the answer was.

Glancing toward her living room window, Maria watched her family. Hank was asleep in his chair. Jonathan, joyful because he'd finally finished his homework, was playing with his sister. Melanie was thrilled with the attention from her brother. Maria had no idea how to tell them that her father, the only male role-model still active in their lives, was gone.

Chapter 5

Avery

A day and a half earlier, a stranger called and informed Avery that her father was dead. It had taken her several hours to wrap her mind around that. He wasn't that old, and he wasn't sick. She'd told that to the man on the phone. Heart attacks can happen even in much younger people, the man had told her, and they usually came without warning. Still, it seemed odd, surreal; her father not being in this world. It made her feel alone and small.

In front of Avery, her computer screen glowed, highlighting a page of listings from the yellow pages. She focused on one in particular: Exotic Escorts. Her father's funeral was in two days. Maria had worked it all out that morning and let her know by phone. It would be the first time she saw her sisters in over a year.

She didn't want to call the number that stared at her in what looked like bold print. It seemed wrong to have an escort take her to her father's funeral; to any funeral.

Avery got up and paced the room, pushing sandy blond hair back from her shoulder. She looked out the window; saw the people walking around below, each of the men standing out in her vision as if they were giants. She felt the inevitable stab of panic. She couldn't be out there by herself for too long, but who could she trust? At least an escort was happy to leave when you wanted, as long as they got their money … Still, it felt wrong—dirty.

Walking to the computer, Avery closed the window on the screen. She went to the door of her apartment and stopped in front of it, staring at it like Superman might do if he was using his x-ray vision. Then, after a couple of deep breaths, she slowly unlocked all the deadbolts and opened the door. Closing it tightly behind her, she took two steps and found herself staring at another door—Mike's door.

Avery knocked and waited for the sound of footsteps. When she heard them, she felt both relief and panic. Then the door opened and Mike's bright blue eyes were looking at her while the smile on his face brought forth a dimple in his right cheek. The smile vanished as soon as he looked at Avery.

"Are you okay?" Mike asked.

Avery meant to say that she was fine, but the words wouldn't come, and seemingly without her consent, her head began to shake side to side.

"What's wrong?" Mike asked. Then he put his hand behind her and gently urged her forward. "Come in and tell me what's going on."

Looking down, Avery realized that her toes were very close to the threshold of Mike's door. *No, don't go inside! Never go inside!*

"No!" She snapped as she pulled back from his touch.

Mike jumped at her abrupt motion, and confusion clouded his face. "Okay," he said holding his hands up in surrender.

"I'm sorry. I didn't mean to act so crazy … It's just …," she stopped as emotion clogged her throat. Tears slid down her cheeks.

"Avery, what's going on?"

"My father's dead." She spit the words out like vinegar.

"Oh. I'm so sorry." Avery could see that he didn't know what to say, and she couldn't blame him. How do you find words to console the woman who has been rejecting you for months? "Is there something I can do?"

Avery nodded. "Would you go to his funeral with me?"

Chapter 6

Maria

Maria stared at her father's house as it loomed in front of her. The yard was perfectly cut, the porch swept, and a row of pansies stood along the sidewalk, so straight they reminded Maria of soldiers. No different than the last time she was here … except for one thing.

She didn't want to go inside. Facing the house without her father's presence was too difficult.

I shouldn't have to do this alone!

Her sisters had made their excuses—as if she didn't have a job, too.

Maria willed her feet to move, pushing forward in slow motion until she reached the front door. Sliding her key into the lock, she opened the door and went in. She tried not to look as she passed through the living room. Too many memories lived there that she wasn't ready to face. She was here to select a suit for her father's burial, and that was all she could handle today.

When she reached the bedroom, Maria went straight to the closet and looked through the clothes. His blue suit was nice with the blue and green striped tie, but the sadness she felt drew her to the black suit and the gray tie.

Then something caught her eye. On the shelf was a small jar with a pink piece of paper taped around it. The faded letters read, "The swearing jar." Maria smiled in spite of her mood and touched the jar with the tips of her fingers as a memory came alive in her mind.

She was about twelve years old, Lauren was nine, and Avery was five. It was in the morning before school and they were running late.

"We can make it, girls," Dad said.

"But, Daddy, I need my bows in," Avery whined.

"Not to worry, sweetie. Lauren, you do Avery's hair. Maria, you do Lauren's hair. I'll do Maria's hair. Line up."

"Why do I always get the short end of the stick?" Maria huffed as they lined up.

"The short end of the stick? I do a damn fine braid if I say so myself," he retorted.

Avery's chubby little hand slapped over her mouth as she gasped. "Daddy, you said a bad word!"

"So I did. I'll have to find a quarter."

"Yes!" Lauren shouted.

"So now you're happy when I say a bad word?" Dad asked.

"Of course. It's my turn to spend the money in the swearing jar, and I'm saving up for a poster of Tom Cruise with his shirt off."

Dad shook his head. "Dear Lord! I'd better watch my mouth, hadn't I?"

Maria's smile faded as the memory left her mind and was replaced by the bitterness of the present. She pushed the jar behind some boxes and selected the blue suit.

The church was completely filled with an additional row of people standing along the back, a sign of her father's impact on the community, Maria supposed. He had been a strong Christian, who believed in helping others. Brushing a few stray dog hairs off her simple black dress, she glanced around at all the faces; friends, neighbors, and members of Arthur's church, all with teary eyes. He'd been well loved.

Hank sat next to her, hands in his lap, fiddling with the program that was handed to them as they'd walked in. Maria wished he would put his arm around her, offer a little comfort.

Is that too damn much to ask at my father's funeral?

Maria looked at him. He had dressed the part. It was the most effort she'd seen him put into his appearance in the last two years. He wore a gray suit with a dark blue shirt and a blue paisley tie. His blond, wavy hair was combed back, every hair in place. He looked so handsome. For a moment, as she watched him, Maria was reminded of what they used to be like. They had once been the type of couple who drew stares and sighs of envy from lonely women. "That's what love is supposed to look like," people would say.

No one said that anymore, Maria thought, as a feeling she believed long dead filled her heart and tears began streaming down her face. Her father's death was not the only one she'd be mourning today.

After a moving eulogy from the pastor of Arthur's church, as well as a few chosen speakers, they moved to the cemetery across the street for the graveside service. Arthur's beautiful mahogany casket was closed now and propped up on a metal scaffold over the already dug hole.

Maria's chest felt tight. The closed casket seemed more final somehow. She would never see her father again.

When Melanie's small hand reached up and grabbed hers, Maria latched on tightly. She needed the contact with another person, someone who loved her.

She looked at her sisters. Avery wore a black and white, knee-length dress with black spiked heels that were slowly sinking into the soft ground. Her hair was drawn back into a French braid. She had on a string of pearls and pearl earrings. As always she had a good-looking man on her arm, and as always, Maria had never seen him before. She was sure she'd never see him again either … but looking closer, there was a difference with this one. He appeared to care for Avery. He had his arm around her, and she wasn't pushing him away. Maria hadn't paid much attention before, but now that she saw this man touching Avery, she realized it was unusual. Hand holding was typically the only touching Avery allowed from her dates, in front of watching eyes anyway.

Lauren stood alone, wearing a dark navy pants suit with a white button-up blouse and no jewelry. It suited her tall, willowy frame. Her sandy blond hair hung free around her shoulders and her sky blue eyes were brimming with tears; hands shoved into the pockets of her jacket. Maria wished she could go to her sisters, hold onto them, but she was fairly certain she would be unwelcome. Instead, she held onto Melanie's hand and reached for Jonathan, pulling him close.

When the graveside service was over, everyone was invited to Maria's house for finger foods. Maria milled around, talking to other mourners about her father, listening to their funny stories. She looked for her sisters, thinking they might be ready to talk again. But by the end of the day, she realized that Avery had never shown up, and Lauren had managed to spend time with Melanie and Jonathan while avoiding Maria altogether.

It didn't matter, Maria told herself, because they would all be in the same room for the reading of the will the next day—no way around that one.

Chapter 7

Lauren

Lauren arrived at the office of her father's lawyer ten minutes early. She realized that she'd done so, not because she didn't want to miss anything or keep the lawyer waiting, but because she didn't want her sisters to see her arrive late. How odd, she thought, to be concerned with that now. Why it even mattered to her at this point, she didn't know. What she needed to worry about was her job. She'd had to take another day off for this meeting. Len wouldn't fire her for taking time when her father had just died. He wouldn't want to look so callous. But the more time she asked for, the thinner the ice she was skating on at this job. And she couldn't afford to lose it.

Lauren checked in with the receptionist and then took a seat. Maria was already there; perfect Maria was always the first to arrive. Lauren sat across from her sister, laying her purse in her lap and tucking her hands in behind it. She glanced at Maria for a moment. Neither of them spoke.

Lauren looked around the reception area. There was powder blue carpet on the floor, oak chairs along three of the walls interspersed with tables that held a variety of magazines. Lauren's throat began to tighten as she realized how much it looked and felt like a doctor's waiting room. It gave her a sense of imminent doom and the ten minutes she had to wait ticked by painfully slow.

Avery arrived just before they were called back. Lauren envied her not having to wait in this claustrophobic room.

As they were escorted down a narrow hallway, Lauren stayed behind her sisters. That way no one would see if she stumbled over her own feet. They were led into a conference room with a long, oval table and several cushiony, high-backed chairs on wheels. Lauren pulled one out and sat down. Maria sat on the opposite side and Avery took one end. They were sitting as far apart as possible, and Lauren felt the distance between them as if it were tangible; like metal rods that held them apart.

At least she could breathe again. This room was no larger than the last, but it was a conference room, not a waiting room. It felt vastly different because it did not remind her of any part of a doctor's office.

After five long minutes of sitting with her sisters in silence, trying not to make eye contact, the lawyer arrived.

"Hello, I'm Max Fisher. I was your father's attorney." He was a short, stout man of about fifty with thinning hair. He wore an expensive tailored suit and a sober expression but seemed very friendly. He walked to Maria's seat, reached a hand out to her. "Mrs. Clark," he said, shaking her hand.

Next, he walked to Avery's seat. "Ms. Anderson," he said reaching for her hand. Then he walked to Lauren's seat and did the same.

Avery gave him a suspicious look. "How do you know our names? I've never met you before."

"Your father was a very friendly and talkative man. He talked about his girls all the time and often showed me pictures of the three of you as well as his grandchildren."

"I see," Avery said, her expression unchanging.

"Well, let's get right to it," Mr. Fisher said. "It's fairly simple as far as what he wants to be done with his estate. He left one item to each of you. Maria, he wanted you to take the china cabinet. Lauren, for you he left your mother's antique dresser. Avery, you are to take the dining room table. The rest of his belongings will be liquidated and added to his existing account. He wants it split evenly between the three of you."

"Okay," Maria spoke up. "I'm sure it can't be much. So are we done then?"

"Actually, Arthur has left a significant estate behind. … But he did leave a stipulation as well."

"A significant estate? How is that possible? He was a high school principal," Maria said. "I mean there's the house ... but ...,"

Lauren's interest was piqued—but what kind of stipulation?

"Arthur made some very good investments, and he managed his money carefully. With the added value of the house and his possessions, the estate will be worth around six hundred thousand."

Lauren's jaw dropped. She had no idea.

"What's the stipulation?" Avery asked. She seemed to have recovered from the shock faster than Lauren.

"Well, your father left a letter explaining that," said Mr. Fisher.

He pulled a hand-written letter out of his pile of papers and slipped on a pair of reading glasses. Holding the letter out in front of him, he cleared his throat and began to read.

Maria, Lauren, and Avery—my beautiful girls,

If you are reading this, then I am gone. Do not be sad for long, girls. I am with our Father in Heaven, and I will always be looking down on you.

For a while now I have watched you three avoid each other. It pained me to have to select time slots for each of you to come and see me separately on Christmas day. What hurts me, even more, is seeing each of you going through difficulties and refusing to lean on each other. But you might remember that, on the day when you all decided to go your separate ways, I told you someday you would need each other. Well, that day has come. I have made sure of it. I have worked hard, saving and investing, so that I could leave an inheritance for the three of you. But you must come together to get it. If you wish to inherit the money I have left you, you must all spend two weeks together in a cabin near Lake Allatoona. Mr. Fisher will make the arrangements if you all agree to go. If you do not, you will still get the items I selected for each of you, but the money will go to charity. It is my hope that you girls will get to know each other again and mend the rift that has formed between you. It may seem impossible to you, or maybe you think it is too late, but all things are possible with God, and I have been praying for the healing of your relationship for a very long time.

Love,
Dad

Lauren was stunned. Her father had money? She had expected a couple thousand, not two hundred thousand. She would most likely lose both her jobs if she decided to do what the will stipulated. But how could she not? Two hundred thousand would be enough to catch her up on her bills and there would even be some left over. She'd just have to find another job … or two.

Lauren looked up at her sisters. Maria looked very torn. Avery looked scared but recovered quickly when she realized Lauren was watching her. Then Lauren looked down at her hands on the table and shoved them into her lap, hoping her sisters hadn't noticed them.

"Is it okay if we think this over?" Avery asked.

Maria's eyes shot up with this question. Neither of them was sure about taking the trip. Lauren would have to hope they would decide to go.

"Of course," Mr. Fisher said. "I know it's a big decision. Let me know as soon as you decide, and in the meantime, I'll get the ball rolling on the liquidation of the assets."

Chapter 8

Avery

When Avery got home, she was restless. She paced the floor of her living room, glancing often at the row of locks on the door. She didn't like this, not one bit. She didn't feel safe anywhere but here. The idea of going to a cabin in the woods for two weeks overwhelmed her.

On the other hand, two hundred thousand was a lot of money. How could she possibly walk away from that? Not to mention that this was her father's last request. She didn't know how she could turn away from that either. The guilt would eat her alive.

She paced some more, looking for an excuse. There was work, but she could take that with her. She looked at her cat. Rocket! Yes, she would have to stay home with Rocket.

Avery shook her head. That excuse sounded stupid even to her. Mike would be willing to watch the cat even if she was still refusing to go on a real date with him. It would be just like when she'd asked him to take her to the funeral. He'd look at her with hurt and confusion in his eyes, wondering why she'd ask favors of him, but wouldn't even allow him past her apartment door. Still, she knew, he'd do it.

There was no reasonable excuse. She'd have to go.

Chapter 9

Maria

Maria didn't talk about the reading of her father's will when she got home, and Hank didn't ask. He probably assumed, just like Maria, that the house was Arthur's only real asset.

She planned to tell Hank about the meeting, the money, and the stipulation as soon as the kids were in bed. But before she had a chance to bring it up, he picked up his jacket and walked to the front door. "I'm going out for a bit," he said.

Maria felt a stab to her heart. No matter how often she heard those words, it never stopped hurting.

The rest of the evening, Maria lay on the couch with Sadie, eating a large bag of potato chips. The TV was on, but she couldn't have answered a single question about the show flickering on the screen. She wasn't even sure what show it was, and it didn't matter. All she could think about was the will and what she could do with that kind of money. *Start over!*

However, leaving her kids for two weeks was not appealing. Sure Hank would feed them, but that might be all he'd do. Who would help Jonathan with his homework or make time to read Melanie a bedtime story? Not to mention all the activities the two of them needed to be taken to. Hank had stopped being an involved father a long time ago.

Hank—the thought of where he was traveled through Maria's mind. She pushed it out. The will was enough to think about right now.

When eleven o' clock rolled around, Maria turned off the TV and went to bed—alone. Two hours later, Hank came home. He stripped off his clothes, and shooed Sadie from his side of the bed. The dog grumbled as she moved to her own bed. Then, as Hank got into bed with Maria, she breathed in his scent. Turning away, she pressed her face into her pillow and let hot tears flow.

Chapter 10

Six weeks later—June
Avery

Avery got out of the taxi, accepted her suitcase from the cabbie when he pulled it from the trunk, and set it down on the ground. She looked in front of her. The lake house was simple, but not shabby—a wooden house, stained rather than painted. Trees surrounded the front of the house, and in place of grass, leaves and pine straw covered the ground. A dirt path led to the front door, lined on both sides by pink and white impatiens. There was a covered front porch with a wooden swing. It was pretty in an odd way; like a pig wearing a dress.

Avery's stomach began to churn as she turned back to the taxi and paid the man with a few bills from the purse she was clutching tightly in her hands. When he drove off, she picked up her suitcase and took slow deliberate steps toward the front door.

She wished she could have brought her own car. Not having one here made Avery feel trapped, but that was spelled out in the fine print of her father's stipulation; no cars were to be brought. They could only leave the house on foot, it seemed. Groceries would be delivered and they could call for take-out with a special cell phone that had only a few numbers programmed into it. No personal calls were allowed. They were supposed to talk to each other.

There were also no computers allowed or internet of any kind. That meant Avery had to take the two weeks off work, which she hadn't expected when she first decided to do this. It was something she'd never done before. There's no need for a lot of time off when you're afraid to go anywhere.

It was only fair though, she supposed. After all, Lauren and Maria couldn't bring their jobs with them.

So she was stuck here without her phone, her computer, her work, her cat, or her locks. It was going to be a long two weeks. She hoped there would at least be a television.

Time to find out.

Avery got to the door and pulled out the key she'd been given, unlocked the door and went inside. She breathed a sigh of relief when she saw that it was a nice enough place, clean and well kept. One fear was alleviated.

Avery stood her suitcase up and closed the door, turning the one deadbolt. Looking around she saw a small but pretty living room filled with bamboo furniture and cream-colored cushions. There was a TV. Thank God. Beyond the living room was a kitchen with white countertops that wrapped around a corner, an island that had bar stools on one side, and a breakfast nook in the other corner with a booth-style table. Avery would call it cute, but it wasn't really her style. It reminded her of Maria though.

The only things left to see were the bedrooms and the bathroom. Avery was the first one here, so she figured she'd go check them out and pick the best for herself. Two of the rooms were very much alike, almost identical. They were fairly small with full-size beds that had white wicker headboards and pastel comforters that reminded Avery of Easter eggs. Across from the bed in each room was a matching wicker dresser with a mirror atop it. And each room had a wicker chair in the corner.

The larger bedroom had a queen size, four-poster bed made of cherry with a dark green and white quilt. There was a matching cherry dresser with mirror and a rocking chair with a cushion that matched the bed's quilt. The room was only a little larger and Avery wasn't that fond of either the country motif it had or the beachy look of the other two. But the bigger room had its own bathroom, and that made all the difference. She pulled her suitcase into that one.

After parking her suitcase, Avery walked back through the kitchen and stopped at the back door. She stood there a moment, talking herself into moving beyond the threshold. Gathering her courage, she slung the door open and stepped out. There was a decent sized deck on the back that was only two steps higher than the ground. On the deck sat a glass top table with an umbrella and four chairs with thick cushions. The umbrella was open and Christmas lights were strung all around it.

Beyond the deck, the ground gently slopped down toward the lake, then stopped at a small retaining wall that held the water back. Steps went up over the small wall to a wooden walkway that led to a floating dock. It looked so much like the place she had vacationed with her father and sisters growing up that Avery was tempted to hurry to the end of the dock and dangle her feet in the water. But somehow the idea of being outside with no shoes on frightened her. It was ridiculous, she knew that, but the same thought kept echoing in her head. *What if I have to run?*

Staring at the dock, deep in her own thoughts, Avery was startled when the back door opened and closed again. Placing a hand over her heart and taking a deep breath, she steadied herself before turning around. At the door, Maria stood looking at her.

"I'm sorry. Did I scare you?" Maria asked. Avery studied her big sister. She was a bit rounder now than she used to be, but still beautiful, with curly, chestnut hair and caramel brown eyes. Avery suddenly felt like a little girl again, looking up in total awe at the sister who had also been a mother to her.

Avery had only been two years old when their mother died of cancer, leaving Avery with nothing more than a sketchy memory of a faceless woman singing her a lullaby. When she was eleven, she had studied an old family photo and memorized every detail of her mother's face. Then she had tried desperately to insert that face into her memory, but she couldn't do it. The woman singing the lullaby remained faceless, and Maria remained the closest thing to a mother Avery had.

Maria had been a good surrogate, for a time. Lauren, on the other hand, had been helpful only occasionally, wrapped up as she was with her art. Perhaps that was why Avery had become so unruly when Maria had gone on to college, eventually becoming out of control. She'd been left behind with a father who, while loving, was overwhelmed with the responsibility of looking after an entire high school. He saw through every one of her stunts but was a little lost when it came to fixing the problem. There were times when a girl needed a woman to guide her.

"Yeah, I guess I was wrapped up in my own thoughts."

Maria nodded. She looked distracted and perhaps even less thrilled to be there than Avery was.

"The house isn't too bad," Avery said trying to make conversation. "At least it has a TV."

"Yeah, it's ok. I guess Lauren's not here yet."

"Fashionably late as always."

Maria made a small sound of acknowledgment, then moved to the table and sat down in one of the chairs.

"Did you look around the house yet?" Avery asked.

"Only the living room and kitchen," Maria said without looking up. She put her hand to her chin and began to chew on her pinky nail.

"What's bothering you?"

Maria looked up now. "It's just the kids, that's all," she said in a tone that was supposed to be dismissive, but fell short.

"They'll be okay. Hank's with them." Avery tried to sound encouraging but wasn't sure if that was what was required in this situation. Avery had never been very good at being an aunt. When Jonathan was born, she had tried to play the part, but in truth, his arrival had made her feel like she'd lost something.

"Yeah, Hank's with them," Maria said with not even a shred of confidence, then she got up and walked out toward the dock. Avery started to follow her but stopped when the door opened again and Lauren walked out.

Avery turned to look at Lauren. She was smiling, her blue eyes sparkling. "It's a beautiful day, isn't it?"

Avery looked up as if to verify Lauren's comment. The sun was shining brightly in a cloudless sky. "I guess."

Chapter 11

Lauren

When they went back into the house, Lauren began to look around. Maria was right behind her, checking out the bedrooms.

"It's nice enough," Maria said glancing around. "Is this your suitcase?" she asked when they walked into the master bedroom.

"No. Mine is still in the living room. It must be Avery's."

Maria turned on her heel and stalked back to the living room where Avery was lounging in a chair. "Avery, why is your suitcase in the master bedroom?"

Avery looked up, shrugged. "I was the first one here, so I picked a room."

"Just because you happened to get here first, you get the best room?"

"How would you suggest we decide?"

"Well … I'm the oldest."

"No, no, no." Avery sat up straight in her chair, fully with the conversation now. "You can't use that for the rest of your life. We're not kids anymore. Just because I'm the youngest doesn't mean I get the last pick of everything. I'm not sitting on the hump anymore."

Lauren didn't speak up, but she felt no sympathy for Avery. The middle child is the one who always gets shafted. She, for instance, only got to have her own room for the three years after Maria went to college. Both of her sisters had gotten far more time in a room all their own. Not to mention the fact that the middle child is never first to do anything, nor are they ever the last.

"Fine," Maria said with tight lips, "We'll draw straws. Is that fair enough for you?"

"I guess. What are we going to use for straws?"

Maria walked out the front door and returned with three small sticks, one a little shorter than the other two. She turned around and when she turned back, she had all three in one hand with the bottom ends concealed so that you couldn't tell which was the short one. "Whoever gets the short one, gets the master bedroom. Why don't you go first, Avery," she said with a bite in her tone.

Avery pulled out a stick and Maria turned to Lauren and she pulled one out, then Maria opened her hand and they compared the sticks. Lauren's was the short one. She felt a sudden burst of elation. She had never won anything before. But she looked at her sisters without smiling and said, "I guess it's settled then," after which, she picked up her suitcase and took it to the master bedroom, grinning the whole way.

Chapter 12

Maria

Slightly disappointed about getting one of the smaller rooms, Maria threw her suitcase down on the bed and began to unpack. At least she had a window that was on the side of the house where no one was likely to go. This allowed her to open the window, lean out, and smoke a cigarette without having to go outside and find a place to hide.

As she glanced out, she saw that the sun was beginning to lower in the sky. It would be dinner time soon, she thought as she opened a drawer and placed a stack of shirts inside. When she opened the next drawer, she saw a small slip of paper inside. A note was scrawled on it. Maria stared for a second at the familiar handwriting, her heart racing a little as she read the five words in front of her. She thought about the letter Arthur had written to them with his will. Did he really think God could help her reconnect with her sisters? It didn't seem likely, but she supposed that she had to try. It was, after all, her father's last wish. She ripped her eyes from the slip of paper, shoved it back into the drawer, and placed a stack of shorts on top. As she opened the third drawer, Maria was interrupted by the sound of the doorbell followed by her sisters' voices.

"What are you doing?" Avery asked in an alarmed voice.

"It's called answering the door," Lauren's voice sounded sarcastic.

"But you don't know who it is."

"I'll find out when I open the door."

Maria heard the door open and the voice of a man saying that he was delivering groceries. Something worked out by Mr. Fisher, she had no doubt. Out of curiosity, Maria left her room and went out to see what had been delivered. After all, her stomach was beginning to growl.

By the time she got there, the bag had been left on the counter and the man was gone.

"Nice looking guy, huh?" Lauren said to Avery.

Avery gave her an annoyed look. "It could have been a murderer and you would have just let him in. You didn't even look out the window first."

"Relax, Avery, it's not even dark out yet."

"Lots of home invasions happen in broad daylight, you know."

"All right, all right!" Lauren raised both hands in surrender, then quickly slipped them behind her back. "I'll look next time, okay?"

Rather than respond, Avery let the subject drop and walked over to the bag. Maria was already taking things out. There was a box of breakfast cereal, Cap'n Crunch, the one they had loved as children; a gallon of milk, coffee, creamer, sugar, a box of pastries, and a carton of orange juice.

"Well it looks like we have breakfast for tomorrow," Maria said.

Avery scowled. "What about dinner?"

Shrugging Maria said, "That's all that's in the bag."

"Mr. Fisher didn't say we needed to bring our own dinner," Lauren said walking over to inspect the bag herself. "And I'm getting hungry." Lauren peered into the bag, then reaching her hand in, she drew out an envelope.

Inside the envelope were two pieces of paper. The first was from the store. On it was the number to call in the morning to order more groceries. The second was a letter.

Darling girls,

I hope you like the house. And now that my delivery has arrived, I'm sure you are wondering what you are supposed to do about dinner. It's time for you to start getting to know each other again. My first task for you is to go out to dinner together.

"Go out to dinner? How are we supposed to do that?" Avery asked, interrupting Lauren who was reading the letter.

"Hold on. Let me finish reading."

I know you are wondering how you can go out to dinner without a car. Remember, girls, there are other ways to get around. Go out to the shed in the backyard. Inside, you will find three bicycles. These are your wheels for the next two weeks. You will be living life in a slower fashion. If you take a right at the end of the driveway, there is a little restaurant about a half mile away. Order whatever you want. Mr. Fisher has already taken care of the bill and included a generous tip. Have a nice dinner, my girls, and don't forget to talk to each other.

Lauren looked up. "I guess we should head out to the shed."

They walked out to the shed and opened the door. The last of the sunlight that remained was streaming in the little window on the left side, giving them just enough light to look around.

"Is there a light in here?" Avery asked.

They all looked around. Three brand new bikes were parked in a row and there was a workbench with some tools behind them.

"There's a flashlight on the workbench," Maria said. "But I don't think there's a light otherwise."

"Great. This is just great," Avery complained while Lauren stepped past the bikes and picked up the flashlight.

"At least it works," Lauren said flipping the switch. "Looks like Dad thought of everything." She put the flashlight into the bag she was carrying and took hold of the handlebars on the first bike in the row. Then she kicked the kickstand up with one foot and got on the seat. "Let's go. I'm starving."

With a shrug, Maria hopped on the second bike. There was no fighting it. They needed to eat and tonight this was the way that had been provided for them. She could worry about the kids here and be hungry or worry at a restaurant and be full.

Avery grudgingly got onto the last bike, still griping under her breath, and they rode off toward the place their father's note had suggested.

Maria's legs were on fire. She hadn't realized she was this out of shape. But when did she have time to exercise? She continued to pedal hard toward the restaurant, seeing nothing but trees along the road as twilight turned into darkness. They had to be getting close to it now.

Lauren was riding at a leisurely pace several feet behind Maria. Always the carefree sister, she seemed to be enjoying herself in all this nonsense their father had set up for them.

Avery, on the other hand, was wound up tight. She was riding her bike in such a way as to stay between Maria and Lauren at all times. It was as if she were afraid of being alone, which seemed very odd. Avery had always been a spitfire—brash and opinionated. She had been in constant trouble during her high school years and had learned countless different ways of sneaking out of the house. But since arriving at the lake house Maria had noticed a distinct difference in her sister.

Maria breathed a sigh of relief as she went around a bend in the road and a building with lights on appeared on the right side of the road. They were finally there! And not a moment too soon, she thought as her stomach growled.

They turned into the parking lot, parked the bikes in a parking space near the front, and walked in through a heavy wooden door with an oval glass pane in the middle. Right in front of them was a long bar where a few lonely middle-aged men sat spaced a few stools apart from each other. Maria headed for a booth on the left side of the entrance and her sisters followed.

"I haven't done that in years," Lauren said.

"You're not the only one," Maria responded.

"It was nice, invigorating," Lauren said.

"I'm glad you enjoyed it. My legs feel like rubber." Maria looked at Avery, who was looking out the window, eyes darting around as if to get the lay of the land. "What about you, Avery?"

Hearing her name, Avery's head snapped around to look at Maria. "Huh?"

"How did you like the bike ride?"

Avery shrugged. "I'd prefer a car."

"Yeah, me too." Maria picked up one of the menus that were wedged between the ketchup bottle and the salt and pepper shakers. "Since it's already paid for, I think I'll get the steak," she said after looking over the selections.

"Pasta sounds good to me," Lauren said laying her menu down on the table. "What about you, Avery?"

"Chicken, I guess." Avery turned her attention back to the window.

Moments later a waiter came and took their order, then they sat in total silence until the food arrived, barely even looking at each other. It was amazing, Maria thought, how long three people could sit together and pretend to be alone. It reminded her of being with Hank when the kids weren't around and suddenly she wanted to cry.

She was relieved when the waiter placed a plate in front of her. *Thank God!* At least now she'd have something to focus her attention on.

For the first several minutes, all that was heard at their booth was the sound of forks and knives on plates. Maria's mind wandered to thoughts of her children. She wondered what they were doing right now and hoped that Hank had fed them a decent dinner. She hadn't wanted to leave them, but when she'd told Hank about the stipulation in her father's will, he had insisted that she honor Arthur's wishes. Maria knew he really just wanted the money. Still, she was here. The funny thing was, every time she'd found a free moment for a fantasy in the last year or so, she'd dreamed about time to herself. Now here she was with no husband, no kids, and no job responsibilities, yet all she could think about was getting back.

Maria snapped back from her reverie when Lauren spoke. "We should talk. Dad wanted us to talk to each other."

"Dad wanted a lot of things that aren't likely to happen," Avery said curtly.

Lauren shrugged. "He's dead, and he asked us to talk. We should try at least."

"Okay," Maria said, looking up. "What do you want to talk about?"

"Yeah, what do you want to talk about?" Avery gave Lauren a challenging look.

"Me?" Lauren's eyes widened in surprise as she laid down the fork she was holding in her right hand. "I don't know. I was hoping one of you would start us off."

"Of course you were," Avery said.

"What's that supposed to mean?" Lauren asked.

"Just that you always expect someone else to do the hard part."

"I just don't have a topic in mind right now and I was hoping one of you would."

Maria, for some strange reason, wanted to blurt out that she missed her dog, but she held back. She didn't know why, but she didn't feel like helping Lauren out of this.

"Right," Avery said, "just like always." Suddenly very agitated, she began to slide from her seat. "Excuse me," she spat out at Lauren who moved aside, letting Avery exit the booth. Avery stalked to the door and reached up to push it open, then stopped short as she looked through the glass pane. She reminded Maria of a caged animal who, when the door was finally opened, refused to go out for fear that what lay outside was worse than the cage.

After a moment at the door, Avery walked off toward the ladies room and Maria looked back at Lauren, whose eyes were downcast.

"I was only trying to honor Dad's wishes," she said.

Despite the sadness in Lauren's voice, Maria suspected that her sister's motives for "honoring their father's wishes" were the same as Hank's. Still, Lauren's sad eyes made it impossible for Maria to say that.

"You never were good at it," Maria said.

Lauren looked up at her. "Good at what?"

"Taking the lead."

"I guess you're right. You used to be good at it though."

Maria caught the accusation.

"Yeah, well, once in a while it's someone else's turn."

Chapter 13

Lauren

The ride back to the lake house had been quiet and tense. When they arrived, it stayed that way until an argument broke out between Avery and Maria when Avery stormed through the house locking every door and window. Maria didn't want her window locked, or closed either. Lauren knew it was wrong, but she liked it a little when her sisters fought with each other. At least then they weren't ganging up on her.

Glancing around her room, Lauren's eyes stopped on the large blue bag that sat in the left front corner. Inside were an easel, and her painting supplies. She hadn't wanted to bring them, but her sisters would expect her to have them. They were going to expect her to paint also. She'd brought her almost finished painting with the plan of sitting it out on the easel after pretending to paint for a few hours. But one partly done painting wouldn't fool them for a whole two weeks. At some point, she thought, feeling the anger rise up, she would have to try and paint. And that, she knew, would be a disaster. Maybe Avery and Maria would believe she was experimenting with abstract art.

Willing herself to let the anger go, Lauren grabbed her suitcase and laid it on the bed to unpack. She placed all her clothes in drawers, then grabbed a smaller bag and headed into the bathroom—her private bathroom. She opened the bag and pulled out several small pill bottles. Having her own bathroom was going to make keeping certain things private a little easier. That was one plus.

As Lauren lined the bottles up in the medicine cabinet, a small piece of paper fell out and fluttered to the floor. Lauren gingerly reached down and picked it up. On the paper was a note written in her father's handwriting.

Remember what we talked about.

That was all it said, but Lauren knew immediately what it meant. Her mind slipped back to a moment more than two years before. It was just after one of the family gatherings that ended badly. Just like their final gathering, and many others before, Lauren asked for financial help from her sisters. It wasn't the first time they refused, and it wasn't the first time they accused her of being irresponsible, but it was the first time it stung so badly. It was the first time their words weren't true. It was also the first time she truly felt like a burden and knew she always would.

"Why won't you tell your sisters what is really going on?" her father asked.

"Why should I? They think I'm irresponsible, and they're right."

"No, they're not. You aren't that person anymore."

Standing in her father's kitchen, Lauren shook her head and moved away toward the window over the sink. She stared out at the pristine backyard. "That's how they'll always see me."

"Sure, if you never tell them different. Lauren, give them a chance. They've changed too."

When she turned back to face her father, Lauren's cheeks were streaked with tears. "It doesn't matter that I've changed. They see me as a burden. If I tell them the truth, they'll know that a burden is all I'll ever be."

Arthur wrapped her in his arms and assured her that he loved her and her sisters did too. But she didn't feel love from them. She hadn't in a long time.

Her father gave her the money she needed to get by that time, and a few other times along the way. He was the one person she was always able to count on. She didn't know how she was going to get through the coming trials without him.

Glancing at the note one more time, Lauren carefully placed it in one of her dresser drawers. "I'm sorry, Dad," she whispered, "I still can't tell them."

Chapter 14

Avery

Early the next morning Avery awoke with a scream in her throat. She wiped sweat from her forehead with the back of her hand and sat still in her bed for a few minutes until her heartbeat slowed down, and the horrifying images faded from her mind. It was a dream about attackers chasing her, and though she'd tried to run, her legs refused to move. The same kind of dream she used to have all the time. It rarely happened now. Her routines and staying behind locked doors most of the time made her feel safe, keeping the nightmares away. Here she didn't feel safe.

As she sat in bed, she found herself thinking about Mike. Somehow having him across the hall made her feel safe, and yet threatened at the same time. He'd been a comforting presence at her father's funeral, but when he'd brought her back home she could neither go into his apartment nor allow him into hers. There was a part of her that very much wanted to start a relationship with him, but at the same time, the thought terrified her. So what was she supposed to do with him if she couldn't get across the threshold of his door, but couldn't get *him* out of her thoughts?

When she felt steady, she got up, gathered her toiletries and padded down the hall to the bathroom to get in the shower. Maria and Lauren were still asleep. By the time they got up, she would look fresh even if she didn't feel that way.

After a shower, Avery went into the kitchen and started a pot of coffee brewing. As she waited for the coffee maker, she went to the cupboard and looked inside. She reached for the pastry box, then stopped short and picked up the Cap'n Crunch instead. She dumped some in a bowl and poured milk on top. It had been a long time since she had eaten this cereal. Closing her eyes, she savored the taste, missing her father with every bite.

By the time she finished her cereal, Maria had walked into the kitchen. “Oh, good,” Maria said, “the coffee is ready.”

“Yeah, pour me a cup while you’re at it,” Avery said, taking her bowl to the sink.

Avery rinsed her bowl, then went to the cupboard and got out the creamer and sugar just as Maria came up beside her with two cups of coffee.

“Thanks,” Avery said. “I really need this.”

“Didn’t sleep well?”

“Not really.” A chill went down Avery’s spine as she recalled the terrible dream. “How about you?”

Maria shrugged. “So, so. First night in a new bed.”

“Exactly,” Avery said, choosing to pretend that was her reason as well.

The subject was changed when Lauren stumbled into the kitchen, catching herself with a hand on the table just in time to keep from falling.

“You okay?” Maria asked.

“I’m fine. I just tripped on the edge of the carpet.”

Maria raised an eyebrow at her, then went back to her coffee, pouring creamer into the cup.

Avery kept her attention on Lauren, watching her sister walk gingerly to the coffee pot. She seemed very unsure on her feet and stayed close to the counter as she walked across the kitchen to get sugar and creamer.

“What the hell is wrong with you?” Avery snapped out the question, feeling irritable from lack of quality sleep. But it wasn’t fair to blame her irritation totally on tiredness. Her sisters always brought out this side of her, Lauren most of all.

Lauren turned to her and gave a smile that was obviously forced. “Nothing’s wrong. I just got up. I’m still getting my bearings, that’s all.”

"It's more than that."

"I'm fine," Lauren said with an uncharacteristic amount of force. "And I think you should worry more about what's wrong with you, miss lock every door and run in fear of the man with the groceries."

"I'm reasonably cautious. There's nothing wrong with that."

Maria, who was sitting at the table, snickered at this comment. Avery gave her a pointed look, "You got something to add?" she said.

"Nope. But whatever your issue is, stay out of my room from now on. I'll worry about my own window."

"I'm very sorry for concerning myself with everyone's safety," Avery said before stomping off to her room. She was angry and agitated. If those two had any clue about what could happen when you're not careful, they'd thank her for her trouble instead of making fun. Who knew what might happen out here in a secluded house in the woods.

Chapter 15

Maria

The following day, Maria sat in her room next to the open window, allowing the smoke from her cigarette to waft out with the breeze. The first full day at the lake house had passed quietly. She and her sisters had interacted very little after breakfast. Avery spent the day sitting in front of the television watching soap operas and sulking. Lauren spent the day in her room, presumably painting, and only came out to eat. Maria spent the day sunning on the dock with a good book and a bottle of sunscreen, trying not to think about her family at home, trying not to worry.

It wasn't what her father wanted. They were supposed to talk, get to know each other again. She had come here fully expecting his hope for them to be impossible, but somehow she felt guilty for not even trying.

Looking down at the cigarette burning between her fingers, Maria thought about the beginning of this particular habit. When she'd left home to start college, she was eager to get away from the responsibility of being a mother to her sisters. She wasn't wild and crazy, didn't cause trouble, but she was ready to try new things, be a little carefree. She began spending time with a young man who introduced her to smoking. She had never meant for it to become a habit, but the way the nicotine calmed her nerves was too amazing to give up. She'd finally quit when she got pregnant with Jonathan. She'd started up again three years ago when Hank had begun to look at her differently, and the habit picked up speed when he'd begun to avoid looking at her at all.

After taking one last, long pull on the cigarette, Maria extinguished it in a small glass ashtray. Then she stashed the ashtray in a drawer and sprayed some air freshener around the room. Picking up a pack of strawberry flavored gum, she took a piece out and put it in her mouth before leaving her room.

As she passed Lauren's room, she heard a clatter and then Lauren's voice mutter, "Damn it!" Maria was curious about what her sister was working on, but Lauren was keeping her door shut at all times.

In the living room, Avery was curled up in a chair watching *Days of our lives*. Maria walked past her and went into the kitchen for a glass of water, then she walked back into the living room and tried for five minutes to become interested in the show on TV. It was so overdramatic.

"You watch this all the time?" Maria asked.

"Usually," Avery answered without diverting her eyes from the screen.

"You record it or something?"

"No."

"Don't you go to work during the day?"

"I'm a web designer. I work from home most of the time."

"Oh." Maria looked down. She wasn't sure how to continue this conversation, but she was trying. She thought about her sister alone at home all day, tried to imagine what that was like. "Don't you get lonely and stir crazy?"

"No. I like being at home."

"Well, how do you meet people then?"

"I do go into the office sometimes."

"But you were always bringing new guys with you to family gatherings. Do you go out a lot at night?"

"No. I don't like bars or crowds."

That seemed an odd statement coming from the sister who had long been considered the family party animal. She was the one who had been so wild during her youth.

"Surely you didn't meet all of them at the office."

"I meet them online, okay," Avery snapped.

Maria wondered why Avery was so sensitive about this subject. She opened her mouth to ask what dating site

Avery used to meet all these men but was cut off by the doorbell ringing.

Avery instantly tensed up and looked at the door with concern. "Don't worry. I'll look out the window before I open the door," Maria told her, feeling an odd maternal pull.

Pulling back the curtain, Maria glanced out the window. A man in his early twenties, with light brown hair, was standing on the stoop holding two brown paper bags in his arms. "It's the grocery guy."

Maria opened the door, greeted the handsome young man, and took the bags from him before closing the door again. She walked into the kitchen and set the bags down on the counter. After unloading and putting away all the food they had ordered, she pulled a note from the bottom of the bag.

"Avery," Maria called. "Get Lauren, please. We have another note from Dad."

A few minutes later Avery came into the kitchen with Lauren just behind her. Lauren looked agitated and tired, but she forced a smile and said, "What's Dad got to say now?"

Maria looked at the note and began to read.

Darling girls,

It is my hope that you are beginning to talk to each other, but I am no fool. A rift like yours is going to take time to mend. I know this because it is not the first time I have seen this happen between siblings. So my guess is that you each have spent the past two days in your own separate corners, doing your own things. You probably think I sent you three here out of some foolish hope, my own desire to have you all get along. And I bet you are all here expecting my plan to fail. Maybe it will, maybe not. I can only ask you to try, but I want you to understand where this request of mine is truly coming from.

In the cabinet under the television, there is a DVD that I want you to watch. It is an old home video I made, and a few years ago I had it put on DVD. Watch it all the way to the end and you will see why this is so important to me.

Love,
Dad

Maria put the note down and followed her sisters into the living room. They found the DVD and put it into the player. Lauren and Avery each took one of the two chairs, so Maria picked a spot on the sofa. After getting seated, she pointed the remote and clicked 'play'.

The video began in a hospital room, and Maria knew instantly what she was seeing. It was her mother's hospital room. Her mother sat on the bed, thin and frail, her head wrapped in a purple bandana. A nine-year-old Maria was sitting next to her while Lauren, six years old, sat in Mom's lap and two-year-old Avery was in Maria's lap. Lauren was holding a picture book and reading it while Maria helped her with the hard words. Avery was pointing at the pictures with a wide smile on her little face.

To the side of the bed, in the corner, Maria could see her father's brother, Uncle Harry, sitting in a chair. His long legs were crossed and his head had more hair than Maria could remember him ever having.

When Lauren finished reading the book, Mom kissed her head. "That's wonderful, girls. I love the way you help each other," she said with a teary smile. "Look at me girls." Lauren and Maria did as their mother asked and Mom reached for little Avery's face and turned it to her. "Promise me, girls … promise that you'll always be friends."

Maria and Lauren nodded, and Avery copied them. Then Mom looked at Maria and said, "Take care of them, Maria."

Maria nodded with tears running down her face. Then Mom looked at Uncle Harry. "Take the girls out to the cafeteria for snacks, will you, Harry?"

He nodded and stood up. "Come along, girls," he said as he scooped Avery up in his arms.

When the door closed behind them, Mom looked at the camera and said, "Arthur, put that down for a minute and come over here."

Dad put the camera down without turning it off and walked over to the bed. He sat down on the side and kissed Mom's forehead. Maria was startled by his appearance. It was hard for her to remember him this young, and yet he didn't look as young as he should have. He was forty-one when her mother died, only three years older than she was now. But she could see in this video that he already had quite a bit of gray hair and his face looked tired and creased with lines, much older than forty-one. Watching this she realized she had never, over the years that followed her mother's death, thought about the extreme stress her father must have suffered. Now she felt so sorry for him.

"Did you hear from Carol?" Mom asked.

Dad shook his head. "She won't even answer or return my calls."

"Did you tell her, Arthur? Did you tell her I'll be gone soon?" Mom's voice was almost desperate.

"I told her in the messages I left, Eve."

Mom began to cry, pulling Dad closer, and burying her head in his arm. "I'm so sorry," she sobbed.

"You've got nothing to be sorry for." Dad stroked her back.

Mom lifted her head and looked Dad in the eyes. "Yes, I do. I was always so hard on her. I didn't let things go. And none of it matters now, none of it. I just want her here with me. I want my sister and she isn't going to come. I'll die without seeing her, without telling her that I'm sorry."

For a couple of minutes, all that happened in the video was Mom sobbing and Dad trying to soothe her. Then Mom looked up at Dad, turned his face to look at her, and said, "Don't let this happen to our girls, Arthur. Make sure they know that they need each other."

Dad nodded as tears flowed down his cheeks. "I will, Evie."

Maria's attention was torn from the video when Lauren jumped up from her seat and hurried off toward her room. She was crying, but Maria hadn't noticed it until she got up.

Just after Lauren's exit, the video cut to static. Maria glanced at Avery, who was still staring at the screen as if there was something more to see. Maria wasn't even sure Avery had noticed that Lauren left.

"Avery, are you okay?"

Avery looked up at her, stared for a second, then said, "I don't remember being there. I don't remember any of it."

"Of course you don't. You were two years old."

"It's not fair."

"It wasn't fair for any of us." Maria was thinking of her father, feeling guilty that she had never thought about what he'd gone through.

"It's not fair that memories fade away when you're a child." Avery looked at Maria now. "It's as if she never even existed for me. That should make it easier, but instead, it's like a hole that can't be filled."

That was another thing Maria hadn't thought about before. She *had* always thought of Avery as the lucky one. Maybe she was wrong about that.

"I don't remember an Aunt Carol, do you?" Avery asked.

"Vaguely. I think I met her once when I was really little."

"She never came then, when Mom was sick."

"No."

After a moment of silence, Avery gave Maria a probing look. "Would you come for me? If I was dying, would you come?"

Maria was stunned by the question. Maybe she hadn't ever really thought about what their separation from each other could lead to. When she answered, her voice was small and thick with emotion. Avery was her sister, but in a way, she was more than that. Maria had had a hand in raising her. But she hadn't, she realized, been that mother figure to Avery in a long time. In truth, since coming here, she was beginning to realize she didn't really know her sisters any longer. "Of course I would."

Avery didn't respond. She sat in the chair with her legs pulled up, knees under her chin, and arms wrapped around her legs. She looked vulnerable, like the little girl she once was, and Maria wished she'd followed through as that mother figure. Maybe she could have done a better job filling the hole.

After several long seconds of silence, Avery said, "Well that's one." She didn't look at Maria, didn't seem to be talking to anyone but herself. Then she got up and walked to her room.

Maria sat alone for a few minutes, trying to process what she'd just watched. She didn't want to end up like her mother and Aunt Carol. But how were she and her sisters supposed to get to know each other again? How could they get past the bitterness?

Chapter 16

Lauren

Lauren was in her room, lying on the bed. She'd cried for a while after leaving the living room. She wasn't sure if she had, in fact, watched the DVD to the end, but she couldn't take any more. Seeing her mother's pain was excruciating. Knowing she might be in that same place someday was more than she could bear. Of course, she wouldn't be in the same place. Her mother had a husband, children, and even a few loving in-laws. What did she have? She had her pride. That was all.

But how could she tell Maria and Avery the truth? How could she go to them and say, "Hey, remember what a burden I used to be? Well, that was only the beginning."

Of course, if she didn't tell them, what would she do when things got bad? Who was going to help her, take care of her? The day would come when she wouldn't be able to work any longer. What then?

She sat up and glanced at the canvas she'd been working on since the day before. It looked like something she would have been proud to bring home in grade school. Now the best she could do is try to pass it off as an abstract, and it made her sad and angry to look at it. She had tried the 'special' brush her therapist gave her. It did little good. She could barely keep from dropping it every thirty seconds.

Staring at the canvas, Lauren deeply wanted to take a knife and destroy it. It was beyond painful to look at the evidence of what she had lost. She had thought from the beginning of this that losing her ability to paint was the worst part. And yet, she was now realizing that it was even worse to think about dying without a soul at her bedside. It was too bad, she thought, that pride was such a hard enemy to beat.

Chapter 17

Avery

It was quiet at dinner that night. Everyone was sullen and it was obvious Lauren had been crying. Avery sat at the table wrapped up in her own thoughts. The loss of her mother was something she didn't like to think about, but that DVD ... It was far worse than just thinking about it. She couldn't get her mother's face out of her head, couldn't believe how much that face looked like hers. Why hadn't she noticed that before? It made her wonder, was she anything like her mother? She would never really know. She had never asked her father, and now he was gone too—another parent to miss.

Stop thinking about this! The nightmares and constant fear that dominated her life was more than enough pain for one person. She didn't need to remind herself of the missing piece. She glanced at Maria. Felt a brief stab of anger. *It would always be missing.*

Looking down at her plate, still filled with the meatloaf and vegetables that Maria had cooked for them, Avery willed herself to stop thinking about her mother. She told herself to think happy thoughts, and somehow that led her mind to her cat, Rocket. Sad as it was, he was the only real companion in her life. She wondered how he was doing. Then, of course, she found herself thinking about Mike. She imagined him playing with Rocket, taking care of him. Then a very strange thought entered her mind in which Mike was playing with two children. The children looked like her and like him and, as she saw these things in her mind, warmth seemed to wrap around her. *What was that?*

When she pulled herself away from her thoughts and looked up, her sisters were both staring at her. "What?" she said.

"Well, I don't know about Maria," Lauren said, her face starting to look better, less blotchy. "But I was just wondering what you were thinking about."

"Why?" asked Avery.

"Because you looked almost angry and then, all of a sudden, you had this goofy grin on your face."

"You must be imagining things. I didn't have a grin."

"No, it was there," Maria stepped in.

"Thinking about someone special?" Lauren asked, looking a bit more animated now.

Avery felt her face get hot. "No! I was thinking about my cat. I miss him."

Maria responded with a raised eyebrow.

"Well, if that's the look you get for your cat," Lauren said, "Then you must be in some kind of slump, and you need to get out and find yourself a man."

Avery was embarrassed and needed to put Lauren in her place. Most of all, she needed to end this topic and escape. "*I* never had any problems finding men. You were the one that always came to everything alone."

Avery began to stomp off toward her room, but Lauren's voice followed her. "That doesn't mean I didn't get dates, it means I won't bring just *any* guy home."

Hurrying into her room, Avery shut the door behind her. She hated being here, hated dealing with her sisters, and hated all the feelings that were waking up inside of her. She didn't want to feel hurt over losing her parents and she didn't want to lust over Mike. But no matter how hard she tried to push the feelings away, they just kept coming back.

After pacing the floor for a few minutes, Avery walked over to the nightstand next to her bed and opened the bottom drawer. She pulled out an object that was wrapped in cloth and, sitting down on the bed, laid it in her lap. For a few seconds she just sat there and stared at it, then she slowly unwrapped it and looked down at it. In her hands was a picture of her mother. Avery always kept this picture near, but she almost never looked at it. Now she stared at it. Her mother was smiling warmly. She looked a lot like Avery, blond hair, bright smile, but she had blue eyes that sparkled like Lauren and her nose and chin were like Maria's.

Avery felt intensely sad as she looked at the photograph. Why did it hurt so much to not remember someone?

No! She wasn't going to do this. She wasn't going to feel this way any longer and she wasn't going to look at this picture for another second. Avery carefully folded the cloth back around the picture frame, then tucked it away in the drawer, promising herself she wouldn't get it out again until it was time to pack her bags and leave this place.

Chapter 18

Maria

After Avery left, Maria and Lauren finished eating with little more to say to each other. When they were done, Maria began to wash the dishes while Lauren cleared the table and cleaned up the mess from cooking. Maria watched her sister out of the corner of her eye. When Lauren was clearing the table, she carried every single dish with her right hand, always managing to keep the left one concealed. When she wiped down the table, she used her right hand, never the left. *Curious ... very curious.*

When the dishes were almost done, Maria decided to try a little conversation. "I wonder what Avery was really thinking about."

Lauren shrugged. "One of the many men in her life, I assume."

"I guess. She hardly ever leaves home, did you know that?"

"What are you talking about? Avery is the family party animal."

"She used to be. She told me earlier that she works from home most of the time and rarely goes out at night."

Lauren gave a skeptical look. "How is that possible? She always has a new guy."

"She meets them online."

"On a dating site?"

"I don't know. I was about to ask when the grocery guy got here."

Lauren sat back down at the table and Maria dried and put away the last dish before joining her. They were quiet for a few seconds, then Maria said, "You're certainly getting brasher."

"I am?"

"I'm sure Avery thinks so. You didn't use to fire off witty quips like you did tonight."

Lauren looked down as if ashamed. "I shouldn't have done that."

Maria was confused by Lauren's reaction to her comment. She wasn't sure why, but for some reason, she felt proud of Lauren. Perhaps it was a little of that surrogate mother from the past coming out again, or maybe she was just missing her kids so much she needed someone to push her motherliness onto.

After their conversation, Lauren went back to her room, and Maria headed into the living room. She watched TV for an hour or so, then headed to her own room to get ready for bed.

Closing her bedroom door, Maria went to the window that was still open and enjoyed a cigarette and the cool night air. When she was done, she gathered her PJ's and toiletries and headed down the hall to the bathroom.

Thankfully the bathroom was empty. It looked like Avery had already gone to bed. Maria went in, stripped off her clothes, and took a shower. When she was done, she wrapped the towel around her hair and went to the sink to brush her teeth. As the fog began to clear from the mirror, Maria, standing there naked, took in the sight of herself. Her skin was a little less firm than it had once been and her belly, hips, and butt were a little plumper.

Maria ran a finger across the scar that went along the bottom of her belly, Melanie's scar. It was from the emergency C-section she'd needed to save her little girl's life when it was discovered that the umbilical cord was wrapped around the baby's neck. She remembered the fear she'd felt and how Hank had soothed her, telling her that everything would be fine and he loved her.

Then another memory came to mind. Hank running a finger along that same scar, several weeks later when it was still fresh, all bright red. Maria had been so unhappy about the scar. It made her feel less pretty. But when Hank had touched it that way and then made love to her, she felt beautiful again.

Weeks after that, when Hank had turned off the light before they made love, telling her that he wanted a little mystery, Maria had thought nothing of it. As time went on, a few pounds were added to Maria's already larger frame, and Hank continued to want "mystery" in the bedroom. For a while, she didn't worry about it, but as Hank began to turn her away more and more, she realized that he was no longer attracted to her. She thought at that time, nothing could hurt more. She was wrong.

Over the next few years, Hank continued to pull away from her. Eventually, he started going out at night after the kids were in bed. Maria was no fool. She knew what he was out doing. But what hurt the most, more than she could ever have imagined, was seeing him pull away from the kids. Sure, he was there most of the time, or at least his body was. His heart and mind, however, rarely were. He didn't make any effort to go to ball games or dance recitals. He didn't play with them. He talked to them very little.

Maria had watched her children change as their father lost interest in them. It was like seeing a part of her kids wilt away, and it broke her heart. For a long time, she'd been angry with Hank, and she'd let him know. She had yelled and, when that didn't work, she'd begged. Then she stopped. Between working and raising the kids by herself, she just didn't have the energy to be angry. After all, what good had it done? She would stay with him, put up with his rejection, at least until the kids were grown. They'd have both their parents that way. That had to be best. A divorce would only hurt them more and their father would probably never even bother to see them.

After putting on her purple flowered pajamas, shorts with a tank top, Maria gathered her things and started back to her room. She stopped dead in her tracks, startled, when she heard, "No! Please! Stop!" in a mumble that she recognized as sleep talking, coming from Avery's room as she passed. In a motherly movement her hand went to the doorknob, but then she stopped herself. Avery was a grown woman. She didn't need her big sister to soothe away bad dreams. Maria kept going.

When she got to her room, she put her things away and crawled into bed. She felt very alone. The empty space on the left side of the bed loomed like a black hole. Why, she wondered, did the presence of another person feel comforting even when that person was miles away from you on an emotional level? When Hank was there in bed with her, she could remember a time when he loved her and pretend it hadn't ended. Hell, even sleeping with the dog was better than being alone.

Chapter 19

Avery

When Avery woke up, gasping for air, she could still feel the monster on top of her, his weight bearing into her flesh. She could still feel his hot, putrid breath on her cheek. Sweat beaded on her skin. Tears escaped her eyes and fell softly on her pillow. Still feeling paralyzed, she forced her arm up to wipe away the moisture on her face.

After lying there for several minutes, Avery got up, put on her bathrobe and padded down the hall to the kitchen. She opened a top cabinet and pulled out a box of hot chocolate packets. This was what soothed her after a bad dream, a tradition Maria had started when Avery was a little girl. When she went to open the box, she noticed that it was already opened and had been taped shut. Had one of her sisters opened it?

Avery pried up the tape and lifted the flaps on the box. Inside, on top of the packets of hot chocolate, there was a folded up piece of paper. She pulled it out, curiosity filling her head, and unfolded it. No surprise, it was written in her father's handwriting. This was becoming an everyday occurrence.

The note was written to her. She read it silently.

My darling Avery,

I knew you would be coming for this box sooner or later because I know that nightmares plague your life. I do not know the reason, but I see your fear. I see it in your eyes and in your actions. Beautiful girl, you cannot spend your whole life hiding from the world, and you cannot live it always in fear. The way to ending this fear, the only way I know, is to face it. I imagine you are spending just about all of your time inside. Go out, Avery! Remember how you used to love to swim? You were like a fish. Outside the door, there is a beautiful lake. Cast off your fear and go swimming.

Your loving father

Avery stared at the note. Her father was right, she had gone outside very little and only for short intervals. She hadn't even been willing to take off her shoes and dip a toe in the lake. It made her feel too vulnerable.

She didn't want to do this thing her father was asking of her, couldn't imagine it. But somehow her father's words made her feel obligated. It was frustrating really, how much power he had over her without even being here. It had been so much easier to turn away from his words when he was alive.

She could ignore the note. It wasn't like anyone would know.

I'll know!

She squeezed her eyes shut, closed her fist around the note, and she knew she had to try.

Avery slept in the next morning. When she emerged from her room at eleven, she was wearing a brand new blue swimsuit. She had bought it, internet shopping of course, just for this trip. It had been years since she'd worn one. She wasn't even sure what had prompted her to think she'd need one for this trip. Over it, she wore a matching blue striped cover dress and on her feet, she wore flip-flops, another thing she hadn't worn in years. Her blond hair was twisted up on top of her head and she carried with her sunglasses and a towel.

Placing her towel and sunglasses on the table, she fixed herself a bowl of cereal. She ate it without tasting it, her nerves so active she couldn't register anything else.

When her bowl was empty, Avery washed it out, went to the table, and picked up her stuff. She walked to the back door feeling as if her feet were made of lead. At the door, she stood for several minutes looking through the window. It was a beautiful day. The sun was shining, the birds were singing, and the lake water was lapping against the retaining wall. It was already eighty degrees outside, perfect for swimming.

Avery wrapped her sweaty hand around the doorknob. Her heart was pounding like the hooves of a stallion. She wasn't sure how her chest was able to contain it.

She closed her eyes and, in her mind, went back to a time when this would have been easy. She remembered how much she used to love swimming, how excited she would get when they went to the lake. She could hear her own little girl's voice resounding with anticipation saying, "Let's go swimming, Daddy! I can't wait!"

Then she did it. She turned the knob and walked out into the brilliant sunshine. Looking around, she didn't see anyone outside. She closed the door behind her, and hesitantly started toward the dock.

When Avery reached the dock, she glanced around again. Her stomach was fluttering with butterflies. She laid her towel down on the dock and sat down, keeping her feet dry. She watched the ducks swimming on the surface of the water, their graceful bodies gliding along. She wondered if they ever felt fear when nothing was chasing them. For Avery, the chase was never-ending, always alive in her mind. She was sure it was only a matter of time before the monster would catch her … again.

The way to ending this fear is to face it! Her father's words resonated in her head. *Okay, okay!* She shucked off her flip-flops, then slowly extended one leg and reached her foot out toward the water. Just as her toe dipped in, Avery heard voices coming from the left side of the yard. She jerked her foot back and pushed the flip-flops back onto both feet.

Heart racing, she glanced toward the sound. It was Lauren and some guy. *Who was he?*

Avery watched as Lauren chatted with the man for a couple more minutes. As her heart slowed, she noticed the way Lauren was smiling, the slight blush in her cheeks. Her sister liked this guy.

When the conversation was finished, the man walked away in the direction they had come from. Lauren waved at him as he went. When he had disappeared, Lauren looked around, noticed Avery on the dock and walked toward her.

At the end of the dock, Lauren sat down next to Avery, taking in her attire. "Going swimming?"

Avery gave a shrug, trying to look casual. "Maybe. I haven't decided yet."

"It's a nice day for it," Lauren said pulling off her sandals and letting her feet sink down into the cool lake water.

"Yeah, I guess it is."

Lauren looked at Avery again, taking in the way she was almost huddled up. "You should put your feet in at least. The water is so nice."

Avery glanced around. There was no one in sight. She looked at Lauren, and began to relax, comforted by her sister's presence. She took off her flip flops and slowly dunked her feet into the water. It was nice and cool on her feet and it reminded her of being a child.

She was proud of herself. She had gone this far at least, and that was something.

After a couple of minutes, she looked at Lauren and said, "So … who was that guy you were talking to?"

"Oh, that's Blake. He owns the house next door, on the other side of that row of trees," Lauren said, pointing in the direction the man had walked off in.

"He lives here?"

"No, not year round. He's here for a couple of weeks getting the place ready for summer renters."

Avery nodded. "He's not bad looking."

"Well, he's no Evan, but he's ok."

"Who is Evan?" Avery asked, perplexed. Had Lauren been making rounds or something?

"He's the grocery guy."

"Oh. You know his name?"

Lauren looked at Avery for a few seconds, as if searching for something, then she said, "Yes, I know his name. That's what happens when you talk to people instead of hiding from them." Lauren's voice was soft, not a hint of sarcasm. And Avery realized that her sister felt sorry for her, and that made her feel like a victim again.

Well to hell with that! Avery let out a little huff, pulled her feet from the water, shoved on her shoes, and stormed off toward the house.

Chapter 20

Lauren

Lauren watched, feet still in the water, as her sister stomped off. She turned back to face the lake just as the back door to the house slammed shut. It didn't seem to matter what she said to Avery or how she said it, nearly every word seemed to upset her sister. Of course, Avery appeared to be living on edge anyway, always hiding, always afraid, always with her guard up. Lauren had to wonder why. What had caused her sister to become this way?

Her mind shot back to the note she'd found in her bathroom and the memory it had evoked, the conversation with her father. *They've changed too*, her father had said. He was right about that.

Lauren swished her feet in the water. A smile crept across her face. She was sorry her conversation with Avery had gone so poorly, but damn if she wasn't happy. Blake seemed nice. They had only talked for a few minutes, but she was feeling things she hadn't felt in a very long time. Giddy. She was giddy, like a little girl with a crush.

She knew it was silly. In a week and a half, she'd be back to her regular life and Blake would be back to his. Nothing was going to come of their time together. Even so, Lauren had every intention of enjoying it while it lasted.

Lauren thought back to their conversation. She had been walking along the edge of the lake, enjoying the warm, late morning sunshine and the sounds of nature when a voice startled her from behind.

"You the new owner?"

Lauren turned, gave the man standing behind her a blank look. "huh?"

He pointed to the house she was staying in with her sisters. "I was wondering if you are the new owner of that house."

"No, I'm just staying in it for a couple of weeks."

"Oh, I see. I didn't think it would be rented so soon. Did you meet the owner when you rented it?"

"No. I didn't do the renting."

The man looked down, his dark blond hair falling over his forehead. He was only medium height, but broad, and his skin was a nice tan. When he looked back up, Lauren noticed his eyes. They were bluer than hers. They reminded her of the Caribbean Sea, so clear and mesmerizing. They made her want to paint an ocean, and for a moment that thought made her blood boil.

"Sorry to have bothered you," he said and started to walk away.

Lauren didn't want him to go, though she couldn't explain why. Something about him was just drawing her. She called out, "Are you staying in one of these houses?"

He turned back to her, pointed to the house next to the one she was staying in. "I own this one here."

"Oh, you live here?"

"No. I come a few times a year and stay for a week or two. In the summer I rent it. Right now I'm here getting it ready for the high season, a little late, I'm afraid. And I was hoping to meet the new owner of the house next door. Mrs. Stanfield sold it last winter so she could move into a retirement community. She wanted to pass it on to one of her kids, but neither one of them wanted it."

"That's hard to believe. It's a cute little house."

"Well, they both live far away and didn't want the bother of keeping the place up."

"I see."

"You're enjoying it then, the house?"

"The house, yes."

The man furrowed his brow at her. "Is there something here you're not enjoying?"

"I'm staying here with my sisters at the request of my father's will. We have some trouble getting along."

"But you came."

"Yes, and so did they. My name's Lauren, by the way."

He stepped forward and reached out his hand. "I'm Blake. I'll be here for a while longer if you need anything."

Lauren nodded, feeling a tingle where Blake had touched her hand. It was silly, like a little girl with an instant crush. Lauren couldn't remember the last time she'd felt that way. "I guess I'll be getting back now." She started back and Blake walked with her until they were past the narrow row of trees that separated his house from her rental.

"It was nice meeting you, Lauren," he said, "I hope I'll get to talk to you again."

Lauren felt her cheeks warm. "I'm sure you will," she said before he started back toward his own house.

Still smiling at the thought of her handsome neighbor, Lauren pulled her feet out of the water, put on her sandals, and started back toward the house. As she neared the back door, she detected a faint smell of smoke in the air. She sniffed the air in different directions and determined that the smell was coming from the right side of the house. She followed it and found herself looking at a tiny drift of smoke wafting out of Maria's window.

Sneaking up to the window, Lauren stepped lightly and tried not to lose her balance. Maria's face registered shock when she saw that she was being watched.

"What are you doing?" Lauren asked.

Trying to look nonchalant, Maria shrugged. "What does it look like?"

"If I remember correctly, you quit smoking eleven years ago."

"Yeah?"

"So what happened?"

Maria's voice was indignant when she answered. "I started again."

It was clear Maria wasn't interested in talking about this subject and Lauren wasn't sure what else to say. She stood there staring for a minute or so, then Maria put out her cigarette and slammed the window shut.

Stunned, Lauren stood frozen for a second, staring at the window. She had managed to anger two sisters, in the course of two different conversations, in less than fifteen minutes. That must be some kind of record, she thought as she walked to the back door of the house. Unfortunately, it wasn't the kind of record she was going for.

Chapter 21

Maria

Maria was in the living room, flipping through channels when the doorbell rang. She went to the door, looking out the window on the way. There was a man standing on the porch with a paper bag in hand, but it wasn't the guy from the grocery store. Maria put her hand on the knob, then stopped before opening it. "Who is it?" she called out. Avery's paranoia must be rubbing off on her, she thought.

"I'm Josh Stanton from the liquor store in town."

Maria furrowed her brow at the door. The liquor store? What was he doing here?

"What do you want?"

"I have a delivery for Maria, Lauren, and Avery from Max Fisher."

Interesting. Maria opened the door, a hint of suspicion still on her face. Josh handed her the small bag. "It's already paid for," he said before turning and walking back to his car.

Maria called out to her sisters. "Hey, we just got a delivery!" Then she walked into the kitchen and put the bag down on the counter.

Moments later Lauren and Avery sauntered into the room, curious looks on their faces.

"I thought the grocery guy didn't come again until tomorrow," Avery said.

"This delivery didn't come from the grocery store," Maria said.

"Really? Then who's it from?" Lauren asked.

"The liquor store," Maria said, looking at her sisters. Avery looked very uneasy.

"The liquor store? What did we get from there?" Lauren wanted to know.

"And who sent it?" Avery chimed in.

"I don't know what it is yet, but it was sent by Mr. Fisher, and that means it's from Dad," Maria answered.

Lauren shrugged. "Open it up," she said.

Maria unfolded the top of the bag and looked inside. She pulled out a blue velvet bag, three shot glasses, and a note, then glanced at her sisters before reading the note.

Darling girls,

I assume you have at least had enough time to begin seeing that you don't really know each other anymore. I'll bet you've all been a little surprised with each other and I know you each have questions to ask. But you probably aren't asking them yet. Getting to know each other again takes time, but we need to speed up the process just a little. Remember when you were kids and you used to play that game, truth or dare?

Maria looked up. "He wants us to play truth or dare? What's next, spin the bottle?"

"Only if we get to invite some men," Lauren said.

Maria gave her an annoyed look. "Some of us are married."

"Yes, yes, I know. Some of us have it all," Lauren retorted.

Maria chose to ignore the last comment, though this new snarky attitude of Lauren's was a bit irritating when turned in her direction, and continued on with the note.

Tonight, after you finish dinner, I want you to play that game. But instead of truth or dare, we're going to change it to truth or booze. You will take turns choosing a sister to ask a question, if she chooses not to answer, she will be required to drink a shot from the bottle of liquor I sent you. You each get to ask five questions. They say, "Loose lips sink ships," but sometimes you need to loosen lips in order to save the ship. Play nice, girls. I hope you learn something about each other.

Maria pulled a bottle of crown royal out of the velvet bag. "Well, Dad," she said, "you never cease to surprise me."

Chapter 22

Lauren

When dinner was over and the table cleared, Lauren sat down with her sisters to start the game their father insisted they play. In front of them on the table sat the bottle of crown royal and the three shot glasses.

For several seconds, the three of them just gaped at each other. This was a strange thing their father had asked of them and yet they didn't know how to say no to a dead man. Lauren held both hands under the table. Her palms were sweaty, so she wiped them on her shorts.

"So who goes first?" Avery asked.

"I don't know," Maria said.

"There are a few old board games in the living room," Lauren spoke up. "We can use the dice to decide."

Avery and Maria both stared at her for a split second. Rarely in the past had Lauren solved even the smallest of problems. She should probably be irritated by their reaction, but she wasn't. It felt good to be the one with an answer, no matter how small the problem, and she didn't care what they were thinking.

Maria went to retrieve the dice and when she came back, she placed one die in front of each of them. "Okay, we each roll one and the highest number goes first."

They rolled the dice and Lauren won. She turned to Maria and asked, "Why did you start smoking again?"

"Wait … what? You're smoking again?" Avery said looking at Maria with surprise.

Maria's expression showed her irritation with the question. "Why does anyone start smoking again?"

"That's not an answer," Lauren said. "It's just another question. You have to answer."

"I don't *have* to answer."

Lauren tilted her head. "Fine, then drink."

Lauren picked up the bottle and filled Maria's shot glass, then met her eyes with a challenging look.

Maria's eyes met the challenge as she wrapped her fingers around the small glass and brought it to her lips. She threw it back in one swift motion and slammed the glass back down on the table.

"Okay, I guess it's your turn then," Lauren said as she glanced at Avery.

Avery nodded and thought for a moment, looking back and forth between her sisters. Her gaze came to rest on Lauren and, tapping her fingers on the table, she asked, "What the hell is wrong with you?"

Lauren felt a stab to her heart. She knew what Avery was asking and why, but it was the last thing she wanted to talk about, and the one thing she knew her father would want her to talk about. Avery's direct hit method of asking was not surprising, it was classic Avery, but it hurt none the less.

Pretending she didn't understand, Lauren looked at Avery and said, "I'm not really good with schedules, but something tells me that isn't what you mean. So I'm afraid you're going to have to be more specific."

"You've been stumbling all over the place since we got here, and you always look tired, so … *what* is wrong with you?"

Lauren felt her stomach roll. She did not want to answer this question. She slowly reached out her right hand and picked up the bottle, poured some into her glass. Drinking wasn't great to mix with her medicine, but this one time wouldn't be so bad.

"No, you have to fill it up. Same as you did mine," Maria said.

Reluctantly, Lauren filled her little glass to the brim. She toyed with it for a moment, then picked it up and poured it down her throat slowly. She swallowed and grimaced as it burned going down. Putting the glass down, she looked at Maria.

Maria glanced in Lauren's direction as if a question was on her mind, then, after a brief hesitation, she turned to Avery. "Who's Mike?" she asked.

Avery's mouth dropped open, then snapped shut. Her eyes narrowed as she stared at Maria. "He's my neighbor from across the hall. But how do you know about him?"

"I heard you call out his name when I walked past your room last night, on my way to the bathroom," Maria said.

"Ooooh, so there's someone special in your life," Lauren said.

"No, he's just a neighbor and I am *not* dating him."

"Sure. I know I call out the names of my neighbors all the time when I'm sleeping." Lauren mocked. The snappy retorts just kept coming out of nowhere.

"He's a friend," Avery said in a sharp tone, "and that's all I have to say right now. I believe it's your turn, Lauren."

Lauren's gaze stayed on Avery. "What's with all the obsessive door locking? What are you so afraid of?"

Without so much as a blink of the eye, Avery said, "That's two questions, so I'm only obligated to answer the first."

Lauren mentally kicked herself. The second question was the one she should have asked, but she'd get back to that one later.

"It's very simple," Avery said as if she were talking to a group of children. "I like to be as safe as possible. There's all kinds of bad stuff going on out there, ya know."

Sly Avery had managed to answer two questions without giving much up. Lauren had to hand it to her.

"So, now it's my turn," Avery said. "Maria, why are you so worried about leaving the kids with Hank?"

Lauren raised an eyebrow. "You're worried about leaving the kids with their father, mister perfect?" Lauren stopped for a second, considered Maria's behavior since they all arrived at the house. "You have seemed nervous."

Maria tried to brush it off, "Every mother worries."

"Once again, that is not an answer," Avery said.

Maria glared at Avery as she picked up the bottle and filled her glass.

Lauren had to wonder why Maria was being so secretive. She was the one that had everything, the perfect husband, two beautiful children. So what was she hiding?

After throwing back the shot, Maria turned to Lauren. Raising one eyebrow, Maria asked, "Why have you been doing everything with your right hand?"

Trying to hide how much that question hit home, Lauren shrugged. "Isn't that the one most people use?"

"*That* is not an answer," Maria said. "Not for you. You're left-handed and we both know it."

Lauren swallowed hard, reached for the bottle, with her right hand, and filled her glass. She looked up at Maria, her eyes begging for mercy, and drank the golden liquid.

As soon as the shot was down, Lauren turned to Avery. "You used to go out and party all the time. You never worried about who you were with or what kind of crazy things they were doing. You certainly didn't worry about locking the doors. You were the one always trying to get past the locks. So why are you so afraid now?"

There was a pause and Lauren was sure Avery was trying to find a loophole to the question, a way to answer without really telling her anything.

"And don't just say that bad things happen," Lauren spoke up again. "We all know that. It didn't matter to you before. I want to know why it does now."

Avery's mouth opened, but no words came out. She looked almost ashen as she tried to find a way to satisfy Lauren's question. Then she closed her eyes, shook her head, and when her eyes opened again, she reached for the bottle and filled her glass for the first time. As her expression went back to the "no fear" Avery she always projected, she raised her glass in the motion of a toast, then drank the shot.

"Okay, my turn," Avery said after placing her glass back on the table. "Lauren," she began and Lauren grimaced—another one for her. "Why is your door always shut? You never used to close your bedroom door. You said it made you feel claustrophobic. So what gives?"

Lauren took a breath and thought about her answer. She looked at Avery. "My painting hasn't been going very well lately and I don't really want to share bad work." That was an understatement, but it was the truth. Avery hadn't asked why her work wasn't going well and Lauren hoped she wouldn't.

But just as Lauren was feeling like her answer had gotten the job done, Maria spoke up saying, "Maybe that has something to do with you using your right hand instead of your left."

Lauren braced for another question from Maria, sure it was coming, but Maria turned to Avery instead. "Avery, you told me that you meet the guys you date online. What kind of site are you meeting them on?"

Avery took a deep breath. The look in her eyes told Lauren that she did not want to answer, but Maria hadn't given her any smooth outs to the question. It was curious, though, to Lauren that this question was so hard. Surely it was some kind of dating site. Why didn't she want to tell them that?

Avery thought for a few moments, glancing back and forth between Maria and the bottle on the table. Then she looked down at her lap, fiddled with her fingers the way a child in trouble might, and said, "I find them on an escort site. They're not dates, they're escorts." Avery's voice was quiet, her expression sheepish as she lifted her head slightly. Lauren could not remember a single time in the past when Avery had looked this vulnerable. And it seemed odd she had chosen to expose herself that way instead of drinking the shot.

Lauren wanted to ask Avery more questions, but it felt wrong when her sister was looking so small. Instead,

Lauren turned to Maria. For a few seconds, Lauren considered what she wanted to ask, then she gave her sister a quizzical look and said, "What's it like, sleeping with the same man for fourteen years?"

"That's a little personal," Maria protested.

"Dad's note didn't say we couldn't ask personal questions. So tell us, is it nice, like he knows just what turns you on, or is it boring?"

Lauren couldn't read Maria's expression. Her mouth was tight and she looked like she was somewhere between hurt and angry. Lauren knew the question was a little personal, but she couldn't understand why it would be difficult, and she certainly didn't know why Maria was looking so upset by it. She had thought it was the kind of question that might lighten the mood a little.

Maria looked at Lauren, her eyes piercing, then said, "I don't think that's any of your business, so I guess I'll take the shot." She poured the liquid into her glass, putting the bottle back down on the table with a little more force than necessary, and threw back the shot. She didn't look back up and Lauren felt regretful and also confused.

Lauren glanced at Avery, wishing this game was over. "It's your turn."

Avery was still looking into her lap. When she looked up she didn't seem any stronger than she had a few minutes before and Avery had always been the "bounce right back" type. She looked at Lauren. "Why weren't you there for me?" she asked.

Lauren shook her head, confused yet again. "There for you? There for you when?"

"When Maria left and went to college. I was only eleven. I still needed someone to act like a mother, someone to help me understand puberty, someone to warn me about boys and help me deal with mean girls. I needed you and all you could do was paint. You didn't care about me and I want to know why."

Lauren was taken aback. She had never known Avery harbored these kinds of feelings toward her. She hadn't felt like it was her job to step in and be a mother to her sister. Maria had always handled that.

"I … I didn't mean to not be there for you. I didn't know you wanted me to. You didn't ask me for any help and I was only fifteen myself." Lauren shook her head. She was dismayed that Avery felt so hurt, but she had never intended to hurt her.

"That's just it with you, Lauren," Avery said, a little irritation coming into her voice in defiance of the tears that were brimming in her eyes. "You never look past you. You didn't see that I needed you, even when I started getting into trouble."

"How was I supposed to know that you were getting into trouble because you needed me? I thought you just liked to party and make Dad angry."

Avery turned away and, once again, Lauren felt ashamed. She just didn't know how to reach out. She hadn't known what Avery needed back when they were kids and she sure as hell didn't know now.

"I'm sorry, Avery. I really am," Lauren said in a quiet, defeated voice. "It's your turn now, Maria."

Lauren was looking down, feeling sorry for the past, and for the future, when Maria spoke up. "Lauren, what do you do with all your money?"

In a heartbeat, Lauren went from feeling sorrow to dismay. But maybe she could answer this one without telling everything. When she looked up, she put on a calm face. "I pay my bills, buy food and clothes. Probably the same thing most people do with their money."

"But you never have enough," Maria said. "You used to always need money because you'd lost your job, but the last time you asked us for money you said that you hadn't lost your job. So why couldn't you pay all your bills?"

"I just have a lot of debt."

Maria narrowed her eyes at Lauren. She wanted more of an answer, but Lauren wasn't going to give any more. "I answered your question," she said.

"Fine," Maria said, giving in.

It was Lauren's turn again, her last question. She looked at Avery. There was more she wanted to ask, but Avery was already so mad at her. So she turned her attention on Maria, and since they were on the subject of the past, she thought about all the times in the past when the family used to gather. She remembered the sullen, dissatisfied look that always seemed embedded on her sister's face. It had never really occurred to her before. She had always thought that look was just because Maria didn't want to be with her and Avery, but maybe that wasn't the reason at all.

"Why aren't you happy?" she asked Maria.

Maria's face registered surprise. "What do you mean?"

"When we used to all get-together, at least the last few times, you seemed very unhappy. And you seem that way here too. You have Hank and the kids, so why aren't you happy?" Lauren said.

"I didn't want to come here."

"No. It's more than that. It's deeper."

Maria stared at Lauren for a long moment, lips pursed. Her eyes pierced into Lauren's, a desperate look in them. She wanted to tell her sisters something, Lauren was sure of that. But then Maria's eyes faded back to a hopeless, indignant stare. She reached for the bottle and took the shot.

Avery looked up when Maria's glass clinked back down on the table. She looked as fragile as a child. She looked at Maria right away. Her lower lip began to tremble as she spoke. "Why did you stop caring about me?"

Maria furrowed her brow and shook her head.

"You left for school and didn't look back," Avery said. "I waited. I expected you to come home for my dance recital, but you didn't. I thought you'd be back for Thanksgiving, but you went to a friend's house instead.

Then, when you did come home at Christmas, you hardly paid attention to me. You brushed me away like I was just a pest."

Tears were dropping from Avery's eyes. She didn't bother to wipe them away. "You were like my mother, the only one I could remember having and then you just stopped caring."

Maria looked stricken and her eyes were moist. This time she didn't reach for the bottle. When she started to speak, her voice was shaky. "I was trying to be a normal kid while I still could. You were only eleven when I left, but I was only nine when Mom died and I had to stop being a kid and act like a mom for you, for Lauren. No one ever stepped in to mother me. I didn't have time for dance lessons or art classes. I didn't get to be rebellious. I didn't get to go to parties. I got to cook dinner, clean the house, and help you with your homework. I just wanted my turn and I wanted to be a big sister, not a stand-in mother."

Maria stopped. Lauren was staring at her and so was Avery. Maria had never expressed these feelings before.

"I never stopped caring. I loved you. I love you now too," Maria said.

Avery's mouth dropped open a little. She started to speak, then stopped, glanced at the ceiling for a second, and started again. "I didn't ever see things from your point of view."

"You were just a kid. I should have come for the recital. I should have made it an easier transition for you." Maria looked down. There was something more, Lauren thought, but Maria wasn't ready to say it.

For a few moments, there was an uncomfortable silence. Unspoken grievances hung in the air. Lauren decided to interrupt the silence. Maria had one question left to ask. When that was over, they could go their separate ways for the night if they wanted. Their obligation to their father would be fulfilled.

"It's your turn, Maria. Last question," Lauren said.

Maria looked at her. “I guess it is.” She turned toward Avery. “But let’s get out of the distant past.

“Avery, that guy who was with you at Dad’s funeral, he wasn’t an escort, was he?”

Avery looked Maria in the eye. She wasn’t crying anymore, but she still looked vulnerable. “No,” she said. “That was Mike.”

Maria nodded. “I thought there was something different about him. *You* were different with him.”

Avery looked confused. “I didn’t even talk to you that day.”

“But I saw you with him,” Maria said. “He had his arm around you.”

“So?” Avery tried to brush it off.

“You never let your dates do that. You don’t want them to touch you.”

“That’s not true,” Avery said defiantly.

“Yes, it is,” Lauren interjected. “You pretend to be cozy with them, but you only let them hold your hand. Nothing else.”

Avery was shaking her head in argument but seemed at a loss for words to back it up.

“You like Mike,” Maria said. “You should let him be more than just a neighbor.”

“And he’s good-looking too,” Lauren added.

“No,” Avery said, her head still moving side to side. “I don’t want him to be more than just a neighbor. I don’t like him that way. He’s just a good friend.”

Maria persisted. “It looked like he wants to be more than a friend.”

“I don’t care what he wants, or how many times he asks. I only brought him with me to the funeral because it was a weak moment.”

“So he does want to be more and he’s asked you out a number of times.” Maria tilted her head to the side a little, regarding Avery. “You could have gone to the funeral alone, ya know.”

At those words, sudden fear took over Avery's face. "No," she spat out. "I couldn't."

"Why not? Lauren was alone. Lauren comes to everything alone."

"Thanks," Lauren said with exasperation. "It's nice of you to notice."

Maria cast an annoyed glance at her to let her know that her feelings were not the ones that mattered at the moment.

"I just can't! Question time is over!" Avery jumped up from the table and stomped off to her room.

Lauren woke up with a start. It was the second time she had awakened and it was only three in the morning. It had taken her over an hour to get back to sleep the first time. Though she was tired, she knew she would never be able to go back to sleep again. Giving a sigh, she sat up in bed and stretched. Inside Lauren's head, a little voice of anger screamed out. *Is it too damn much to ask for a decent night's sleep!* She pushed the anger away. What good would it do? This was par for the course in her life now, sleeping poorly and feeling like shit. A full night's sleep was a rare joy. The doctors had told her it would be this way.

Stepping out of bed, Lauren grabbed her bathrobe and tip-toed to the kitchen to start the coffee maker and wait for the sun. As she entered the kitchen, she noticed light twinkling in from the back door and went to see what it was. When she looked out the window she saw that the Christmas lights around the umbrella were turned on, and sitting in one of the chairs by the table was Maria.

Maria was slumped over, asleep in the chair. The bottle of Crown Royal was on her lap and one of the shot glasses was on the table. It appeared she had drunk herself to sleep. And once again Lauren had to wonder what was driving Maria to such odd behavior. The game had shed no light on that, really. Maria had only answered one question and that was a question about the past.

Lauren shook her head, turned on the kitchen light, and went to the coffee maker. When it was ready, she took her cup and sat down at the table with it, glancing occasionally at her sister on the other side of the windowed door. *What could be going on in Maria's perfect life to drive her to smoke again and drink herself into a stupor?*

A short while later, Lauren moved to the living room and began reading an outdated magazine that she found in the stack of board games. She was in the middle of an article on nutrition when she heard a shrill scream ring out through the pre-dawn silence.

Chapter 23

Avery

Avery was in a strange place. It was cold and dark. The floor beneath her was hard, and shards of glass were digging into her flesh. The smell of liquor lingered in the air. Her head throbbed, but when she tried to reach a hand to it she found that she couldn't move. *Was she tied up?* No, she just couldn't move. *What the hell was going on?* She tried to yell for help, but her voice was a raspy whisper. No one was going to hear her. Then a form came into view above her. It moved closer, inching along, then it split into two … then three.

Avery opened her mouth, desperate to make a sound. This time her voice obeyed.

As the scream ripped from her throat, Avery flew up in bed. Her breath came in short, fast bursts. She searched the darkened room with her eyes. She saw the wicker dresser and the familiar chair in the corner. She was in her room at the lake house. Everything was okay. It had been a dream.

Avery looked at the clock on the nightstand. It read five oh three. She should go back to sleep, she thought, falling back onto the pillow. She laid there for a few minutes, but couldn't even close her eyes. How could she sleep again when her heart was still racing? She needed the hot chocolate. That would calm her down.

She got out of bed, put on a bathrobe, and padded down the hall. She was surprised, when she reached the end of the hall, to see the lights were already on in the kitchen and living room. The smell of coffee wafted in the air. As she walked into the living room, Lauren looked up at her from the couch.

"Bad dream?" Lauren asked.

Avery stared at her.

"I heard you scream."

"How do you know it was me?" Avery tried to be casual.

"Because Maria is asleep on the deck."

Avery gave her a skeptical look and began to walk toward the back door. "On the deck?" she said. When she got to the door, she looked out the window. Sure enough, Maria was sleeping in one of the chairs.

A moment later Lauren was behind Avery, looking out at their sister. "What do you think is going on with her?" Lauren asked.

Avery shook her head, looking at the bottle in Maria's lap. "I don't know."

"She was awful secretive last night. It's hard to imagine why."

"No, it isn't." Avery held secrets that she told no one. Things happened sometimes—dark, ugly things. Things you didn't want anyone to know about. Avery's mind snapped back to the images of her nightmare; the dark figures, the fear. She turned to Lauren, looked her in the eyes. "You're not exactly an open book yourself these days."

For a few seconds, Lauren didn't move or say a thing. Then she stepped away from Avery, went to the coffee maker and filled her cup. "I guess that's what Dad is trying to point out to us with all of this."

There was sadness in Lauren's voice and, Avery thought, a hint of longing.

"Wanna tell me yours?" Avery asked.

Lauren's forehead wrinkled. "My what?"

"Your secret."

Lauren looked down, stirred her coffee and stared into her cup for a long moment. "There's nothing to tell."

Avery nodded. She was not surprised. She didn't want to reveal her secret either. "Right," she said, casting a glance at the coffee pot that was already half empty. "You're up awful early."

Lauren didn't respond. She moved to the table and Avery went to the cupboard to get the hot chocolate. She put a cup of water into the microwave and when it beeped, she emptied the hot chocolate packet into the cup of hot water. Pulling a spoon out of the drawer, she stirred the mixture and carried the cup to the table to join Lauren.

After a moment of silence, Lauren looked up and said, "I really didn't know that you wanted my help back when we were kids. I know I should have. I'm sorry." Lauren's eyes were full of shame and that caused a stab of regret to Avery's heart.

Avery had been angry about this for years. She had heaped blame on both of her sisters for the bad things that had happened in her life. They were supposed to replace her mother, even though she'd never asked them to. They were supposed to give her what she needed, be there for her, keep her on the straight and narrow, even though they were just kids too.

The blame that didn't get assigned to her sisters was given to her father. Avery had never taken any of it on herself, never been willing to think of her choices as solely her own. She didn't want to. How did you live with that much anger directed toward yourself? The fear was more than enough. She'd needed someone else to take the anger. But when she'd confronted Lauren and Maria with her anger the night before, their answers didn't affect her the way she'd thought they would. She was sure she'd feel satisfaction at that moment, but she hadn't. It really all came down to the simple fact that they were just kids then too. And that was something she hadn't considered. They had made choices that hurt her, but they hadn't meant to cause pain. They had been hurting as well. They had been missing a mother, just as she had. She'd never thought about their pain or what they were missing. She had expected too much, been unfair. So where did all her anger go now? She wasn't sure, but she knew it shouldn't all go to her sisters.

"No. You weren't my mother. You were a kid too. I expected too much."

"I could have done more. I could have helped."

"Yeah, and I could have asked for help. I didn't. I wanted you to know what I needed. I thought that you should and I was mad when you didn't. I never looked at it from your point of view. I was wrong to expect so much. I was wrong to never ask for what I needed." Avery looked down, shame filling her heart. "I was wrong to try to get your attention by acting out." Tears began to burn her eyes as she thought about the choices she'd made in years past. Those choices had been a desperate attempt to get her sisters to focus on her … at first, they had. Then, as time passed and Maria and Lauren still weren't stepping in, it was anger that drove Avery's choices; anger that had burned hot inside of her like an unquenchable fire, anger that took her to dark places and changed her life forever.

Avery blinked back the tears and composed herself. She wasn't ready to spill all her troubles, not yet.

For several minutes she and Lauren sat together in silence. Avery drank her hot chocolate and Lauren her coffee. When their cups were empty Avery asked, "Are you going to try and get some more sleep?"

"Are you?"

"Yeah," Avery said. Then she gave a worried glance toward the back door. "But don't you think we should help her inside first? I don't want to leave her out there."

Lauren followed Avery's glance. "Yeah, let's go get her."

The two of them got up from the table and went to the back door. Lauren opened it and, looking out into the early morning darkness, Avery felt her heart speed up. She went toward the opening, but when she got there, her feet suddenly felt like lead weights. *I need to do this. I can't leave my sister out there asleep in a chair.* Inside, Avery was screaming at herself, but her feet refused to obey.

Lauren looked at her with eyebrows knit together. “You okay?”

Avery nodded even though her stomach had begun to churn. She looked at Lauren—she was not alone—and summoned all her courage. Forcing her feet to go, she moved across the threshold and made it to Maria. She focused on the string of Christmas lights twinkling above them and tried not to look beyond the deck. She didn’t want to gaze into the darkness.

While Avery stood there feeling the paralyzing fear, Lauren picked up the bottle from Maria’s lap, tested its weight, and moved it to the table.

“She’s gonna feel this when she wakes up,” Lauren said. “Okay, you get her from the left side and I’ll take the right.”

Avery didn’t move.

“Hey!” Lauren called to her. “I can’t lift her alone.”

Avery looked at Lauren with wide eyes, wordlessly begging for help. She couldn’t be out here like this. The dark was filled with monsters. They’d come for her. They had before.

Lauren’s expression softened. She moved around Maria’s legs and came face to face with Avery. Putting her hands on Avery’s shoulders, Lauren said, “It’s alright, Ave. I’m here with you.” Then she pulled Avery close and held her for a moment. Lauren didn’t ask, *what the hell is wrong with you?* But that’s what Avery would have done if their places had been reversed. Lauren didn’t ask anything at all. She just held Avery until the trembling stopped, trembling Avery hadn’t noticed until she was in her sister’s embrace.

This was not the Lauren that Avery used to know, the one that only thought of herself. And Avery realized just how much Lauren had meant it when she said she was sorry. For a second Avery thought about telling Lauren her secret, letting it all spill out. But the moment was gone in a split second when Maria fell forward, almost tumbling out of the chair.

"Hank … nooo," Maria mumbled as she went. Lauren let go of Avery and leaped to the rescue, catching Maria before she left the chair.

"You were right. It might be dangerous to leave her here," Lauren said. "Can you help me now?"

Avery was feeling stronger. She wasn't looking at the darkness now. She nodded and bent to put Maria's left arm around her neck. Lauren followed suit with Maria's right arm and they lifted her up. Maria's head fell to the side and expelled a pungent breath in Avery's face. Yuck! Avery thought, remembering all the times she'd drank too much. It was a lot less appealing from this perspective.

Maria was not fully awake and she was totally unaware of her surroundings, but she protested the movement. "Caaan't … waaalk … Hank, pleeease." Then she started coughing and gagging.

Lauren looked at Avery. "Get her to the grass!"

They moved in unison and got to the grass just in time for Maria to vomit. Lauren and Avery each held back one side of Maria's head of curls. "Well, at least she did it out here. Let's get her to bed and hope it doesn't happen again," Lauren said.

Avery nodded again and they moved back up the two steps of the deck and into the house.

"Why … Hank?" Maria slurred as they got her to her room and laid her down on the bed. Avery gave Lauren a questioning look and Lauren shrugged. Then Lauren took Maria's shoes off and arranged the pillow under her head.

When Maria was settled, Avery and Lauren left her room and started toward their own. Avery stopped Lauren with a hand to her arm. Lauren turned and looked at her. "Thanks," Avery said, then turned and went into her room.

Chapter 24

Lauren

Lauren didn't expect much when she returned to bed, but to her surprise, she was able to fall asleep again. Of course, it only lasted for about an hour. She was up again before seven. Groggily she shuffled into the bathroom, tripping twice and almost falling. When she got to the sink, she opened the medicine cabinet and retrieved her pills. After swallowing them, Lauren got into the shower.

By twenty after seven, she was standing on the back deck, showered, dressed, and holding a cup of coffee in her right hand. The sun was rising in the sky and slowly burning off a slight fog that seemed to only hover over the lake by that point. Birds were chirping and foraging in the grass and ducks were gliding through what remained of the fog. Despite feeling somewhat under the weather from her poor sleep and alcohol consumption, Lauren smiled at the beauty of the morning. It was like a gift that she'd never unwrapped before her medical issues began. Back then she was always up late painting. She never got up early enough to see the world like this. And, as much as she hated the toll this illness was taking on her, she was still trying hard to find every silver lining she could. If she didn't, the loss would overtake her, rule her life. That was the last thing she wanted. She was going to hold on to every good thing she could for as long as possible.

When her coffee cup was empty, Lauren sat it down on the patio table next to the shot glass and bottle of Crown Royal that were still there. Then she walked down toward the lake, stumbling a couple of times as she went. *Damn these slow feet!* She stood at the edge of the retaining wall and, bending slowly she picked up a pebble from the ground and attempted to skip it along the surface of the water, but instead, it just plunked into the water and sank. Lauren frowned at the ripples that remained on the water's surface. She picked up another pebble and gave it a gentle toss, but the result was the same.

"You've got to throw from the side more," came a voice from behind. A grin sneaked onto Lauren's face. She waited to turn around until it was contained.

"Excuse me?" she asked as she turned to face Blake, her grin replaced by a questioning glance.

"You're trying to skip the rock, right? You need to throw from the side more."

Lauren raised an eyebrow at him and picked up another pebble, attempting to do as he suggested. It was not as easy as he made it sound. The stone sank again. *If only I could do this with my left hand.* But that wasn't possible.

Blake moved closer to the water, picked up a rock and tossed it at the surface of the water with perfect precision. The pebble skipped three times before sinking.

Lauren rolled her eyes at him. "Show off."

"It's not that hard," he said.

Maybe not for you!

Blake moved up behind Lauren and reached his hands around her on either side, causing her skin to tingle. Her pulse sped up as he pushed another stone into her hand.

"Here, I'll show you," he said, taking her right hand into his and moving it across the front of her body. For a moment her eyes closed as she inhaled the light scent of cologne on him. Then, in a perfect, smooth motion, he glided her hand till it was straight out in front of her and whispered into her ear, "Open your hand," at just the right moment. His breath danced across her skin. She obeyed his command and watched as the stone skipped across the water twice and then fell below the surface of the lake.

Blake was still touching Lauren's hand as she turned around to face him. He was so close she had to take a step back. His closeness caused her cheeks to blush, but she didn't look down or try to hide how she was feeling. Life was short and things could change at any time, opportunities could slip away or become meaningless. Lauren knew that now. She had a short time to be here and explore these feelings. She was going to make the most of that time. "I think I'd like to kiss you," she said.

He was surprised. Lauren could see that in the look on his face. "We don't even know each other," he said.

"I'd be happy to get to know you better, but what harm will it do to start with a kiss?"

A smile inched across his face. "You're very forward, aren't you?"

"I wasn't always, but life is short. Besides, it isn't like I'm asking you to take me to bed."

His eyebrows shot up in response, but he moved in, wrapping his arms around her, and gently kissed her lips. "At this rate," he said, "I'll expect that in a day or so."

Lauren was still savoring the feel of his lips on hers. It had been a long time since she'd been kissed. His lips were warm and softer than she expected. And his touch caused butterflies to dance in her stomach. She definitely wanted to try that again. She brought her arms up and grabbed both his shoulders, enjoying the feel of hard muscles under her palms, and pulled him back to her lips again. This time Lauren took the kiss a little deeper, drew it out longer. Then she let go of him, pulled away, and turning to leave said, "You never know."

Lauren hoped she was leaving Blake completely flabbergasted and wanting more, though she had never in her life behaved that way with a man. Somehow being here had brought her a boldness she never knew she could possess. Maybe it was seeing that video of her mom, and realizing how limited her time might be. Maybe it was being here with her sisters and finding out that very little of what she had believed to be true actually was. She didn't know them at all anymore and they didn't know her. She had no reason to keep playing the role she always had in the past.

Chapter 25

Maria

When Maria woke from the alcohol-induced slumber, the first thing she noticed was the dry stickiness in her mouth. Her tongue seemed to be almost cemented to the roof of her mouth and the taste on it made her grimace. She was pretty sure the Crown Royal hadn't left that flavor. When she cracked open her eyes, the light streaming in from the window pierced them like knives. She reached a hand to her head as it exploded in pain. Even the gentle whir of the ceiling fan seemed loud. It had been a long time since she had felt like this, and the instances were few—all long ago.

She knew this would be the result when she chose to keep drinking the night before. As bad as it felt, it wasn't a surprise. She just hadn't cared. After the emotional ordeal with her sisters, she needed the escape, even if for just a little while.

Maria had revealed very little to Lauren and Avery, but the answers to all their questions had swum in her head. Without the kids to think about or even the dog to care for, the flood of emotion was overwhelming. There was no distraction from the pain, nothing to focus on that forced her to be strong. So she had been weak. And now she was paying the price.

Slowly Maria sat up in bed. She glanced at the clock on the nightstand. It was 10:30. Sleeping so late was another thing she didn't do in her regular life. She moved her legs to the edge of the bed and carefully got up, trying not to make any fast movements that would add to her pain. She went to the door, about to put on her robe when she realized that she was still dressed in yesterday's clothes.

In all honesty, she didn't even know how she had gotten to bed. The last place she remembered being was the deck.

Throwing the bathrobe over her shoulder, Maria grabbed her toiletry bag and headed down the hall to the bathroom, taking each step with care. She arrived at the door to find it locked and the shower already running. *Great! Just perfect.* As she started to leave the door, she almost ran into Lauren, who looked perfect and even perkier than usual.

Lauren gave a little gasp as she looked at Maria. "Oh, wow," were the words that came out of Lauren's mouth.

Maria grunted in answer. She didn't want to talk if she could help it.

Lauren looked her over. "I think Avery just got started in there. She slept late too. Why don't you use my bathroom? Just let me pick a couple of things up first."

Maria tried to nod. Pain seared through her head with every movement.

Lauren went into her room and Maria could hear her moving some things around. Then she returned to the hallway saying, "Okay, go on in."

Maria gave another short grunt that was meant as a thank you and went into Lauren's room. It was still a mess. Clothes were strewn about all over. Lauren always had been a slob. The thing that was odd was that all her painting supplies were picked up and stashed away. Lauren really didn't want anyone to see what she was working on.

For a brief moment, Maria was curious and the thought occurred to her to snoop and try to see Lauren's latest painting. But she was in no condition for that. She moved into the bathroom and turned on the shower. Catching sight of herself in the mirror, she could see why Lauren had gasped at her appearance. Her mop of chestnut curls was matted with sweat and sticking out in all directions. Her face was pale and deep, dark circles were entrenched under her eyes. She looked worse than the bag lady she saw on the street every day. Turning from the mirror, she stripped off her day-old outfit and stepped carefully into the steaming water. A sigh of relief escaped her lips as the water pelted down on her skin.

Maria stood against the wall of the shower, letting the water run over her until it started to get cold. It made her feel a little bit more human. When she got out, she decided that some aspirin would be a good idea and looked to see if Lauren had any in her medicine cabinet. She saw several prescription pill bottles inside the cabinet. Maria turned each one so she could read the label. Her heart sank as she looked at them. She was not surprised by what she saw—it confirmed what she already suspected. But seeing the proof, knowing it was true, was still a heart-wrenching blow.

Maria lowered herself onto the toilet lid and sat for a moment. She thought about the signs she'd seen in Lauren since arriving here and tried to remember if they had been there before. The truth was, she just didn't know. She hadn't been watching before, hadn't tried to see. How long, Maria wondered, had Lauren known herself?

Maria lifted a hand to her head. It was pounding like a drum beat in there and she'd found no aspirin in this bathroom. She stood up, wrapped her hair in a towel and put on her bathrobe. Bending down to the floor, she gathered her clothes. She left the bathroom and went back to her own room to get dressed and take the medicine that would help her head.

After pulling on her clothes, Maria headed down the hall to the kitchen and poured a cup of coffee from the half-full pot that sat on the counter. The invigorating smell of the brew helped her head a little. Fresh air might help even more, Maria thought and headed out the back door to sit on the deck.

Still on the table were the reminders of the previous night; the bottle of Crown Royal and the shot glass. Maria groaned, pushed them aside, and sat down where she could face the lake. Avery was sitting down on the dock, a blue striped towel beneath her. Maria might have thought her sister was enjoying a beautiful day at the lake if it had not been for the ridged way Avery sat. She was not there to enjoy the blue skies and birdsong. Maria doubted her sister even noticed them. She watched as Avery slowly slipped off her flip-flops and set them aside, then glanced around like a rabbit looking for predators.

Maria took a long sip from her coffee and continued to watch as Avery inched the toes of one foot toward the rippling surface of the lake. *What could be so hard about putting her feet in the water?* Avery got her toes just to the water, then pulled back quickly and held her knees to her chest like a frightened child.

Maria thought about the night before, how vulnerable Avery had been. It had been a pretty raw and unnerving experience for all of them, Maria was sure, but Avery had been the one to begin the process of opening old wounds, allowing her sisters to see a side of her that hadn't come out since childhood. And, watching her now, Maria realized what she'd seen the night before was more the "real Avery" than what she usually saw. Avery tried to be what she'd once been, a headstrong, willful spitfire. But, even though that part of her still existed, this fearful, vulnerable persona was the one that most ruled her life now, strangling away what was left of the strong one.

Maria drank down the remainder of her coffee, then left her mug on the table and headed down toward the dock. Avery jumped and threw a hand over her heart, startled when Maria stepped up behind her.

"Mind if I join you?" Maria asked.

Avery's body immediately relaxed from its former rigid state. She was still pretending, playing the part. Shaking her head, Avery scooted over to make room for Maria on the towel. For a few moments, they sat together in silence.

"It's a pretty day," Maria said, breaking through the quiet.

"Hum? ... Oh, yeah." Avery said. She looked over at Maria and studied her. "You look better today than I thought you would."

"You saw me last night, I take it."

"Yup. You were really drunk. Lauren and I helped you get to bed."

"I was wondering how I got there."

"You threw up in the grass."

"Oh, I'm sorry about that." Well, that explained the taste in her mouth when she woke up.

Maria slipped off her sandals and dipped her feet in the water. Avery watched her and slowly, tentatively followed. Maria noted a look of satisfaction, pride almost, cross her sister's face. How long had Avery been trying to do this small thing?

"Lauren let me use her bathroom to shower, but when I came out I didn't see her. Do you know where she is?" Maria asked.

"I think she went on a bike ride with our neighbor … She likes him, you know."

"You mean … romantically?"

"Yeah. She blushes and gets giddy when she talks to him."

Maria was a little surprised, but also happy for Lauren. She might not get any more chances to be loved that way. Maria knew that for sure now. Then again, it was doubtful Lauren had told this guy her secret. Who knew what would happen when and if she did.

"It's been a long time since Lauren had that kind of interest in anyone as far as I know."

"Yeah, but it's not like she's gonna have a real relationship with him. I mean we'll be here for less than a week and a half now."

"True, but you never know."

"I guess," Avery said. She swished her feet in the water and a smile played at her lips. A moment later that smile turned to a frown. "Do you know the grocery guy's name?"

"You mean Evan?"

Avery's brow knit together in a look of frustration. "You've talked to him?"

"A little, why?"

"It's nothing," she answered in an irritated tone, her body going rigid again. A few seconds later she pulled her feet out of the water, put on her flip-flops, and got up. "You can bring my towel back in when you're done with it," she said and headed for the back door.

Maria wasn't sure what had set Avery off, but one thing certainly hadn't changed; when Avery got upset, she stomped off to find solitude.

Maria stayed by the lake for a while, allowing the peacefulness of nature to surround her while she waited for the aspirin she'd taken to quiet the drumbeat in her head. A short while later, she saw Lauren return and put the bike back in the shed, looking like a teenager who had succeeded in sneaking out to a party. Maria stayed quiet and pretended not to notice her sister. She was, however, going to have to get a look at this neighbor.

When Maria finally went inside, she spent the rest of the day in her room recovering from the previous night. Her sisters also seemed content to do their own thing. There were no deliveries that day and no messages.

Chapter 26

Lauren

Day six at the lake house started great for Lauren. She slept better than she had in days and wasn't dragging too much. When she got out of the shower, she realized that her left hand was more under her control than usual. She decided to wait on breakfast for a while and try to paint while things were good. It was the first time in months she had actually been reasonably happy with her work, and all things considered, that was something to celebrate.

It wasn't like she didn't ever have good moments at home. It was just that she was almost always working when they came. And if she wasn't working, she was trying to get a little sleep or heading to an appointment. Working two jobs and having a regular schedule of doctor's appointments made it difficult to make good use of her very fleeting good times. But at the lake house, for the two weeks allotted, there was no work and no appointments. And if the time she'd spent there so far had taught her anything, it was to use her good moments to her advantage as much as her father's requests allowed. That meant painting, and when she wasn't doing that, spending time with Blake.

When Lauren's hand stopped obeying her and her feet became wobbly, she decided to go to the kitchen for breakfast. When she got there, Maria was at the table with a crossword puzzle. She looked up at Lauren and smiled. "Good morning," she said looking at her watch as if to make sure it was still morning.

Lauren smiled back and returned the greeting. She pulled a bowl out of the cabinet and filled it with cereal. Then she poured milk over it and sat down next to Maria. "Where's Avery?" she asked.

"She's sitting out on the deck."

Lauren nodded and began to eat her cereal. Then Maria spoke up again. "We got another delivery from the grocery store this morning."

Lauren looked up from her bowl. "There was a note, I take it."

"There was." Maria scribbled some letters into her crossword. "I hope you packed some good walking shoes. It looks like we're going hiking."

Lauren's good mood faded a little and she let out a sigh. She wondered if her father hadn't planned this little outing with her in mind. It was going to be very hard to seem okay in front of her sisters if she had to go hiking. Uneven surfaces and tripping hazards were not her friends when it came to keeping her condition a secret.

Maria was looking at Lauren, but instead of curiosity, Lauren saw what looked like sympathy on her sister's face. Lauren scrunched up her face in response. "You okay?" she asked.

Maria nodded, but the look she was giving Lauren still made her feel like a lost puppy in need of a home. She looked away. Maybe it was something she'd said during the truth game. But she couldn't think of anything she'd said that should attract this kind of sympathy. Avery was the one who had done that.

Lauren tried to focus on her breakfast, eating and not looking up at her sister. When she was done, she carefully made her way to the sink and rinsed her bowl. When she started toward the back door, Maria spoke up again, "Dad's note calls for us to leave here with a picnic lunch. And he was very specific about us eating that lunch after we walk for about an hour. There's a place where he wants us to stop. He gave a description in the note. So I guess we'll need to leave here sometime in the next hour or so. Avery and I ate breakfast a lot earlier than you. We'll be getting hungry soon."

"That's fine," Lauren said as she opened the back door and walked out into the sunlight, closing the door behind her. She looked up at the sky that was deep blue with only a few fluffy, white clouds floating along. The lake water was lapping at the retaining wall, making little splashing sounds, and sunlight glistened off its surface. The birds were chattering and singing in the tree branches. Lauren smiled. Even if she had to go hiking, she was going to enjoy this day to its fullest. Maybe it would be a good thing if she couldn't keep her secret anymore. She'd already thought about telling her sisters. The video of her mother had served to get her thinking in that direction. But for some reason, when the opportunity was clearly there during the truth game, she hadn't been able to do it. The words had dried up on her tongue. Maybe it would be easier if they figured it out on their own.

Lauren glanced to her right. Avery was sitting in one of the chairs looking out at the lake through a pair of sunglasses. She looked up at Lauren. "It's a pretty day," Lauren said.

Avery nodded, then looked back at the water. Tension was clearly visible on her face even with the dark glasses on. Lauren wondered if she was worried about the hike they were going to take or if it was because Avery was still trying to muster up the courage to dangle her feet in the water without anyone sitting next to her.

Lauren thought for a moment about the past, when Avery had been an incorrigible party girl without a care in the world. At least she had seemed to be. Then, at some point in time, she had begun to pretend to be that person, but in reality, had become a hermit who passed escorts off as boyfriends to her own family. Something had happened, and Avery wanted it kept a secret. Lauren thought back to two nights before, when she and Avery had found Maria asleep on the deck. Avery had opened a door to her that night. She'd offered to share her secret if Lauren would tell hers. A part of Lauren wished she'd had the courage to walk through that door with her sister. But she was unable to say the words.

Allowing her gaze to leave her sister, she looked at the row of trees to the left of the yard. Smiling, she walked off the deck and headed toward the row of trees. She moved past them and looked around. Blake was inside his house. She could see him through an open window. He was painting one of the bedrooms. There was music playing—she could hear that now. She watched for a minute as his strong arms went up and down with the paint roller. He wasn't wearing a shirt. His muscles rippled under a sheen of sweat.

A few seconds later, Lauren realized her mouth was hanging open. She closed it without taking her eyes off Blake. She didn't have much time, but she was going to spend whatever time she could with him.

Hurrying back past the trees, she went into the house and straight to the refrigerator. She pulled out a can of soda and started back for the door. Maria glanced up from her crossword and watched, but didn't say a thing as Lauren rushed back outside.

Without even looking at Avery again, Lauren started back to the tree line. When she tripped on a tree root and had to catch herself, she slowed her pace and began to walk more carefully.

She went to Blake's front door and rang the bell. There was no answer. She knocked. No answer. He probably couldn't hear over the music. She checked the knob and found the door unlocked. She felt her cheeks blush as she opened the door and went in uninvited. She hadn't even done anything like that as a teenager. She had cared little about teenage rebellion, unlike Avery. Lauren was always too wrapped up in her art to think about much else. Some of her art class friends had used spray paint to act out their rebellion, but Lauren had always preferred her canvas and brush.

Lauren stepped into Blake's house and called out to him. "Blake? I brought you something." He didn't respond. She walked through the living room and kitchen and headed for one of the bedrooms at the back of the house where she'd seen him through the window, following the sound of the music.

When she reached the door, she peeked in and saw Blake standing on a ladder, painting the top of the back wall. He was wearing an old pair of khaki cargo shorts that were speckled with the pale blue paint he was using on the wall. Paint brushes and other tools were sticking out of the pockets. His hair was ruffled and sweaty and Lauren couldn't look away from him. For a moment she wished she'd used her good time that morning to spend with Blake instead of painting.

Lauren stood there staring at Blake on the ladder until her hand lost hold of the soda can and it fell to the floor with a loud thud.

"What the hell?!" Blake shouted, almost toppling off the ladder.

"It's okay. It's just me," Lauren said scooping up the fallen soda can and moving into the room where Blake could see her.

He looked at her for a long moment and she wasn't sure how he was feeling about her being there. "I don't suppose anyone ever told you that it isn't nice to sneak up on someone, especially when they're on a ladder. Not to mention the whole breaking and entering thing."

Lauren looked up at him sheepishly. "I didn't mean to startle you. You didn't hear me knock or ring the bell and the door was unlocked. I saw through the window that you were painting in here and I wanted to bring you a cold drink." Lauren held out the can. "You should probably wait to open it now though."

A smile spread across Blake's face. He shook his head. "I just never know what to expect from you, Lauren." He stepped down from the ladder. "Keeps things interesting. How about we go to the kitchen and get some lemonade?"

Lauren smiled her agreement and took hold of Blake's paint flecked hand as he got to her. He led her into the kitchen and took the soda can she was holding. He placed it in the refrigerator and took out a jug of lemonade. Sitting it, along with two glasses, on the small round table that stood in the center of the room, he motioned for Lauren to sit down.

She sat and jammed her hands under the table as she began to feel the trembling begin. Blake poured lemonade in both glasses and sat down. "I wasn't planning on a break until lunch, but it is nice to sit down."

"I wish I could bring you lunch today too, but I have to go hiking with my sisters."

"You have to?"

"Well if you know how to say no to a dead man, let me know. So far none of us can do it." Lauren raised her glass with her right hand and took a sip.

"I'm glad you can't say no to him. After all, that's the reason I met you."

Lauren nodded. "I'm glad of that too. And it's a nice day for a hike, I guess."

Blake squinted his eyes at the sunlit window. "Is it? I haven't been out there today."

"It's hot, but there's a light breeze and the sun is shining brightly."

"I can see the sun is bright. At least when you're hiking, you'll have the shade of the trees to keep you from getting too hot."

Lauren nodded. "I enjoyed our bike ride yesterday." She thought about how free she'd felt riding that bike. Somehow turning the pedals was far easier for her than walking. She could just move her legs in circles. She didn't stumble or miss steps. And the feeling of freedom she experienced was almost as good as being a kid again.

Lauren's smile faded when she noticed Blake's gaze. She'd made the mistake of putting her hands on the table, both of them, and he was staring at them. She jerked them off the table and shoved them in her lap, looking down so he wouldn't see the fear in her eyes.

It felt like eons went by in silence before Lauren heard the scrape of Blake's chair on the linoleum floor. She looked up as he was bending down in front of her. "It's okay. It's not the first time I noticed," he said.

All she could do was stare at him. Tears were welling in her eyes and she didn't know how to stop them.

"I know what this is," he said.

She tried to read how he felt about it as tears snaked down her cheeks. Her feelings fell somewhere between a punch in the gut and relief. She wondered if this is how it would feel when her sisters knew the truth or if this was entirely different.

"My step-father had it," Blake said tenderly. "You don't need to hide it from me."

Lauren still couldn't speak. She had no idea what to say, but for some reason, tears continued to fall from her eyes. It was as if she'd been saving them up for a really long time. There had only been one other person in Lauren's life that knew about her condition other than her doctors and that had been her father. Now he was gone and maybe she needed someone to share the burden of this knowledge with her, even if it was someone that would only be temporary in her life.

As Lauren remained silent, Blake leaned forward and began to wipe the tears from her cheeks with his thumb. She stared into his Caribbean blue eyes with amazement. She was feeling things for this man that shouldn't be possible after such a short time. But his compassion was drawing her heart in fast. She wrapped her arms around him and sagged onto his shoulder, letting all the tears fall.

The next thing Lauren knew, Blake was kissing her. His lips were warm on hers and his hands were gentle on her back as he held her close. His tongue moved between her lips and began to tangle with hers—then the doorbell blared.

"Lauren! Are you in there?" came Maria's voice. "Lauren? Did you forget about Dad's note?"

Lauren pulled back slowly and looked into Blake's eyes one more time. "I guess I have to go hiking now."

He nodded. "I guess I should get back to work."
Lauren smiled at him as she slowly got up from her chair and walked to the door. "See ya later," she said as she opened the door and walked out. Her smile didn't even fade when she saw the irritation on her sister's face.

Chapter 27

Avery

Avery glanced in the mirror one last time and tucked a couple of loose tendrils of blond hair into her neat French braid. She could see the anxiety in the caramel brown eyes staring back at her. "There's nothing to be afraid of," she told herself. But that did nothing to settle her nerves. Her stomach felt like it was filled with a dozen fluttering butterflies. She rubbed a hand over it. "What are you trying to do to me, Dad? I'm not ready for this," she whispered, wishing he could answer her. She missed him more than she could have ever imagined possible. She hadn't realized it when he was alive, but he'd been her anchor. The one person in her life she could hold onto, talk to. She'd long since pushed everyone else out and built a wall around herself to keep anyone new from getting too close. Mike had gotten closer than anyone else, but she still kept him at arm's length.

She thought about the previous Christmas when she'd showed up at her father's house, at her appointed time, with yet another "date."

Arthur had managed to get her alone in the kitchen and cornered her asking, "Who is this man, Avery?"

"Josh. He's my date." Avery had shrugged her shoulders and tried to sound as casual as she could, though the question had made her profoundly uncomfortable.

"This man is not your boyfriend. Don't you think I can see that?"

"I didn't say he was. He's just a date."

"No, he isn't. You don't know this man." He shook his head, sadness in his eyes. "For years I watched you run wild and nothing I did ever seemed to help. Now you show up with all these strange men. I don't know why you are doing this … Do you?"

For a few long moments Avery had struggled for an answer to give her father—she certainly couldn't tell him who the men really were. Then Josh, her "date," walked in and interrupted the discussion. Avery was saved from having to give an answer.

Coming back to the moment, Avery felt more shame than ever before. She was ashamed of lying to her family for so long. She was ashamed of using an escort service for family events. She was ashamed of the paralyzing fear she couldn't overcome. And she was ashamed of not telling her father the truth. She should have. He would have held her, let her cry on his shoulder. He would have given her the love and support that she so desperately needed. She knew even then that he would. But she hadn't been able to tell him. The words got stuck in her throat. She wanted love and support, but the truth was too terrible to tell anyone, even her father. She didn't know how to talk about it. She tried very hard not to even think about it. But no matter how hard she worked at pushing it from her mind, it forced its way back—like a rabid dog, it held onto her. It came back in her dreams and it haunted her every time she tried to venture out from home.

But now she felt she had no choice. This trip with her sisters, doing all the things her father asked of them with his notes, wasn't just about getting the inheritance money. It was about honoring her father's last wishes.

Avery's last few years with him had been filled with dishonesty. He'd reached out, and she'd turned away. She realized now that she had robbed both of them of the relationship they could have had. She could never get that time back; never change the choices she'd made. But she could do what he asked of her now and maybe somehow he'd know. Even if he didn't, she would.

Chapter 28

Maria

Maria shifted the backpack she was carrying from one shoulder to the other while she waited for Lauren to come out of the neighbor's house. The pack held a blanket and the food she and her sisters would have for lunch while they were hiking.

When Lauren breezed out, she was smiling and hardly noticed Maria's scowl. "I'm ready. Let's go," she said. It was so like Lauren to go off and do what she wanted instead of helping to prepare lunch. It was also like her to keep everyone else waiting.

Maria's scowl deepened as they walked together and joined Avery at the edge of their yard. But by the time they walked the short distance up the road and crossed to the other side where the trail led off, her scowl had disappeared. The day was beautiful—blue sky with only puffy white clouds, birds singing in the trees, green leaves and flowers everywhere. So what if Lauren kept them waiting while she spent time with a man she liked. It was a small thing. And Maria *was* glad to see her sister so happy.

As they moved past some towering oaks, a squirrel ran out and crossed the path in front of them. Maria's mind shot to thoughts of Sadie. The golden retriever would love it out here. The kids would too. She missed them all more than words could say. Even their sibling bickering would be welcome at this point.

Maria lurched forward when Lauren—walking ahead of her—tripped on a tree root and stumbled. Catching Lauren's arm, Maria stopped her fall.

Lauren tugged her arm away. "I'm fine," she said.

Avery was on Maria's other side, staying very close. She jumped at every sound. The first couple times Maria had assured her that the sounds were just the movements of small forest animals. "I know that," Avery had replied with annoyance. Avery was angry with her for not playing the role of a surrogate mother long enough in childhood, but now when Maria played that part she was rewarded with irritation. She hoped she could find the right balance.

When they started climbing a hill, Maria moved in closer to Lauren and kept her hands at the ready for a catch. Within a few steps up the hill, Lauren lost her balance and Maria caught her with a hand to her back.

Lauren turned and glared at Maria. "What is your problem?"

"I'm just trying to help. You were about to fall."

"I was fine." Lauren gave her a quizzical look that didn't match the irritation in her voice, then pulled away and moved further ahead. Maria stayed back but kept a close eye on her sister. She didn't want Lauren to know that she'd seen what was in the medicine cabinet. She hoped Lauren would eventually tell her and Avery the truth on her own. That would be best. Still, Maria didn't want Lauren to get hurt. This trail was full of tripping hazards and uneven ground.

After they had walked for just over an hour on the trail, they came to a small clearing with just a single tree in the middle. Maria stopped cold when she saw it. Staring at the tree, her breath almost stopped.

Eyeing her with a sideways glance, Avery asked, "What's wrong?"

Maria didn't respond. She felt frozen.

Lauren stepped close and touched Maria lightly on her shoulder. "What is it?"

"I know this place," she said walking toward the tree. Its trunk leaned to the left a little and, on the right, it had a large lower branch that came out from the trunk almost parallel to the ground, then turned up in a perfect right angle. It looked like an arm bent at the elbow. Maria ran a hand along the branch. "We've been here before."

"We have?" Lauren asked. "When?"

"The summer before mom died. We hiked this trail. Dad saw this tree and wanted to take a picture of the three of us sitting on the branch."

"I don't remember a picture like that," Avery said. "And I remember them all. I used to look at the old photo albums all the time." Maria knew that was true and now she understood the hole her sister had been trying to fill. She felt a pang of regret and sorrow for Avery. The only way she'd ever had to know their mother was through photographs and stories; always begging for the scraps of other people's memories.

Maria turned and looked at her sisters with moisture in her eyes. "He never got the picture."

"Why not?" Lauren asked.

"Because of me," Maria answered. "He didn't choose this spot for our picnic at random. I know why we're here."

Maria frowned at the gnarled old tree in the center of the clearing, touching the bark and then pulling back as if it had burned her. The memory of a day long ago jumped to life in her mind as if it were just yesterday.

"This is the place where I left my childhood behind," Maria said, talking more to the tree, or to herself, than to her sisters standing behind her. "We came here on a hiking trip the weekend after Mom got the test results following her last round of chemotherapy."

Maria stopped, braced her hand on the loathsome tree, and closed her eyes tight. She was holding back a flood of tears. She could see her mother smiling with a yellow bandana tied around her bald head. And she could see her father, aged past his years by the stress of what was to come. Still, he too was smiling. They were looking forward to a wonderful day together and Maria couldn't understand that.

When her emotion was under control, Maria took her hand from the tree and brushed the dirt away. She kept her body turned so that she didn't have to look either sister in the eye. "The treatment had failed. The cancer was still growing and there was nothing more to be done.

"Mom was feeling better that weekend because the chemo was over and she wasn't sick anymore. She wanted to spend some quality family time with us, so we went hiking."

Lauren inched closer to Maria. She motioned to Avery, who was now carrying the backpack. Avery moved to her, and Lauren pulled the blanket out of the backpack and spread it on the ground next to the tree. Lauren and Avery sat down, but Maria stayed on her feet, unable to relax. She turned her back on the lone tree in the clearing and looked out to a spot at the edge of the tree line. She kept talking as her mind slipped back to that day when she was barely nine.

"Come sit here on this branch with your sisters, Maria," Arthur had said as he placed a squirming two-year-old Avery on the branch next to Lauren. "I want to get a picture." Lauren obediently curled her arms around Avery and made room for Maria.

"No," Maria said, folding her arms across her chest. She turned away from Arthur and stomped off to a spot near the tree line.

"Maria! You come here and ...," Arthur's voice, angry at first, stopped dead. Maria turned to see why, but not enough to let him know that she cared. Her mother was moving toward her and her father was setting her sisters both back on the ground. Then he followed her mother and they both moved in behind her.

Eve, Maria's mother, touched her shoulder lightly, but Maria jerked away from her.

"Sweetheart," Eve began, "what's the matter?"

"What's the matter," Maria parroted back her mother's words in a small voice that was little more than an echo. Then she turned to her parents with tears streaking her face. She shook her head in disbelief. "What's the matter?"

Eve reached for Maria, pulling her into a fierce hug. She kissed the top of her daughter's head. "Oh, baby. I know it's hard." Bending down, Eve pulled the bandana off her head and used it to wipe Maria's tears. But seeing her mother's head with only wisps of hair sent a stab of pain through Maria's heart and she began to sob. Eve always wore the yellow one on days she was happy. "It's the color of sunshine," she'd say. It didn't look like sunshine to Maria. To her, all the bandanas were the same color. They were the color of sadness; of death. And Maria would never say it aloud, but she was afraid to have the bandanas touch her. The bad things that were sucking the life from her mother might spread.

Half a second later, Arthur's arms were wrapped around both Maria and Eve. Maria looked up at him. Tears glistened in his eyes too.

"You want me to act like everything is okay," Maria said. "But it's not. How can you expect me to smile for pictures when I know you're dying?"

"Maria," Eve spoke gently. "I understand how you feel. Do you think I'm not angry?" She stopped for a moment allowing Maria time to consider that question. Maria did not answer. "I saw my three beautiful girls born and I thought I would see them grow up, get married, have kids of their own. I'm not going to see any of that."

Arthur broke into sobs and turned away so Lauren and Avery, standing just out of earshot, would not see.

"This isn't the way I thought my life would turn out. But I can't change it. I tried." Eve smoothed a hand over Maria's curls. "Now I have a choice. I can be angry and waste what time I have left, or I can try to enjoy every last second I have with my family." She paused, looking Maria right in the eye. "I choose to savor every last second with you girls."

Eve pulled Maria close again. "I love you so much, darling. And I need you right now." Releasing Maria from her embrace, Eve turned and looked at Lauren and Avery, who were now squatting down studying something on the ground. "Lauren is only six and Avery is only two." Eve looked back at Maria. "I need you to help your father look after them." She glanced at Arthur who was standing just behind Maria, in control of his emotions again. "He's a great

Dad, but raising all three of you on his own is a big job. Promise me you'll help him, Maria. Someday Lauren and Avery will have questions only their big sister can answer … And," Eve gave Maria a piercing look. "I need you to help them remember me."

Maria stared at her mother, her forehead crinkled as a mix of emotions swirled through her. "You're older," Eve said. "You'll remember me the best. Soon their memory of me will fade. Avery will probably not remember me at all. They'll need you to fill in the gaps, to remind them who I was—they'll need you."

Maria looked into her mother's eyes and saw the need. She placed a hand on Eve's cheek. "Who you are," she said without fully understanding why the distinction was so important.

Eve nodded and Maria looked at both of her sisters. She knew her mother's request meant she'd have to grow up fast and leave her childhood behind. Even so, she would do as her mother asked, she decided. She would not let her mother down.

But she had, Maria realized as she came back to the moment and looked at her sister's watchful faces. Avery felt abandoned by her and had been left with an empty hole in the place where memories of their mother should be. And Lauren wouldn't even come out and tell her about the terrible weight she was carrying. The heaviness of that promise to her mother had sat on Maria's shoulders for nearly thirty years, and yet she hadn't done what her mother had asked at all.

Chapter 29

Avery

Avery sat on the living room couch with a photo album in her lap. She flipped through the pages, looking at the pictures that were taken in the months just before her mother's death. For some reason, she needed to see some evidence of the day Maria had described, something to help her picture it all.

As she flipped another page, Maria came out of the kitchen and moved in next to her. The walk back from their picnic spot had been quiet and so had dinner. No one seemed to know what to say.

"Sometimes I forget how beautiful she was," Maria said looking at the album in Avery's lap.

Avery looked down at the album and ran a finger over the image of her mother's face. "Even more so before the chemo."

"Even during all that," Maria said sitting down next to Avery. "She just had a glow about her. She seemed to always have joy in her heart." Maria released a sigh. "I wish I knew her secret."

Avery glanced at Maria. She hadn't noticed that her sister wasn't happy until Lauren brought it up during the truth game. Now she wondered how she had missed it. The evidence was not hard to see. Maria seemed to have a constant lack of energy as though she was always walking around with a weight on her back. She was a mom and Avery could say she assumed that was the cause, but the truth was she hadn't been paying attention. And even here with the kids away from her, Maria was no better, maybe even worse.

"Me too," Avery said flipping to the next page.

"Oh, look!" Maria pointed to another picture of their mother. "This was the day of the hiking trip. And this one too," her finger moved to the next one that also included all three girls, Maria with a scowl on her face.

Avery smiled at the pictures of her mother wearing the yellow bandana. They had life for her now that she knew what had been happening that day.

She flipped the pages of the album back to an earlier time and pointed to a picture of her mother with a multi-colored scarf wrapped around her head, sitting in a wheelchair. Eve was laughing and had somehow managed to get all three girls on her lap. Avery looked at Maria. "Tell me about this picture."

Maria smiled and glanced at the picture. "That was the day we went to the zoo with Uncle Harry. Mom was weak from the chemo and had to ride around in a wheelchair. She made it fun though. We took turns riding in the chair with her."

Maria laughed as she moved her finger to another picture. "This was Lauren's sixth birthday. She got her first real art set—paints, canvases, an easel. She was so happy."

"The day an obsessed artist was born," Avery said with a smile.

"You got it! She was so happy that day she even let you use her new paints … See here?" Maria turned to the next page and pointed to the photo at the top. It was a picture of Avery, a chubby two-year-old with several colors of paint streaked on her face. "Your version of a self-portrait."

Avery laughed. She could have figured out what was going on in some of the pictures, but it was so nice to hear about it all from someone who remembered. She looked at Maria sitting next to her; the bouncing curls, the caramel eyes that were just like her own scanning album pages. And Avery realized that it was the first time in a very long time that Maria had felt like a sister to her. It was nice. Better than nice. It was like getting back something precious that had been lost. Avery wanted to hold onto the moment for as long as she could. She scooted in closer and, flipping to a new page in the album, pointed at another picture. "Tell me about this one," she said, realizing that she was experiencing the beginning of the very thing her father had hoped for.

Chapter 30

Lauren

The sun was beginning to set when Lauren stepped out the back door of the house. She had her hair down and neatly brushed, and she was wearing a little bit of makeup, which was quite rare.

She stopped on the deck to take in the pink horizon and was startled by a voice.

"Sneaking out to see your boyfriend?" Avery asked. She was sitting at the far end of the deck with her butt in one chair and her feet propped up on another. She was spending more and more time outside, trying to conquer her fears. It was more than Lauren could say for herself.

"He's not my boyfriend," Lauren said in an offhanded tone, but in truth, hearing the word boyfriend in reference to Blake sent a flutter of excitement through her chest. It reminded her of how she'd felt in high school when she found out Tommy Jackson liked her. It was hard to stifle her desire to smile. "I'm just going to see how his work is coming on the house."

Avery gave her a wry look. "Of course you are." She looked out at the setting sun and pulled her legs up against her chest in a protective gesture. "You just met him, you know."

"I know."

Avery looked at Lauren, worry in her eyes. "He may not be what you think."

Lauren nodded. She wanted to say that Blake was a nice guy, but the heartfelt concern she saw in her sister's eyes stopped her. She wondered who had hurt Avery.

"Just—be careful, okay?" Now Avery's face was nothing but serious and Lauren found she couldn't brush off the warning.

"I will," she said longing to know what had happened to so drastically change her sister's personality, to cause violent nightmares and constant fear. She gave Avery a long measuring look, then went on her way. Avery wasn't going to just tell her. If it was going to be that easy, she would have talked about it the night of the truth game.

When she arrived at Blake's house, she stopped at the door and ran her fingers through her hair, checking that it was still neat. Then she knocked and a few seconds later Blake answered the door with a smile. He looked a bit disheveled. His shorts were covered in paint and there were spots of it on his skin and shirt as well. He was a little sweaty and his hair was a mess. Lauren smiled. She liked him this way.

"Care to take a walk?" he asked. "I'm getting light-headed from all the paint fumes."

"Sure," Lauren said making room for him to step out the door, breathing in the mixed aroma of sweat and paint as he moved by.

The sun was all but gone as they walked to the edge of the lake. Lauren tried hard to keep control of her feet moving at Blake's pace, a normal pace, but she still stumbled over her own feet. Blake noticed her difficulty and slowed his steps, giving her time to step more carefully. As they moved along the shoreline, Blake reached for Lauren's hand and grasped it, sending a shiver up her spine.

"How is the house coming?" Lauren asked.

"Fine. If you weren't here, I'd probably finish ahead of schedule."

"Sorry, I'm slowing you down." In more ways than one it seemed.

Blake gave her a playful smile. "Don't be sorry."

Lauren felt a rush of heat in her cheeks. She was glad the sun was all the way down now so he wouldn't see her schoolgirl reaction. It had been so long since she'd felt like this.

They walked for a few minutes hand in hand, but when Lauren's fingers began to spasm, she pulled her hand away and shoved it in her pocket. Blake looked at her with a measure of confusion but didn't say anything. The trembling fingers were a reminder of that morning, of what they both knew but neither seemed able to talk about directly. And Lauren wasn't sure how to get comfortable sharing this with another person.

After a few minutes, Lauren had to break the silence. "Tell me about him."

"Who?"

"Your step-father. He was important to you, wasn't he?"

"He was as much a father to me as my actual father." Blake stopped walking and sat down on the ground, looking out at the water. The sound of crickets filled the night air and, in the distance, an owl was calling out. Lauren scooted in next to him. "My parents divorced when I was ten. It wasn't really anyone's fault, or at least not just one person's. They just couldn't get along anymore in the same house. After the split, my mom was very depressed. She cried all the time and didn't go out much.

"Jerry was my soccer coach. He volunteered because he liked kids so much. He didn't have any of his own. My mother got to know him over time and it was changing her for the better. He brought her back from the sadness. Before I knew it they were dating. I didn't mind. I was glad to see her happy again and Jerry was a great guy."

Blake glanced at Lauren, his face just visible in the dawning moonlight; just enough so she could see the hurt in his eyes.

"None of us kids knew about Jerry's disorder. He did a good job of covering up. But he was straight with my mother. He told her about it on their first date."

Lauren felt shame wash over her. She couldn't even seem to tell her own family the truth. Every time she thought of telling Maria and Avery, she'd remember all the fights, all the times she'd been a burden to them. She had been irresponsible in years past. She hadn't been able to see it then; wrapped up as she was in her painting, in her own little world. But when her diagnosis was given to her and her world was turned upside down, she'd begun to realize how wrong she'd been before. At that point, her life could no longer revolve around painting. It had to revolve around scheduled appointments, medical bills, and jobs she couldn't afford to lose. She had to be responsible. But her sisters couldn't see that because she was still begging money off of them. From their perspective, nothing had changed, and Lauren knew it never would.

Sure, when the two weeks here was over she'd get the money from the will. Then she could pay off her debt and have some leftover, but it wouldn't last long. And she had only one of her jobs to go back to when she went home. Her job as a store clerk was gone. Len had fired her the second she'd asked for more time off. And she knew that getting and keeping jobs would get increasingly more difficult.

"He told her all that could be expected as time went on," Blake said, continuing his story. 'She didn't care and neither did I. Jerry was making our lives so much better. So what if he stumbled a lot. So what if he was grumpy sometimes because he couldn't sleep at night. So what if it was going to keep getting worse. We loved him."

Blake picked up a pebble from the ground and began to toy with it. He was looking down, and Lauren felt sure he was avoiding eye contact with her. "When things got bad, Mom stood right by him. I did too, but it was hard. We watched him deteriorate. He had more and more trouble moving. Then one day he was trying to go up the one step to the front door of our house and he fell. Doesn't sound so bad. But he hit his head on the concrete stoop—hard. That's how we lost him."

Lauren reached out and grabbed Blake's hand again, ignoring the tremors. She held onto him and allowed him to feel what was happening to her body without her consent. When he turned to her, his eyes were moist.

"I haven't talked about Jerry with anyone but my mother since we lost him five years ago."

"How do you feel now that you have?"

"Raw—but—better somehow, lighter." He gave a tiny laugh. "Funny I should be talking about all this with someone I just met a couple of days ago."

"Only fair, really." Lauren smiled at him. "After all, you know my biggest secret." She stopped and considered that a moment. "You know my biggest secret—the thing I can't seem to talk to my sisters about—yet you know next to nothing about me otherwise. And I know all about your step-father, but very little else."

"When you put it like that, it sounds weird."

"It is weird."

"Maybe we should talk about some other things." He squeezed her hand and caressed it with his thumb. Lauren shivered in response. He was awakening things in her that had been buried so deep she'd practically forgotten they existed.

Lauren looked at Blake, his unkempt appearance and clothes splotched with paint. "Here's a start," she said, "usually, I look more like you do right now."

He raised an eyebrow. "So you usually walk around in need of a shower, wearing clothes that should be in the trash can?"

A giggle escaped Lauren's lips. "Not exactly. I have to admit that on a few occasions I forgot to shower for a day or two because I was so wrapped up in my work, but I was really talking about the paint you're wearing."

"You paint houses for a living. Then I need you to come over more often."

"Not houses, canvases. Though that never earned a living for me."

Blake raised his eyebrows and nodded his head in appreciation. "I see." Then he looked at her still trembling left hand. "You're left-handed aren't you?"

"Yes."

"That's why you were having so much trouble skipping the stone."

Lauren nodded. "And it's why I rarely paint now."

"Were you good?" Blake asked, looking into her eyes now.

"I guess that's a matter of opinion, but I loved it."

For a few seconds they were silent and only the sounds of the crickets and lapping lake water surrounded them. The air was cooler now that the sun had gone down, but it was thick and balmy.

"Well," Blake broke the silence, "I feel extremely boring saying this now, but I'm the manager at a bank."

"It doesn't sound boring. It sounds like a job that actually makes a living. And as long as you like doing it…"

"No, it really is boring most of the time. I hate doing it."

"Then why are you doing it?"

Blake drew in a breath considering his answer. "Well, I could say that my dad pushed me into it, but that's not true. I went into it because I was pretty good with numbers and leadership—or so my teachers always said—and, this is embarrassing to say out loud," Blake rubbed a hand under his nose. "I kinda thought that I'd get to be a hero someday. Like someone would try to rob the bank and I'd save the day. Really stupid childhood fantasy."

Lauren smiled. "That's sweet actually. The world needs heroes, but wouldn't saving the day be the security guard's job?"

"With the help of the bank manager," Blake said with emphasis. "But my bank has never been robbed. I mean—that's a good thing, but the job is a lot less exciting than I'd once hoped. I actually enjoy the weeks I come here and work on the house a lot better."

"Maybe you should consider a change of profession."

"And give up the good paying job that pays for this house and the one I actually live in?"

"I guess there's no gain without risk."

"I suppose you're right. I'll have to consider that."

Lauren would have to consider it too, she thought as they sat silent for a few moments. Then Blake turned to Lauren and asked, "Is that enough talking for tonight? Can I kiss you now?" Lauren smiled and nodded, moving into his arms.

After a long, intoxicating kiss, Lauren looked up at the starry sky. "Sleep outside with me tonight," she said, looking at Blake hopefully.

"I knew it!" he said. "Just a couple days and you're asking me to take you to bed."

"I am not! I'm asking you to take me to your deck and sleep under the stars with me."

Blake reached a hand around to rub his back. "I've been painting all day. There's going to need to be something involved that's a lot more comfortable than wooden planks."

"We'll cover the deck with blankets."

"Seriously?" Blake raised one eyebrow.

"Pleeease? The sky is so beautiful tonight."

"Alright," Blake sighed. "I think I have an air mattress in the back closet."

Lauren smiled and kissed Blake's cheek. "Before you get too excited," he said, "I have to take a shower first."

Lauren nodded. "That's probably a good idea. Show me where the air mattress is and I'll get things all set up while you wash up."

Chapter 31

Maria

At ten thirty, Maria sat alone on the deck. A cigarette burned between her fingers and the Christmas lights twinkled above her head. On the table sat the remnants of the bottle of crown royal. She had been staring at it for ten minutes reminding herself of all the reasons she shouldn't drink it. But all the reasons she wanted to drink it kept rearing their ugly heads in her mind—Hank being the main one. Two nights ago, when she'd gotten drunk, she had stopped thinking about him for a while, and that felt good.

A giggle rang out in the distance. It was Lauren. Maria could just catch a glimpse of her and the neighbor—Blake—through the trees. They were lying on his deck, snuggling, talking, and laughing under the stars.

It brought back memories watching them, memories of long ago. As Maria took a long drag on her cigarette, she thought of the time she and Hank went to the beach for their first anniversary. They slept under the stars one night, right on the sand. They spent little time, however, looking at the stars. They were far too wrapped up in each other. Maria remembered it like it was yesterday—the way Hank looked at her that night. She was lying on a green blanket and Hank was propped up on one elbow, looking down at her. The ocean breeze was ruffling his wavy blond hair as the waves crashed on the shore a few yards away. Hank reached out and took hold of a lock of Maria's chestnut hair, wrapping the springy curl around his finger, then letting it fall again. "You are the most beautiful thing I have ever seen," he told her. "More beautiful than all the stars in the sky." Then he cupped her face in his free hand and kissed her. They spent the rest of that night cuddling and talking about the future.

But even that night paled when Maria thought about the day she'd told Hank she was pregnant with Jonathan. Hank had gotten down on his knees in front of her, lifted her shirt just a couple of inches, and planted kisses all over her still flat belly. The love in his eyes overwhelmed her. She never imagined that love could fade, but somehow it had. Now it was gone entirely, Maria thought as she watched Blake kiss her sister.

She tried to remember when it had changed—the moment she'd known for sure that something was wrong in their relationship. The change had come gradually, she supposed, but she could remember the day she knew they were in trouble. It was a Friday three years ago. She'd just put the kids to bed. She and Hank had not made love for over three weeks and that was pretty much the longest they'd ever gone. Hank was in bed already, flipping through a magazine. Maria went into the bathroom and put on her sexiest nightgown and fixed her hair the way Hank liked it. Maybe he wouldn't want the lights off this time, she thought. He didn't even look up when she came back out into the bedroom, but Maria didn't think anything of that. She got into bed with him and eased up close. When he still ignored her, she began to kiss his neck and stroke his chest. He pushed her hand away and said, "Not tonight, okay?"

"But, Hank, it's Friday night, the kids are asleep early, and it's been a while."

At this, he finally looked at her, but not with a smile, with an annoyed expression. "I said, not tonight."

Maria moved the covers down a little so Hank could see what she had on. She was sure that would get him interested. His annoyance didn't disappear as he jerked the covers back up and returned his attention to his magazine.

Maria was hurt, but she tried to push that aside. "Hank, I'm wearing your favorite nightgown, didn't you see? I put it on just for you."

When he looked her way again, Maria was sure she saw a hint of disgust cross his face. This time when he responded to her, he did so with more force. "I said I'm not interested … Maybe if you lost a little weight. That nightgown doesn't even fit anymore."

His words hit her like a slap in the face. Maria sat there stunned for a second, then quickly snapped off the light, not caring whether or not he was finished with the magazine. Then she sank into her side of the bed—turning away from him as bitter tears began to fall. She hardly knew how to stay next to him that night, but she also didn't know what else to say or do in response to his hurtful words. The man who had once made her feel so beautiful now made her feel ugly. She had never felt so humiliated.

The next day Hank brought her flowers as a way to make up, but it was a hollow apology. Their relationship had a few brighter spots after that, but not many. She made some effort to lose weight, hoping to please him, but there was little time for exercise. As Hank pulled back from helping with the kids, even less time was available. So the pounds stayed on and eventually Maria gave up trying to get Hank's attention. She consoled herself with nicotine and settled for snuggling with the dog, she thought as she crushed her cigarette under her foot and then picked up the butt and closed her fist around it.

She looked again at Lauren and Blake. She was happy for her sister but sad for her ruined marriage. And she was feeling far less certain that staying with Hank for the sake of the kids was a good idea. Her resolve to do so weakened every time she looked at Lauren and Blake. But she had been a married woman for almost fifteen years. She wasn't sure she liked the idea of becoming single again; a single mother at that. She also wondered if Hank would even bother to see the kids if she divorced him. Then again, what did spending time with them matter if his heart and mind were never in it?

She toyed with the bottle in front of her, unscrewed the lid and picked up the bottle. The scent of the liquid inside wafted out under her nose. It would be so easy to go ahead and drink—forget her troubles for the night.

Maria's head snapped to the left when she heard Avery's voice at the back door. "If you're going to drink that, could you at least come in and sit in a chair you can't fall out of first?"

Maria set the bottle back down on the table with a sigh. She screwed the top back on. "I'm not going to drink it. I was thinking about it though."

Avery continued to stand inside the back screen door, her eyes darting around. "Well … I'm going to bed now," Avery said.

Maria nodded, but Avery didn't move away from the door. "When do you think Lauren will be back?"

"I don't think she's coming back tonight," Maria said. This news caused Avery to look very worried. "She's with Blake." Maria pointed in the direction of his house. But Avery's expression only seemed more alarmed. "She's fine. I can see them from here. They're sleeping under the stars, I think."

Avery didn't answer, but she didn't appear to have gotten any relief from Maria's words.

"She'll be fine," Maria said with assurance.

"Are you coming in soon?" Avery fiddled with the deadbolt on the open back door. She couldn't go to sleep until she felt safe and she couldn't feel safe until the doors were all locked, Maria could see that. She nodded and picked up the bottle on the table before getting out of her chair and heading to the door.

Once Maria was inside, and the door was locked, Avery headed off to bed and Maria went into the living room with a book to read. Instead of escaping her unhappiness with alcohol, she attempted to do so in the pages of a mystery.

An hour and a half later, she was asleep on the couch. Then she was jarred awake when a scream rang out.

Chapter 32

Avery

Avery was standing on the deck, darkness all around her. Out in the yard, she could just make out Lauren's form near the row of trees that were swaying, casting shadows in moving patterns across the yard. The lake water was eerily still despite the breeze that ruffled the trees. Unafraid, Lauren turned to her and waved. Avery inched her toes forward, dragging them like lead weights. But when she reached the stairs, fear grabbed her so tight she couldn't move any further. She shook her head. She could not go out there. Then, out of the pitch black of the shadows came another form … then another … then another. The forms were indistinguishable to Avery, but they were big and bulky. They were larger than Lauren who did not see them behind her as she was now facing the lake. Avery tried to scream, to warm her sister, but no sound came out. All three forms lunged forward, taking Lauren down to the ground. She screamed. Avery tried to move. She needed to help her sister. But she couldn't move. She was frozen in place. Her feet would not respond even as her brain willed them to move. Lauren struggled, crying for help, but she stood no chance. Why wouldn't Avery's feet obey her? She had to help.

"No! I need to go!" she cried out, but now something was holding her arms too. Panic ripped through her as she fought the invisible hold on her arms. "Let me go!"

"Calm down, Avery. It's just a dream."

Avery's eyes flew open to see Maria leaning over her, holding her arms. She jerked them out of her sister's grip. "What are you doing in here?" she demanded breathlessly, her heart still galloping in her chest.

"I heard you scream ... and … I …"

"You what?" Avery spat the words as she wiped a tear from her cheek. She was flooded with embarrassment having someone see her this way. She wasn't sure why it was so hard to show vulnerability to her sisters. She had done that some on the night of the truth game, more than either of them, but this was about three steps further as far as she was concerned. She wasn't ready to let anyone see her like this.

"I … You said you felt abandoned by me. I heard you scream and I thought I should do something—help somehow."

Part of Avery wanted to accept what Maria was offering; to seek comfort in someone's arms the way she did as a child. Would it be so bad to let someone comfort her? But the words that came out of her mouth betrayed that desire. "It's too late for that. You might have noticed I'm not a little girl anymore."

Maria nodded and stood up from where she sat on the bed next to Avery. She turned and walked toward the door, looking a little stricken. Avery felt some satisfaction from turning her sister away. She felt guilty at the same time. The guilt made her angry. Why should she feel guilty? Maria shouldn't have barged into her room.

When Maria got to the door she turned back, gave Avery a sorrowful look, and said, "I'm sorry I wasn't there for you back when you were still a kid, but—maybe it doesn't have to be too late. We all still need comfort sometimes."

As soon as Maria was out and the door was shut, Avery buried her face in her pillow and cried. This dream had been the worst one ever. Somehow watching her sister get attacked and finding herself paralyzed was worse than getting attacked herself. Added to the fear she always felt for herself there was fear for her sisters and with that, shame. What would she do if Lauren or Maria were really in trouble? Stand there unable to move? Watch them get hurt or … worse?

When the tears stopped, Avery turned over and tried to fall asleep again. But strangely, her mind was now filled with thoughts of Mike. She didn't know where that had come from. She could picture him in her mind—his dark hair, icy blue eyes and the dimple in his right cheek. Somehow thinking of him was comforting, yet frightening. More than anything, she wished he was nearby. How odd to feel such a need for someone she barely ever talked to. And at the same time she wanted him near, she feared allowing him to get too near.

Chapter 33

Lauren

The eighth day at the cabin was a Saturday that started with rain. Lauren was annoyed the minute she woke up and heard the plick-plunk of the drops on the roof. She glanced at the bedside clock. It read five thirty-two. That meant she had managed to sleep for almost six hours, which was a rare happening. She could be grateful for that at least. But she had hoped to follow her morning cup of coffee with a walk by the lake. If she was by the lakeshore at sunrise, it was almost certain Blake would show up. She hadn't gotten to spend any time with him since their night under the stars. The previous day he had been gone all day taking care of some business that couldn't wait till the end of his time off.

She tried to spend that time with her sisters, but Maria was sullen and Avery was downright irritable most of the day. So Lauren had taken one of the bikes out for a ride and treated herself to lunch at the restaurant they all went to on their first night.

Lauren pushed back the covers and dragged herself out of bed. She stumbled into the bathroom and took a shower. Then, after getting dressed in a T-shirt and shorts, she went down the hall to start the coffee. She tripped over her own feet twice on her way down the hall. Then lost her balance and had to catch herself by grabbing hold of the kitchen counter. An image flashed into her mind of a man lying on the ground next to the front stoop of a house, his head bleeding. Was she going to see that image every time she stumbled? Would she wonder each time if the next stumble could be the last? Maybe encouraging Blake to tell her about his step-father was not such a great idea. She'd never even thought about dying like that before.

Lauren steadied herself. It was lucky her sisters were both still asleep, she thought as she turned on the coffee maker.

When the coffee was done brewing, Lauren filled a cup and took it to the table along with a book of crossword puzzles. She picked up her cup, sipped the coffee, then dropped the cup back down to the table. Some of the hot liquid sloshed out of the cup as it clattered on the table. Lauren stared at her right hand. Tears sprang up in her eyes. She swiped at them with her trembling right hand, barely able to manage the movement correctly. It was getting worse.

In an instant, her tears were replaced by a flash of hot anger. *Why?* She thought. *Why is this happening to me?* Her stomach churned at the reminder of all the nevers that now filled her life. She would never be a successful artist—at least not while she was still alive. And not with anything she painted from here on out. She would likely never be able to create a decent painting again. She would never again know what it is like to be a normal, healthy person. It might not be long before she wouldn't even be able to take care of herself. And that made it pretty certain that she would never get married.

Lauren stopped herself right there and pushed the anger back as she reminded herself of the maybes that existed. Maybe she could fix her relationship with her sisters. She was beginning to believe that her father's wish might just be possible. She was even starting to believe they might be able to see her as more than just a burden. And there was Blake. It might be a little silly seeing as they would only be here for a short time longer. But they both lived pretty nearby. And he already knew about her condition—and knew it well—and hadn't run away yet. So, who knew, maybe there was a possibility for a lasting relationship. These were both things she wouldn't have imagined possible a month ago.

There was a part of her that couldn't believe she was even thinking about a lasting relationship with a man whom she had known for less than a week. But it had been an amazing week and she was feeling things she hadn't felt in a very long time. This could be her one last chance to have someone to love. She certainly had to give it a shot.

Chapter 34

Maria

Maria looked out the window at the dreary conditions. It was lunchtime and the rain was still coming down. She took a sandwich to Avery, who was in the living room watching her soap opera. Then she handed one to Lauren, who had been sitting in front of the same crossword puzzle all day. Fixing a sandwich for herself, she joined Lauren at the table. Maria took a bite of her sandwich, then glanced at the puzzle in front of her sister. Only six words were filled in. Lauren had been very distracted and kept looking out the window, presumably to see if the weather had changed.

"It's only water, you know. You could just run right through it if you want to go see him that bad," Maria said when Lauren looked up at her.

"I might just do that later if it doesn't let up."

"Or you could bring him over here for a change and let him meet your family," Avery piped up from the other room.

"I don't think so," Lauren said. "I'm not so quick to bring men home."

"You mean you *never* bring them home," said Avery.

"There haven't been that many. I'll bring a guy home when it's the right guy."

"You don't have to be engaged to let a guy meet your sisters."

"I like to get to know the guy myself first, okay?"

"And I don't need to know them at all, is that what you mean?" Avery was getting agitated.

"You never know, maybe he will be the right one," Maria intervened before things could go any further.

Lauren looked at her for a second, as if measuring Maria's sincerity. "Maybe," she said unable to stop her lips from curving upward.

Maria was just about to ask Lauren what Blake was like when the doorbell rang. She started to get up, but Avery jumped up from the couch and said, "I'll get it," before Maria could even push her chair back from the table. Maria looked at Lauren to see if she was surprised by this too. Lauren shrugged in response.

Maria turned and watched as Avery checked out the window to see who it was. "Grocery guy," she said moving toward the door. She unlocked the deadbolt and opened the door just enough to stand in the opening, bringing her toes just to the edge of the doorframe—a blocking gesture.

"So, you're Evan, right?" Avery asked the young man.

"Yeah, that's right," Evan responded.

"And you work at the grocery store."

"Yeeaaah."

"Well, I'm Avery."

"Okay. Nice to meet you, Avery."

"Soooo, what do you do when you're not working?"

There was a brief pause. Then Evan replied, "I'm usually at school when I'm not working, or doing homework."

"Oh, you're in school. That's great. But there must be something you like to do for fun."

Again Evan was silent for a few seconds. Maria imagined he was trying to figure out why a customer was questioning him about his leisure activities. "Are you flirting with me?" Evan finally asked. "Cause I have a girlfriend."

"N—no, I am not flirting with you," Avery stammered at first, then sounded defensive by the end of her sentence.

"Oh, okay. Can I come in and put this bag down? It's getting heavy."

"I'll take it." Avery jerked the bag from Evan's arms and shoved a few dollars into his hand for a tip. Then she shut the door in his face and stomped into the kitchen. She dropped the bag on the counter and marched off to her room without another word.

Lauren and Maria looked at each other. "Well, that was awkward," Lauren said.

"Yeah," Maria responded. She thought about her conversation with Avery the other day on the dock. Avery had asked if Maria knew the grocery guy's name and when Maria answered that she did, Avery had gotten upset and stomped off. Avery's attempt at conversation with Evan had definitely been a failure, but she was trying to move past the fear that clearly ruled her life. And that was no different than Maria's failed attempt to comfort Avery two nights ago. Maybe they were all trying and who knew, perhaps they could mend the rift between them after all.

Chapter 35

Lauren

Things remained quiet most of the day. When Maria began pulling things out of the refrigerator to start dinner, Lauren offered to help her cook.

"What are we making?" Lauren asked.

"Beef stew," Maria said. "Here, can you chop the vegetables?"

"Sure," Lauren answered with a confidence that she didn't feel. Chopping vegetables was a simple enough task—for someone who's hands didn't tremble. Lauren started with the celery, chopping slowly and carefully, hoping her right hand would behave at least. She stood so Maria would have a hard time seeing her hands, though some part of her wanted her sister to see. The secret was beginning to drive her mad, yet she couldn't seem to just tell her sisters the truth.

When Lauren was done with the celery, she placed a carrot on the cutting board. This would be even more difficult. Carrots were a harder vegetable. She worked slowly, but the trembling in her left hand was getting pretty bad and she was making a mess of the carrot.

"Let me help you with that," Maria said over Lauren's shoulder.

Lauren jumped at the sound. "I'm fine," she said defensively. She jerked her hands away from the counter and out of Maria's sight. The knife clattered down on the countertop. Lauren squeezed her eyes shut for a few seconds. She hadn't meant to react so abruptly. She'd wanted Maria to see, hadn't she?

"I'm just trying to help," Maria said.

"I don't want help. I'm doing fine." Lauren tried to keep her voice calm and even, but there was anger rising up inside her that she was struggling to control. She was angry at the disease that was taking her life away inch by inch. She was angry that she should need help with such a small task. And, though she didn't really know why, she was angry at Maria for offering help. She was also angry at herself for her inability to let her sisters see the truth.

"But—"

"But what? The carrots aren't perfect? So what?"

"I just—"

"You just want everything to be perfect, I know!" Lauren's anger was out and she didn't know how to stop it. She didn't even know where her words were coming from; old feelings that were still unresolved perhaps. "Perfect Maria with her perfect life!"

Lauren stopped short as her sister's expression changed in front of her. First, it was soft, wanting to help, then it changed to irritated, then stone cold. "Perfect? You think my life is perfect?"

Lauren took a deep breath, swallowed, and prepared for what was about to come.

"My life is so perfect that I worry constantly about my son flunking out of school and my daughter getting into trouble searching for attention because I hardly ever have enough time left for her and her father barely acknowledges her existence. Is that perfect enough for you?

"Or maybe you would rather hear about how my husband never touches me and tries pretty hard not to even look at me. How is that for perfect?" Maria's voice had started out steely cold, then risen with anger at the end.

Lauren stood staring at Maria for a few long seconds in shock. "Since when is Hank anything other than madly in love with you?"

The anger seemed to drain out of Maria, and then she looked a little stunned by her own outburst. She answered in a soft voice. "Since I turned thirty-five and put on fifteen pounds."

"But that was three years ago."

Maria nodded, then her composure broke and tears spilled from her eyes. She turned and ran for the front door, slamming it shut behind her.

Lauren stood still in the now silent room for several seconds. How could Maria's life be so very different than she'd thought? She was shocked. She was beginning to feel like she'd been living her life with her head in the sand, missing everything going on around her. She really was as selfish and out of touch as Maria and Avery accused her of being.

She walked hesitantly toward the front door and opened it gently. Stepping out onto the porch that was still wet from the rain which had nearly stopped now, Lauren saw Maria sitting on the swing. She was rocking the swing just a little with her head down. Lauren walked over and stopped in front of her sister.

"If you want to hear more about how perfect my life is, I could tell you how I'm inappropriately attached to my dog because she's the one who snuggles with me at night," Maria said without lifting her head.

"Actually, I wanted to apologize. I don't know what came over me. You were only trying to help."

Maria looked up at Lauren, then scooted over on the seat of the swing and patted the empty side. Lauren sat down. For a few seconds, they were quiet. The last drips of rain and the singing of a few birds were the only sounds.

"I'm beginning to realize how little of what I thought was true, actually is. Dad tried to tell me that once. I didn't listen to him. I was too wrapped up in my own troubles. I'm starting to see just how selfish I've been. I was living in my own little world. I didn't see that Avery needed me, and I didn't see that you were unhappy. It wasn't until the truth game the other night that I realized it. And even then I had a hard time imagining your life as anything other than perfect. Somehow I can't seem to get past the old ideas in my head," Lauren said.

Maria sniffed. "It gets better … Hank's cheating on me."

Lauren was shocked once again. She didn't know what to say in response, so she just sat there staring at Maria's tear-streaked face.

"With his secretary," Maria added.

"Oh," Lauren said, "how very cliché of him."

"She's a slim and trim little redhead with big boobs."

"Does he know you know?"

"He didn't tell me if that's what you mean." Maria pushed the swing with her toes. "And I haven't confronted him."

"Then how do you know for sure?"

"He comes home at least once a week, late at night, smelling like her perfume." Maria's composure broke again, fresh tears spilling from her eyes. "He doesn't even bother to try to hide it. Maybe he's daring me to confront him."

"Why haven't you?" Lauren couldn't imagine how Maria could know this and say nothing.

Maria sighed. "It's hard to explain how it all happened. It wasn't like we were super happy until one day I realized he was sleeping with peppy, busty Carina.

"First, he wanted to have sex with the lights off. Then, he wanted it less and less. Eventually, he didn't want it at all. But I hardly had time to worry about that because I was too busy worrying about the kids, and on top of that, worrying about why Hank was ignoring the kids. After work, making dinner, helping Jon struggle through his homework, and trying to pay some attention to Melanie, I was exhausted. At first, I was angry with Hank for not helping. I mean he was there, every night he was there, but only physically. Mentally he was checked out. He would just sit there in front of the TV and pretend the kids and I weren't there. Eventually, I was too drained to be angry anymore. I was just numb. It seemed easier that way. The anger was draining me even more.

"That's when he started going out at night. The kids went to sleep, and Hank went out. I got to stay home, cuddle with Sadie, and stuff my face with comfort food." Maria looked at Lauren, catching her eyes. Lauren saw the fresh tears welling, ready to spill. "Every night he came home with a smell. Most nights it was peanuts and beer. But once or twice a week it was Carina's perfume."

Maria exhaled deeply. "I didn't want to confront him. If I do that, everything will change. I thought it was better for the kids this way. At least their father is around—sort of. This is the first time I've even talked about it."

Lauren reached a hand over and put it on top of Maria's hand. "I'm sorry," she said. She didn't know what else to say, so they sat silently for several minutes listening to the drops falling from the trees and the creak of the porch swing.

"I've been pretty foolish, haven't I?" Maria asked lifting a hand to wipe the moisture off her face.

Lauren shrugged. "Maybe, but only you can decide that."

Maria turned her head and regarded Lauren with surprise at that answer. "Avery would think I was a fool for staying so long and not confronting him."

Lauren could understand why Maria would think so. Avery had always had the most spunk and the hottest temper. And she didn't mind saying exactly what was on her mind. However, since coming here she had seen a side of Avery that was very different. "She might. Then again she might surprise you. But it doesn't really matter anyway. The only thing that matters is what you think is best for you and the kids."

Maria nodded. "I've been thinking the last couple days that with this money from Dad's will, now might be the time to end this. Maybe it's not best for the kids to stay with their father if all he's going to do is ignore them."

Lauren understood Maria's reluctance. They had lost their mother as kids and grown up with just one parent. Maria didn't want her kids to experience that kind of loss even if it came in another form.

"I'm sure you'll figure it out."

"Yeah," Maria said with a nod. "Thanks, Lauren … for listening. It feels good to talk to someone about it."

This was a chance. Lauren knew that. Maria had opened up to her and now she could do the same. She wanted to—and yet, she couldn't. What would she become in her sisters' eyes when they finally knew the truth? Poor, sick, never-gonna-get-better, Lauren—that's what she'd be. But … what if they didn't see her that way? What if telling them could be a good thing, a great thing? Blake didn't see her that way—did he? She didn't think so. Still, when she opened her mouth to speak, she just couldn't say the words. She closed her mouth again and stayed silent.

"I'm worried about Avery," Maria said after a few moments.

Lauren turned and looked at her sister.

"She's having a lot of nightmares," Maria continued. "I think something must have happened to her—something bad."

"Yeah, I've been hearing her at night too."

Maria looked at Lauren. "I tried to go in and comfort her the night before last when I heard her scream." Maria stopped and looked down into her lap. "She pushed me away. She said it was too late."

Lauren sensed that Maria had more to say, so she stayed silent and waited.

"It's not too late though," Maria finally said. "I don't think it is. I used to, but now I see that Dad's idea of bringing us back together might not be so crazy after all. I've learned so much. I see now that things aren't quite the way I thought." Maria looked at Lauren with that comment in a way that made Lauren wonder exactly what Maria meant. "I see that at least some of—the problems between all of us—are my fault. There's more we need to find out about each other though. You and I need to find out what happened to Avery."

Lauren nodded. "How?"

"The note today," Maria said, speaking of the note from their father that had been in the grocery bag that morning. "Dad wants us to play a game together. Maybe we can get her to open up."

"We can try," Lauren agreed. "But we'll have to be careful. If she feels like she's being ambushed, she'll run away."

"We will have to be careful, but I think she'll stay even if she's upset."

Lauren raised her eyebrows at her sister. Avery was notorious for running away when she got upset.

"It's not about us. The note says we have to stay till the end of the game. Avery will do it for Dad."

Lauren thought about it. Maria might have a point. Avery had stayed the night of the truth game until all the questions were asked and answered—or not. She was upset that night. She had cried, but she hadn't run away. The wish of a parent who was no longer living was powerful. It was strange, Lauren thought now, that he'd had to die to get them to listen.

"Okay, we'll try it. I'll follow your lead," Lauren said.

Maria raised an eyebrow, her expression tired.

"We both know you're better at taking the lead. I'd probably just mess things up."

"Fine," Maria agreed. "Now I guess we better go finish dinner."

Lauren nodded, then looked longingly at the house next door, barely visible through the trees.

Maria sighed. "Fine. Go."

Lauren perked up, smiled, and kissed Maria's cheek. "Thanks, sis." She got up from the swing and started across the porch toward Blake's house.

"Does he know?"

The words stopped Lauren cold. She turned and gave Maria a probing look.

"The morning you let me use your shower," Maria said. "I was hung over. I went looking for some aspirin."

"You looked inside my medicine cabinet?"

"Yes. But it only confirmed what I already suspected. I'm a nurse, remember?"

There was a part of Lauren that wanted to be mad at Maria for snooping. But looking into her sister's concerned eyes, she couldn't be mad. She saw love and concern in those eyes. There appeared to be no resentment. Besides, she'd wanted her sisters to figure it out, right? Now one of them had. Lauren was surprised at the amount of relief she felt.

She smiled. "Blake does know. He figured it out because his step-father had it. It feels kinda good that you know now too. I wanted to tell you and Avery the truth, but I just couldn't seem to do it." She looked down at her feet, then sheepishly glanced at Maria. "I was afraid. I used to be so selfish. I didn't mean to be. I just had a hard time putting anything above my painting." Lauren snickered. "As if it was more important than everything. Somehow I thought it was supposed to be that important to you guys too. I took advantage of you and Avery, and I didn't even see it until suddenly my world changed and something had to be put ahead of painting. I started getting to work on time—always. I needed the money to pay for my medical bills. I got a second job. But it was never enough, so I still had to ask for help. The difference was, I had begun to see myself through your eyes; the irresponsible leach. And the worst part was that I knew I would never be anything else. If you and Avery knew the truth, you would know that things were never going to change." Lauren wanted to look away, but she forced herself to hold eye contact with Maria. "You would know that I'll always be a burden."

Maria stood up and walked over to Lauren. "This doesn't make you a burden, Lauren. You can't help having an illness. It's not the same thing as before."

Lauren's eyes welled with tears. "Dad said I should tell you."

Maria smiled, "Yeah, he said something similar to me once. I didn't listen either." Maria reached out her arms and pulled Lauren in for a hug.

Chapter 36

Avery

Avery sat in her room, staring out the window. She had been there for a few hours. The rain had stopped and there were only drip drops falling from the roof and trees now. The birds were twittering and she could see the ducks swimming on the lake. Her sisters probably thought she was hiding away out of embarrassment. She *was* embarrassed, but mostly she was angry with herself. It seemed she was unable to have a simple conversation with another human being. Even when she knew who the person was and why he was there. Even with her sisters right there, she couldn't stop the fear long enough to act like a normal person.

Of course, she'd had conversations with Mike plenty of times without it being so awkward. Then again, that was only true when he was willing to stand and chat in the hallway. As soon as he wanted one of them to cross the other's threshold, everything changed. That was when the fear took over again. Would she ever get past it?

Avery stood up and walked to her nightstand. She opened the drawer and pulled out the wrapped up picture of her mother. Avery spent lots of time studying picture albums of the past when her mother was alive. She wanted to learn everything she could about her mother and about the happy times in her family's past when her mother was still alive. But this photo she kept wrapped up and stored away, always near, but rarely seen. It was like a piece of her mother that she was keeping just for herself. Perhaps it was a way to replace the picture of her mother that should live inside her memory—but didn't. In there, her mother was just a faceless person. But, just like her sisters could look back in their memories and see their mother's face, Avery could unwrap this photo and steal a glance. That was the idea anyway. But it was a poor substitute for the memory she didn't have.

Avery carefully unwrapped the picture and set the cloth aside. She traced the outline of her mother's face with her fingertip. "I wish I knew you, Mom." She never would know her mother the way she wanted. But she knew her better now than she ever had before. Maria and Lauren had helped with that. Her father's video had shown her a bigger picture too. She could see her mom as more of a real person. And maybe, if she let them, her sisters could broaden that picture.

Spending time with Lauren and Maria would do more than just fill the void left by her dead mother. Avery understood now that she had another void in her life. That void was the missing relationship with her sisters. She hadn't realized just how much she missed them, but she was starting to see that now. She truly wished she hadn't snapped at Maria the other night. Avery wished she had been able to run to the safety of her big sister's arms, take comfort there. Why was it so hard?

She stood up and carried the photo over to the dresser and stood it up. It belonged out in the open now. She didn't need a stolen glance to feel like she had a memory of her mother. She could satisfy that need by hearing her sisters talk about their mother. She was going to try harder to make things work out with them.

Chapter 37

Lauren

Lauren hurried to Blake's house, paying close attention to possible tripping hazards on the ground. She rushed up the steps, her heart beginning to beat a little faster, and knocked on the door. After two knocks, there was still no answer. Lauren stepped off the porch and walked around to the back of the house. She peered through the trees and saw Blake standing near the edge of the lake.

Lauren walked up beside Blake. "My favorite color is yellow," she said.

Blake looked at her and raised his eyebrows.

"We should probably get to know more about each other than our jobs and worst burdens."

Blake nodded. "Okay, why is yellow your favorite?"

"My mother died when I was six. She was sick for a couple of years before she died. Lost all her hair because of the chemo. She used to wear all sorts of scarves and bandanas to cover her bald head. She wore a yellow bandana only on the days when she felt the best. She said it was her happy color. My best memories of her include that bandana. So now it's my happy color."

"Well, I don't have such a story to go with it, but my favorite color is blue."

"Like your eyes?"

Blake moved in close, kissed Lauren lightly on the lips, then said, "No, like *your* eyes."

Lauren's heart skipped a beat, and she felt heat rise up her neck and into her cheeks. Had he really just said that? She fought to retain eye contact and not shy away from his penetrating stare. Time seemed to stop as they searched each other's eyes. His minty breath wafted warm across her face.

Blake cleared his throat. “My favorite food is steak. When I was a kid, we only ate steak when we were celebrating. So every memory I have of eating it is really happy.”

Blake looked down and his expression changed. He looked as if someone had forced something distasteful into his mouth.

“What’s wrong?” Lauren asked.

Blake shook his head. “I never thought about it before, but I haven’t eaten a single steak with my mother since Jerry died.”

Lauren nodded. She knew what it was like when a good memory suddenly turned sour. She moved forward with the conversation, hoping his mood would come back to happy. “My favorite food is fudge. I love the way it melts in my mouth.”

He looked up at her and smiled. “Fudge isn’t a food, it’s a dessert.”

“Dessert is food.”

Blake laughed and moved back from her. He bent down and picked up a pebble, then skipped it across the water with an ease that seemed unfathomable to Lauren.

“Show off,” she said, smiling, as she sat down in the grass. It was still wet from the rain, but that didn’t bother her.

“Favorite holiday?” Blake asked ignoring her comment.

“Christmas for sure. Even after Mom died it was the best time for our family. Dad had time off. We were all together, and lingering on sadness was not permitted. What about you?”

“Halloween. My cousins and I used to have a crazy good time together.”

“Going out and causing trouble?”

Blake winked at her. “Sometimes when we were older, but even when we were just kids dressing up and begging for candy, it was a great time.”

Blake tossed another pebble into the lake and then sat down next to Lauren on her right side. He picked up her hand and held it in his. She kept her left hand out of sight as best she could. Blake knew about her condition, but she still wasn't comfortable with him seeing it all the time. He stroked her hand in silence for a few seconds, then he said, "So, we talked. We know a little more about each other. Can I kiss you now?"

"You already did kiss me," Lauren said playfully.

"That was just a peck. I can do better."

A smile spread across Lauren's face. "Can you?"

"Sure, I'll show you." Blake reached his right arm around Lauren's shoulder and met her lips with his own. He took the kiss deeper and before Lauren knew it, they were on the ground necking like a couple of teenagers, water from the grass soaking into their clothes.

When was the last time she had done this, or anything remotely similar? She couldn't remember. She wasn't even sure when she'd last been out on a date. Her life had become so consumed with her medical situation that she didn't even think of such things anymore. She hadn't thought of them much before her diagnosis either. Back then she was too consumed with her painting. She was thinking about dating now, or whatever this was, and wondering why the hell she had ever put finding someone to love on the backburner.

Chapter 38

Avery

Avery emerged from her room just in time for dinner. She had come out briefly for lunch and was told about their father's note. It seemed they would be choosing a board game to play after dinner. She almost rolled her eyes when the information was given to her. What did her father think playing a game together would achieve? She, for one, was not looking forward to it. *Aren't all these things Dad is asking of us making a difference?* A little voice inside her asked. She internally shouted at it to shut up. She had tried to broaden her horizons this morning and got smacked in the face for her efforts. She wasn't ready for another try just yet.

Avery planted her butt in a chair at the table where her sisters were waiting for her. She looked at their faces. They both looked happy. No, Lauren looked ecstatic. Maria looked refreshed like a weight had fallen off her shoulders. Avery scowled at them.

When she began to eat, the scowl fell away. Maria really was a great cook. She had inherited that from their mother. *I should cook more*, Avery thought. After all, with no social life, she had plenty of time to develop that skill. At least then she'd have something to show for all her time alone.

She sighed, drawing some attention from both of her sisters. She pretended the amazing food was the cause, but it wasn't. Cooking was not something she had ever enjoyed and it wouldn't fix her loneliness. After this trip, it would be impossible to lie to herself about how lonely she really was. It was eating her up inside. So was the fear. But how did she fight that? The fear was so intense as to be paralyzing. Staying home, safe behind a row of deadbolts, was the only thing that stopped the fear.

Avery paused in mid-chew. That statement wasn't true either, not anymore. She had gotten a little better, hadn't she? She was sleeping in a house with only one lock on the door, and without knowing for sure that all the windows were locked, or even closed. She was going outside every day. She was very close to putting her feet in the water even without one of her sisters sitting with her. There was no way in hell she would have even thought of that a few weeks ago. It *was* possible to overcome her fear. She was just going to have to do it one baby step at a time.

"What do you think, Avery?"

She snapped her head up and looked at her sisters. Maria had asked the question. "What do I think about what?"

Maria looked annoyed by Avery's lack of attention to the conversation. "About what game to play. Lauren wants to play *Monopoly* and I thought *Life* was a better idea. What do you think?"

"Are those the only choices?"

"No," Lauren spoke up. "There's also *Clue*, *Uno*, and *Candy Land*."

"*Monopoly* is so long. I hate *Life*. I say, *Uno*." Avery said.

Maria shrugged. "I guess we're drawing straws again."

Chapter 39

Maria

Avery won. They would play *Uno*. Lauren found the cards and dealt the first hand. Maria looked at the cards in her hand. She wasn't thinking about how to win so much as how to draw the game out. She wanted to play a few hands, let Avery get comfortable before she started actively trying to get her talking. She had spent some time already thinking about the best strategy. She considered it likely that Avery would not open up easily. But on the other hand, when they played the truth game, Avery had been more open than she or Lauren. So maybe it wouldn't be so hard. But, the night of the truth game, Avery had mostly opened up about the past. Getting her to talk about more recent events might prove difficult.

The first three hands went by with idle chit-chat being the only conversation. Lauren eyed Maria a few times. Maria knew her sister was wondering when she intended to start working on their plan.

Maria's turn came. She laid down a blue four, then she said, "I had a terrible dream last night."

Avery's head snapped up. She gave Maria a sharp look. Maria continued to talk. "It's the first time in a while I've had one of these dreams. I used to have them all the time."

Lauren played a wild card. "Red," she said.

"It started after I lost Melanie in the grocery store when she was three. The store manager found her after fifteen minutes. She had wandered into the employee area and was hiding under a table. It was the longest fifteen minutes of my life. I thought something horrible might have happened to her. I felt like a terrible mother," Maria said. "After that, I started having these nightmares about losing my children. They weren't all the same, but they had that one thing in common. The worst part was they felt so real. I would wake up gasping or screaming or crying."

Avery laid down a red six and then Maria followed it with a red reverse card. The play went back to Avery and Maria stayed quiet for a couple more plays, letting her story set in. Then she looked up at Lauren and asked, "Have you ever had a dream like that?"

Lauren gave Maria a wide-eyed look, like a deer caught in headlights. "N—no. I've never had a recurring dream."

So much for following my lead, Maria thought. You'd think Lauren could at least make something up. It wasn't that hard. But clearly, Lauren was not going to be any help. Maria moved on by herself.

"It wasn't the first time for me." Maria laid down a green seven. "Uno," she said. Avery scowled at her. She didn't like to lose. "Back when I was in college I had some recurring dreams. It happened after I went to this frat party." Avery looked up at Maria with interest. She wasn't worried about losing the game anymore. "I drank too much; *way* too much. I got sick, and then I passed out."

Maria looked at Avery. She was white as a sheet, and a tear streaked down her right cheek.

"I woke up the next morning in bed with one of the frat boys. I knew him. We were in some of the same classes."

Lauren played a draw two card. Maria gave her an annoyed look as she picked up the required cards, but inside she was smiling. At least Lauren was doing something helpful. The hand would continue.

"He said nothing happened. He told me that he found me passed out and moved me to his room to make sure no one took advantage of me. He was a nice boy, so it's probably true. And we were both wearing clothes when I woke up. But I wasn't wearing my own clothes. I was wearing some of his sweats. He said he helped me change because I had thrown up on my dress. That *was* true.

"Still I had to wonder what, if anything, had happened to me when I was passed out. Even if *that* boy was totally honest, someone else may have found me before he did. I didn't know because I had no memory at all of that time. It's frightening to realize you have this chunk of time when you have no idea what was going on. I had nightmares about it for a couple of years. I never got drunk like that again … until a few days ago that is."

When Maria stopped talking there was a moment where everything seemed to stop. No one spoke and no one played a card.

"It's your turn, Avery," Lauren said breaking the silence.

Maria looked up. Avery wasn't responding to Lauren. She didn't put down a card, she just sat there. She seemed frozen except for the tears rolling down her face. *Did I go too far*, Maria wondered; *poke her soft spot a little too roughly*.

Then Avery spoke in a near whisper. "I have dreams like that." Her lips trembled as she tried to find the words to reveal her most painful secret. "But it isn't because I don't remember what happened to me … it's because I do."

A couple of seconds ticked by, then Lauren reached out and wrapped her hand around Avery's wrist. That was when Maria realized she was literally holding her breath waiting to hear what Avery would say next. She released the air from her lungs and took a breath. Then she reached out and held onto Avery's other wrist. Avery glanced at each sister.

Maria decided it was time she acted like the stand-in mother she once had been. "It's okay, Avery. We're here for you. You can tell us what happened."

"A couple of years ago," Avery began shakily. "I was out—at a club as usual. I met this guy, and he seemed really nice. We talked a little, but the club was noisy so we left and went to his place. That was stupid, I know." Avery looked up sheepishly. "I never thought about those things back then;

never worried. I was reckless at first because I was looking for attention. Then it just became a part of who I was.

"When we got to his place, he offered me a drink, and I took it. We talked for a while, and I started to feel funny. My arms and legs were sluggish. Then, they wouldn't obey my command at all. I couldn't move. At first, I didn't get what was going on. I asked the guy, Greg was his name, for help; told him something was happening to me and I needed him to call 911. He sat there and looked at me, smiling. My glass dropped out of my hand, and crashed on the floor. Glass shards flew out from it, and amber liquid sloshed all over the hardwood." Avery shook her head. "I guess that's not important, but for some reason, I can't recall that night without seeing that glass breaking."

Avery stopped for a moment, gathering her courage to keep telling the story. Maria watched her. She knew where this was heading, and it wasn't entirely a surprise. She had wondered if something like this had happened to Avery. But seeing her baby sister hurting like this, knowing what she'd been through, was heartbreaking. Maria could feel the sting of tears forming in her eyes. She wanted to reach out to Avery and somehow make this terrible thing go away. Of course, that wasn't possible.

"After the glass fell, he came toward me. He dragged me to the floor where there was a rug covering the hardwood. The pieces of glass on the floor dug into my skin as I went across them." Avery stopped, broke off from her sister's grasp, and covered her face with her hands. She sobbed for a few seconds before regaining control. "I couldn't fight him. I knew what he was going to do, but I couldn't move. I wish to God he'd given me something that would have knocked me out." She glanced at Maria with blotchy, red eyes, and her voice broke with her next words. "If only I didn't remember."

Avery broke into sobs again, and Maria jumped off her seat, wrapped Avery in her arms, and stroked her hair. Lauren grabbed Avery's hand.

"I'm so sorry," Maria mumbled in Avery's ear.

Avery cried for only a few seconds, then she pushed away from Maria and said, "I need to finish."

Maria nodded and returned to her chair.

"He raped me. I think you already know that. But after he was done with me, he called out, 'hey guys, it's your turn.'" Avery's face scrunched up as she fought to control the emotion. A disobedient tear streaked down her cheek. "A bedroom door opened and two other men came out. They raped me too."

"Oh, Avery," Lauren said. "I'm so, so sorry I wasn't there for you when you needed me. If I was, maybe that wouldn't have happened to you. I'm so sorry." Lauren was crying now.

Avery got up and went to Lauren, wrapping her arms around her. "No. I blamed you—and you," she said looking at Maria. "But I was wrong. It wasn't your fault. I was the one who was foolish and irresponsible. I see that now. Maria, you had to take over as my mother figure when you were only nine. You had every right to want a life of your own. And Lauren, you didn't even know what I expected of you."

"But that's just it," Lauren argued, "I should have been paying attention. I should have seen that you needed me. I was too self-absorbed."

"Maybe," Avery said. "But you were fifteen when Maria left for college. I think being self-absorbed is actually pretty normal." She looked at both her sisters and smiled a little. "I don't blame either of you anymore. But now you know why I'm so afraid—of everything." She stopped, took a deep breath, and smiled through the tears that were still glistening in her eyes. "I'm glad you know. I didn't think I wanted to tell you. It seemed too painful to talk about, but I feel a little better now that you know."

"I'm glad you're feeling better, but I don't know if I can forgive myself. I was fifteen when Maria left, but I didn't stay fifteen. I should have seen your behavior for what it was. I should have been there for you," Lauren said.

"I should have too," Maria said. "I'm sorry I made you feel abandoned. I wish I had done better."

"Me too," Avery said. "I should have asked for what I needed instead of acting out. We all made mistakes."

Maria and Lauren both nodded. Then Maria looked at Avery and said, "I want to tell you something too. I spewed it all out to Lauren earlier today. It came out in anger, but then we talked, and I was glad I told her. Now I should tell you as well." She paused. It wasn't easy to say, but what Avery shared was far more difficult. Taking a deep breath, she continued. "Hank is having an affair. I think I'm going to leave him when I get home."

"Oh, my God! Really?" Avery said.

Maria nodded. "It's been going on for a good while now."

"Since we're all sharing," Lauren said, "I want to tell you something too, Avery."

"Is it about how you've been tripping all over yourself and not sleeping—or painting?" Avery asked.

Lauren looked surprised. "I tried to paint since we got here, but before that, I hadn't painted in months. How did you know that?"

"Your door is always closed. You don't do that when you paint. You always liked sharing your work."

Lauren nodded in agreement. "Not anymore," she muttered. "It is about—what's going on with me. You see ..." Lauren paused, looked at Maria, searched her eyes for help. Maria nodded for her to continue. "I—do you remember Aunt Emma?"

Avery's forehead scrunched up. "Dad's older sister? The one that had … You don't mean?" Avery stopped short, shaking her head.

Lauren nodded. "Yes, that's what I mean. I have Parkinson's. I'll never get better, only worse. I'll never be the artist I dreamed I'd be."

"Oh, Lauren," Avery said, leaning in, and wrapping her arms around her sister. When she pulled back, Avery said, "That's what all the money was for. And I was so terrible to you when you asked for help."

"You didn't know," Lauren said. "You didn't know I was working two jobs and getting to work on time every day. You thought I was being the same old irresponsible Lauren you always knew. Why wouldn't you? I didn't tell you any different."

Maria took hold of a hand from each sister. "It will be different now. We have Dad to thank for that."

Maria sat in her room by the open window. A cigarette slowly burned between her fingers. She blew smoke out the window and watched as it wafted away in the breeze. She was feeling something strange. Ever since the talk with her sisters had ended, she'd wanted desperately to talk to Hank. Strange didn't even seem a strong enough word. She hadn't engaged in a real conversation with her husband in over three years. But no one had ever filled the void that was left. It wasn't just her husband she had lost, it was her best friend. She and Hank used to talk about everything. She had girlfriends, but none of them had ever compared to the friend Hank had once been to her. She missed that now. Learning so much about her sisters, Maria wanted to tell someone. But not just anyone … Hank. She missed him, missed what they used to be together. She had once thought of him as the kindest and warmest man she'd ever known. Then he changed. Her Hank seemed to fade away and this other Hank took over. The new Hank didn't look at her with warm eyes like the old one had. He didn't ask about her day or offer to help with the kids, or the dishes, or the laundry. He didn't really talk to her anymore at all. Maria only wished she knew what had happened to cause the change in him. She often wondered if it was her. Was it really the weight she'd gained? Or was it something bigger than that? She wished she knew because her marriage had fallen apart, and she didn't feel like she'd ever had a chance to fix things. How do you fix what is broken if you don't know what it is?

Maria snuffed out her cigarette in the glass ashtray on the window sill. Could she really leave Hank? She still loved him. There was no denying that. But it had been some time since she'd felt like he loved her back. Didn't she deserve better? Lauren and Avery thought she did. They had encouraged her to leave him. They were probably right, but it still stung when they called him a scumbag and other choice names. They were trying to support her, but it was an insult to her as well—or at least she felt like it was. Hadn't she chosen him? Built a life with him, and had a family with him? If he was a scumbag, then that is what she chose to be with. But he wasn't always that way. Maria wanted desperately to see some sign that the man she married was still there, buried beneath the new persona. She wanted to believe that he could be that man again. Was she being naïve?

She closed her eyes and tried to remember what his touch had once felt like. She tried to remember what it was like to be held in his arms and share all her thoughts with him. In her mind, she saw the two of them walking down a quiet street hand in hand. The glow of the street lamps softened the angles of Hank's face as he looked at her with adoring eyes and listened to her talk about all the patients she'd worked with during the day. Her heart fluttered with the image, but then it changed, and he was the man that sat in the recliner with his eyes closed until the kids went to bed. He was the man that didn't talk to her or look at her or touch her. He was once again the man that ignored their children and went out late at night. Worst of all, he was once again the man that came home smelling like Carina's perfume.

Maria got up, closed the window, and gathered her pajamas and toiletries. She swiped away a few tears on her cheeks impatiently, then headed for the bathroom to take a shower. She knew what she had to do.

Chapter 40

Lauren

Lauren sat quietly by the lake. She was showered, and she'd finished two cups of coffee. She was still tired, but that was normal for her now; always tired, always stumbling with feet that didn't quite move the way they were told.

The sun was just beginning to rise, coloring the water with gold at the horizon. Lauren thought for a moment what a beautiful painting it would make. She closed her eyes, and, in her mind, placed the image on a canvas. If she added a few clouds to the picture, the water would be colored with shades of pink. She wanted so badly to have that brush in her hand, putting what was in her head onto a canvas. But it wouldn't come out right. Her hand would start to tremble and mess everything up. Even in her good times, her work came out sub-standard, like something she could have painted in grade school. Her therapist had given her a special brush to use and insisted painting, even when it didn't come out as good, was good for her well-being. Though she was usually just too busy, she had tried since coming here. But how could it be good for her to keep reminding herself that she wasn't what she used to be? Without her ability to paint she didn't even feel like she was *who* she used to be. Maybe that was her fault. She had decided long ago to make painting the center of her identity. She had allowed so little else in her life. She was Lauren the irresponsible painter. Now she was neither of those things. So where did that leave her? Who was she? When she got home, would she even have time to try and find out? She'd need to find a second job to replace the clerk job she'd lost. And once again life would be an endless parade of work shifts, doctor appointments, medication schedules, and trying, desperately trying, to sleep.

Lauren picked up a pebble in her right hand. It wasn't trembling, hadn't again since yesterday morning. It would start again, and it would get worse until she had little control left over her own body, she knew that. But today, for now at least, it was obeying her commands. She rolled the pebble in her hand a moment as she got to her feet. Then she moved her arm as if Blake were there guiding it, and tossed the stone at the lake. She smiled when it bounced once before sinking.

"See, I knew you could do it," Blake said from behind her. She turned around and grinned at him.

"It's crazy that a rock bouncing on the water can make me this happy, but I'm not even going to give you a hard time for sneaking up on me again."

Blake shrugged innocently. "Who's sneaking?" He moved closer and pulled her into his arms, kissing her. "I just wanted to say good morning."

"If you're going to say it like that, you can say it again."

"Okay." He kissed her cheek. "Good morning." He kissed her neck. "Good morning."

Lauren smiled at his playful way of greeting her. She could get used to this. Perhaps it would be a part of her new identity; loved by a handsome man. Of course, it wasn't love—not yet, but someday it could be.

Blake loosened his embrace and they both sat down on the edge of the retaining wall. "I told my sisters," she blurted out.

Blake gave her a measuring look. "How was it?"

"Wonderful—and terrible."

Blake's face turned to confusion as he continued to watch her. "I learned things about them too," Lauren continued. "Nothing is what I thought when I came here a week and a half ago. I wasn't even close to knowing who Maria and Avery are and what they've been through." Blake nodded, urging her to continue. "I should have known my dad would be right about that. He told me we didn't know each other any longer and that they had both changed. If we had talked to each other more before, Dad wouldn't have needed to go to such great lengths with his will in order to make us see." She looked at the lake down below her. "And he wouldn't have had to spend the last year of his life seeing us each separately. He hated that."

"I take it they were supportive," Blake said softly.

Lauren nodded. "They were wonderful. And I feel a lot lighter now. They're going through things too. I think we can help each other."

Blake smiled his radiant smile, Caribbean blue eyes flashing. He pulled her into a hug. "That's wonderful."

Lauren pulled back from the hug. "Yeah, and you've been wonderful too. I would never have imagined I'd meet someone here, someone I think could be really special. Someone who knows all about what I'm dealing with and doesn't care. I can't wait to see what you are like when we both go back to our real lives. I bet you look amazing in your suit for work."

She glanced at Blake's face. His smile seemed to have tightened. Maybe she was pushing things too fast. She stopped talking and they sat in silence. Lauren wanted to kick herself for letting too many of her thoughts out. She should know better. But then again, she hadn't been in a relationship for quite a while. Remembering all the rules was tough. She'd come on strong right after they met, but that was different than this. Demanding a kiss could not be equal to placing herself squarely in his regular life without an invitation. It just seemed like things were going so well. She had made an assumption.

After ten minutes of awkward silence, Blake got up and dusted off his pants. "I better get started," he said. "I have a lot to do today." He kissed the top of her head and walked away.

Chapter 41

Maria

Maria was in the kitchen with a cup of coffee and a book when the doorbell rang. Evan smiled at her when she opened the door. She took the bag of groceries he was holding and gave him a tip, then carried the bag back into the kitchen with her. She set it down on the counter and unloaded its contents. At the bottom of the bag, there were three envelopes. Maria lifted them out and looked at them. Each envelope had a name on it; one for her, one for Lauren, and one for Avery.

Maria set the letters for her sisters on the counter where they would be seen and took the one with her name on it back to the table. She sat down and carefully opened the envelope, and took out the letter inside.

Dearest Maria,

It is my hope that by now you and your sisters have talked, and, in so doing, have learned some things about each other. I hope you are seeing each other through different eyes. All of you have been hard on each other, holding onto grievances, and also hard on yourselves—you especially, Maria. You have always carried such a heavy load. I know you carry the burdens now that should be shared with your husband, and, before you were married, you carried the weight of acting as a mother to your sisters. That is my fault. I let you take on that role even though I knew that was not what was right for you. It was hard losing your mother and becoming a single father. I went to work and gave all I had to other people's kids all day. Sometimes it was hard to find anything left at the end of the day to give to my own. But putting it on your shoulders was wrong of me. I know you think that is what your mother wanted, but it's not. She never intended for you to carry that burden. She wanted you to help your sisters and to help me, but she didn't want you to take on the job of a mother when you were just a child yourself. It was unfair of me and caused bitterness between you and your sisters. Your mother wanted the opposite and I failed her. I hope now this bitterness can end. I want to ask that you start that process in a small way today. Go swimming together.

Maria smiled as she finished reading the note. A lot of the guilt she felt about failing to uphold her mother's wishes when it came to her sisters had already begun to fade. Telling Lauren and Avery how she felt and listening to them had made a big difference. But this note from her father gave her even more peace. It wasn't really because he didn't blame her. In fact, she hated that he had blamed himself so much. What really gave her peace was knowing that, while her mother's wishes were somewhat failed by all of them, it was not too late to fix it. She could still be the big sister her mother wanted her to be. She and Lauren and Avery didn't have to turn out the way Eve and her sister Carol had.

Her father's request might sound silly to most. What could swimming in a lake do? But Maria knew why he wanted them to do it.

Chapter 42

Avery

Avery wiggled into her blue swimsuit. She had read her father's note to her. He wanted them all to go swimming and, of course, it was for her benefit. She stepped to the full-length mirror that was hanging on the back of her bedroom door and glanced at her reflection. The bathing suit looked good on her, though it would look even better on Lauren with her blue eyes. But the color suited Avery's blond hair and light complexion. She wondered for a moment what Mike would think, and found herself blushing with the thought. Sometimes she would lie in bed at night and imagine what it would feel like to kiss him. The idea made her heart flutter, but she couldn't move beyond the kiss in her mind. She simply could not bring herself to think of his hands on her. When she did, she went instantly back into her nightmare. She wanted to fall in love, just like anyone, but she didn't think she could ever let a man touch her again. If the thought of it was too painful, how would she ever handle the reality? And what man was going to want a relationship with someone he could not touch?

This time the bathing suit was going to get wet. She would make it into the water with her sisters' help. They understood her now, as well as anyone could, and she understood them much better also.

Avery picked up a hairbrush from the nightstand and brushed her hair, pulling it into a ponytail with the rubber band that was around her wrist. She gave the picture of her mother a quick glance. *I'm stepping forward, Mom*, she thought. *You'll be proud of me.* Then she picked up her towel and headed out to the kitchen.

Her sisters were there waiting for her. Maria was wearing a burgundy one-piece suit that looked amazing with her chestnut hair and caramel eyes. Lauren was wearing a green and yellow striped bikini that was faded and worn. Avery was hit with the realization that Lauren was, in a sense, poor. Her bathing suit was probably a few years old. She couldn't afford a new one, something Avery hadn't even given a second thought to. Lauren spent all her money on necessities and medical bills.

Avery dropped her eyes away, feeling ashamed of all the times she had treated Lauren badly. She had more than enough money. Why had she been so resistant to helping her sister? She told herself that she would have acted differently if she had known Lauren was sick, but would she have? The truth was, she didn't know. There had been such a chasm between them before this trip. She had blamed her sisters for so much of what hurt inside. She'd never considered their side of things.

"Let's go, Avery," Lauren said. "I can't wait to get into the water."

Avery looked up and gave her sister a half smile. She nodded, and they all headed out the back door. The day was beautiful. The sun was shining high in a deep blue sky. The lake was shimmering in the sunlight, and the ducks were easing their way across the water.

The three of them walked to the dock and put their towels down. Maria turned to Avery and asked, "Do you want to sit for a while and just put our feet in?"

Avery nodded. That would make this easier. She wanted to swim, but, even with her sisters here, it was still a little scary. It was hard to let her guard down and put herself in what felt like a vulnerable situation.

They spread their towels and sat down, allowing their feet to dangle in the water. It was only a little bit cold under the warmth of the sun.

"It's a beautiful day," Avery said.

"You should have seen the sunrise," Lauren said.

Avery glanced at her with a smile. "I suppose you watched it with our hunky neighbor."

"Blake showed up," Lauren said without taking her eyes off the lake.

Maria turned and raised her eyebrows at Avery. "Everything okay with the two of you?" Avery asked.

"Sure. Why wouldn't it be?"

"I don't know. Just asking."

Several seconds elapsed in silence, then Lauren spoke up again. "It's not like it matters, right? It's just a vacation fling. It was never going anywhere."

"You never know," Maria said. "My friend, Jessie, met her husband on vacation."

"Jessie was probably a lot smarter and cooler than me," Lauren said.

"What does that mean?" Avery asked, looking in Lauren's direction.

Lauren sighed. "I think I screwed it up."

"Why do you think that? He looked pretty into you the other night when you two were star gazing." Maria said.

"This morning I made the mistake of assuming this was more than just a vacation fling. I invited myself right into his regular life … stupid."

"Why? What did he say?" Avery asked.

"He didn't say anything. We sat in silence for several minutes and then he excused himself. He got tense as soon as the words came out of my mouth."

"Oh … I see," Avery said. She looked back out at the lake. The ducks had come closer, probably hoping for an offering of food. One of them was quacking at them.

A few moments later Lauren spoke up again. "It shouldn't bother me. We're having a good time here. I should be happy with that."

Maria and Avery both looked at her but said nothing.

"It's just that I really like him, and I thought he really liked me. Then again, it's been so long since the last time I dated, I'd probably jump at any opportunity."

"Are you seriously trying to say that you're just so desperate you don't know your true feelings?" Avery asked, a little edge coming into her voice. "Because that's not you at all. You have never been that person. Whatever you feel, I am sure it's real."

Lauren shook her head. "Well, I'm glad you know who I am because I'm not sure about that anymore."

Avery looked at Lauren again. A tear was running down her cheek. She swiped it away and tried to recover. Avery reached over and grabbed her hand. "You're the same person you've always been. This disease doesn't change that."

Maria took Lauren's other hand. "She's right, Lauren. You're still you."

"No, I'm not. I used to know exactly who I was, an artist, a painter."

"That's still you, Lauren," Avery insisted.

"No, it's not. I can't paint anymore."

"You can still paint," Avery said.

"No, it comes out terrible. My hand shakes. Even when it is only trembling a little, it's a problem."

"Maybe you need to find a way to make that work for you," Maria said.

"How?"

"I don't know. You're the artist," Maria said. Then with emphasis, "You are. Maybe landscapes aren't the right outlet for your creativity anymore. Perhaps you should think in broader terms."

Lauren was quiet for a few seconds, then she nodded. "Maybe you're right … I'll think about it."

"And you know, Lauren, maybe Blake was just surprised. Give him some time. But if you think he's right for you, then don't question yourself. Go for it. At least you'll know one way or the other," Avery said.

Lauren nodded and smiled in Avery's direction. "Thanks, Ave. I'll think about that too."

"How about we forget the men and get to swimming. The water is looking pretty good to me," Maria said.

Lauren and Avery smiled and nodded in agreement.

"Okay, then, time to hop in," Maria said before getting up and jumping into the water. The ducks scattered as the water splashed. "It's great! Come on in."

Lauren stood up next and hopped into waist deep water. Avery felt her heart clench a little at the thought of following. She looked around, checking the perimeter.

"Come on, Avery, you can do this," Maria encouraged. She and Lauren both stepped to the edge of the dock and reached out their hands. Avery took their hands and eased off the edge of the dock, inching into the water at a slow pace. Maria and Lauren were patient with her, allowing her to go as slowly as she needed.

The water splashed as Avery dropped the rest of the way off the dock, and some of the ducks quacked in protest of the continued invasion. "I'm in," Avery said smiling. "I did it."

Lauren and Maria smiled back at her, still holding her hands. "It's a big step," Maria said. "Now let's see if you can swim."

Avery followed as Maria led her out into deeper water. She was afraid and continued to glance around. Each time she did, one of her sisters grabbed her attention and reminded her that she was not alone. As she ventured out further into the lake with them, she felt a sense of freedom, as if chains were falling off her. It was scary, but freeing. Could it be like that with Mike too? Could it be possible to get past the fear? It was hard to imagine, but a few days ago jumping into this lake seemed hard to imagine. Now she was standing with water up to her shoulders ... and she was thrilled, exhilarated. Maybe, with the help of people who loved her, anything was possible.

Chapter 43

Lauren

After they were done swimming and had eaten lunch, Lauren indulged in a nap. She awoke three hours later, at four in the afternoon, feeling the best she had in days. Saying she was refreshed and energized was probably a bit of an overstatement, but she was as close to that as she had been in nearly two years.

When she sat up, the first thing to catch her eye was an empty canvas that she'd left sitting atop her easel. A feeling of anticipation filled her chest as she thought of what Maria had said. Maybe there was still a way for her to be an artist. Perhaps she didn't have to let this disease take that, her greatest joy, away from her. She jumped out of bed, then stopped short, grabbing the nightstand to stop her from falling. *Damn!* In her excitement, she had forgotten that some limitations did still exist, her problems with balance being a primary example. She steadied herself and got her bearings, then went into the bathroom to brush her hair and pull it back.

Lauren went to her easel and got her colors ready. Then she picked up her brush and stared at the empty canvas. She tried to visualize the picture she wanted to put there; the sunrise over the lake, with a gold reflection on the water. No, she had to think of something else. Landscapes required attention to fine details, and that was no longer possible for her. She closed her eyes, trying to imagine something broader to paint on the canvas, but it was no use. Everything that came to mind was impossible. She couldn't paint her passion, landscapes, she couldn't paint people, that would be even harder. She struggled to think of something that stirred her emotions, something with less detail, but her mind kept coming back to the sunrise. *Damn it! Damn, damn, damn!*

Lauren threw down the brush in frustration and paced the room. She just couldn't do this. She dragged her toes across the carpet, not picking them up high enough, and lost her balance, fell, and landed on her bed. *That was lucky*, she thought. Then she pounded her fist into the mattress. *Lucky?* No, none of this was lucky. It shouldn't be this way!

She got up from the bed and left her room, storming through the house and out the back door. Then forced herself to slow down. There was nothing soft to break her fall out here. Moving gingerly, she walked to the edge of the lake.

Lauren heard something splash into the water and looked up to see what it was. There was only a small ripple on the water's surface. She glanced to her right and saw Blake standing there with a handful of pebbles. He raised his other hand and waved at her. "Hi," Lauren said in return.

Blake threw another pebble, and Lauren watched as it skipped across the lake. She thought about sitting down, but her frustration level was still too high. It was taking all her willpower not to pace in front of Blake. She wished he wasn't there. She really wasn't in the mood to talk to anyone, especially him, and watching him skip stones so easily was only adding to her aggravation. There was no rational reason to be upset with him, she knew that. It wasn't like he was at fault for being capable of such things while she was not. But it didn't really matter right now that it wasn't his fault. She was angry at her situation, and she felt like lashing out.

Blake took another stone from his left hand into his right and prepared to toss it. Then he stopped and regarded Lauren. "What's wrong?"

"Nothing," Lauren said defensively, her voice holding a sharp edge.

Blake raised his eyebrows. He laid his pile of tiny rocks down on the ground and walked closer to Lauren. Then he sat down and waited.

"I said I'm fine," Lauren said.

"Okay." Blake stayed where he was.

Lauren moved to the edge of the lake. "I don't want to talk about it."

"Sure, okay."

Lauren looked back at him. He just sat there, watching her. "I can't paint, okay? Are you happy now?" she yelled.

"You can't paint … or you can't paint what you want to paint?"

She squinted at him. How did he know that was the problem? "It's the same thing. I thought I could paint something different, something with less fine detail, but the only things that come to mind are impossible for me now." She huffed out a breath. "You know what they say about teaching old dogs new tricks."

"That's a terrible metaphor. You are not old, nor a dog. How long have you tried to paint something different?"

Lauren felt a little silly suddenly. She looked away from him so he wouldn't see the rise of color in her face that came from a combination of embarrassment and irritation.

"How long?" he persisted

"I don't know, twenty minutes or so," she barked.

"A whole twenty minutes and it's a lost cause, huh?"

Lauren glared at him. How dare he judge her so smugly? What did he know about it anyway? Had he ever had to try and change virtually everything about the way he did things because of a disability? "I'm sure *you* could never understand."

Blake sighed. "Probably not," he agreed, and for a moment Lauren was angry at him for daring to agree with her. "So it would be easier if you explain it all to me."

Lauren turned back to the lake and watched it ripple as the ducks swam across. She didn't want to talk to him, but, for some reason, the words began to flow out of her anyway. "I was talking to my sisters today and they suggested that I try to make my disability work in my favor somehow, paint different things that didn't require the fine details. I thought it could work, maybe, and I started to feel really excited about it." She turned and looked at him pleadingly as if he had the power to fix what was wrong. "If I could paint again, that would mean everything to me."

Lauren looked back to find Blake watching her intently. "This is going to sound a little strange to you, I think," he said, "but, in a way, I envy you a little."

Lauren crinkled her nose up at him. Was he crazy? Why on earth would anyone envy her right now?

"You have an absolute picture of who you are. You are an artist—simple as that. I guess it's impossible for me to imagine what it would feel like for you to feel like that identity is slipping away. I'm still wishing I knew exactly what my identity should be. My job is a job. It is not my identity, and I don't know what is."

Blake paused for a moment and looked at Lauren. "But maybe I can still help you." He stood up and walked to her, placing his hands on her arms. "What are you feeling right now, when you think about not being able to paint what you would like to?"

Lauren shook her head. "Angry."

"Just angry?"

She didn't want to, but she let her mind go back to the easel for a second, allowed herself to touch that moment, that feeling again. "Furious," she said.

Blake looked into her eyes. "Yes. Now you're getting to the truth … Paint the fury."

Lauren searched his face as if a better explanation could be found there. Could she do that, paint an emotion? She had never even thought of such an idea before. Of course, there were artists who did it, but she had always painted what she could see or imagine. Could she imagine a feeling, put it into shape and form, give it a color?

"I don't know if I can do that," she muttered. "I've never painted that way before."

"I guess you won't know until you try."

Lauren nodded as the hint of a smile emerged on her face. The fury had faded for the moment and she was feeling lighter. She leaned in and hugged him. “Maybe you should consider counselor as a possible identity. If nothing else, you got me thinking in a new way.”

Blake smiled at her. “I hope it really does help.” Then he walked back to his pile of pebbles and picked them up again before turning back to look at Lauren. “Sit with me a while?” He said.

Lauren nodded and walked over to him. They sat down at the water’s edge and talked about their favorite places and where they would go if they had the money to travel anywhere, while Blake casually skipped stones. Lauren wondered how Blake was feeling now about their conversation that morning—when she had let him know that she was interested in a relationship that went beyond their time at the lake. She thought about bringing it up, but she was afraid it would take them back to the uncomfortable silence that had followed before. She decided to let it go and see what happened. Avery told her to go for it—tell Blake what she wanted and see what he said. Part of her wanted to do that. Then at least she would know one way or the other, but she decided to let things happen naturally instead of pushing it. If nothing else, she could enjoy the next few days with him.

Avery

It was almost time for dinner, and Avery was helping Maria cook. Realistically, she was watching and assisting with small tasks that Maria gave her. That was better for everyone. She watched Maria prepare a chicken to bake, and helped by cleaning up behind her with Clorox wipes. Then Maria started some vegetables on the stove, and Avery wrapped potatoes in foil to be put in the oven with the chicken.

Avery was feeling great, better than great. She had known getting into the lake would be a step forward for her, just as her father had known, but she didn't realize it would make this much difference. She felt like chains had been pulled off her. No, it wasn't the end of her issues, and she knew that. She would still struggle with irrational fear, but, for a while, she had been free of all that. The fear had slid away to the bottom of the lake, and she'd been able to enjoy some time outside like a normal person. She had been able to talk to her sisters without a constant eye sweep of the perimeter. She had been able to let the worry go. For thirty minutes she had been outside without looking for escape routes or calculating possible dangers, and it was blissful.

Lauren was in her room and had been in there quite a bit since they came in from swimming. She had spent a little time out by the lake, presumably with Blake. Avery wondered what Lauren was doing all that time in her room, and hoped she was painting. Avery had given Lauren a hard time about her singlemindedness over the last several years, and painting was the object of that, but, in truth, Avery was proud of her sister's artistry. She had never wanted to see Lauren lose that. Now, knowing what Lauren was facing, Avery hoped and prayed she would find a way to keep painting in her life.

Maria turned from the simmering pot on the stove. “Everything is cooking and there’s really not much to do except stir and baste once in a while. We could do something else for a while, play a game, watch TV...” Maria shrugged.

“Let’s look at some more pictures. I like to hear the stories.”

Maria smiled. “Sure. Go get the book.”

Avery went into her room and looked at the photo albums she’d brought. It was odd to take something like this on a trip, she understood that, but somehow she couldn’t imagine going anywhere without them. It would be like leaving her past behind. There was so much about her family, her mother especially, that she couldn’t remember, so these books of pictures seemed like her only link. Maybe she wouldn’t need them anymore once she’d heard all the stories. She would have something else to hold onto.

Avery selected an album that contained older family photos, from before she was born, and went back out to the kitchen. She placed the album on the table, and Maria joined her there. They both looked in awe at pictures of their mother with hair, before she was sick. Maria told Avery about camping trips and family events; the Christmas when Lauren lost a tooth and it fell in the dough for the cookies, the fourth of July picnic when mom announced she was pregnant again (with Avery) right as the fireworks started. Avery cherished every second of this time, hearing these stories. She was like a starving child finally getting food, and everything tasted wonderful.

By the time Lauren came out to join them for dinner, Avery was feeling joyful, enjoying all the new memories she could now hold onto. They weren’t her own memories, of course. No one could change the lack of real memory she had of her mother, and of their family while she was still alive, still healthy, but the stories were almost as good. Maria did such an amazing job of telling them. She really put Avery in the moment, and Avery was fairly certain that Maria was trying to do exactly that.

Lauren did not look very happy. She looked like she was stuck in a state of deep concentration, working on a problem that was far too difficult, and her jaw was tight. Avery angled her head in Lauren's direction. "What's up?" she asked.

Lauren looked at her for a moment as if she were looking at a stranger. A few seconds ticked by, then Lauren said, "Nothing. I'm fine."

"You don't look fine, and you've been in your room for a long time."

Lauren shook her head and tried a little smile. "I'm just trying to figure something out."

Avery regarded her closely. "You were working on painting."

Lauren sighed. "I was trying to work on painting. I didn't get anything done. I'm just trying to figure out how to paint in a new way. I thought it would come easier. I'm not sure why."

Avery reached out a hand and laid it on Lauren's. "You will figure it out. I'm sure about that. Don't give up."

Lauren gripped Avery's hand and nodded. "I won't give up this easy. It's just difficult to accept that something that used to come to me so easy is now so hard."

Maria joined them, setting the baked chicken down on the table. She placed a hand on Lauren's back. "We're right here with you, sis," she said before sitting down. "Avery, I'm terrible at carving a chicken. Would you do it, please?"

"Oh, yeah, sure." Avery picked up a large fork and a carving knife and began carving the bird.

They ate quietly for a while, then Maria broke the silence. "Lauren, I've been thinking—about your situation, and ..."

"My situation?" Lauren interjected.

"Well ... I don't know a better way to put it. It's just that I wanted to suggest that you move in with me."

Lauren dropped her fork, noisily, on her plate. "Move in with you?" She sounded flabbergasted.

Maria laid her fork down carefully and looked up at Lauren with an earnest expression. "You shouldn't be working two jobs. You need more time to rest. And I want you to have some time to paint. Besides that ..." Maria stopped. It was obvious that the next words on her mind were ones she didn't think Lauren would like.

"What, Maria? Just say it," Lauren said.

"I could help you. I'm a nurse and eventually—well, you'll need some help."

Lauren looked down at the table and fiddled with her napkin. "I don't think it's that bad yet."

"I'm sorry. I'm not trying to make you feel worse. I just don't want you working so hard. It's not good for you. You shouldn't have to when I can help."

"I know you just want to help, but you've got the kids—and Hank."

"I don't think Hank and I will be in the same house much longer," Maria said tightly.

"Even so," Lauren looked up, "You don't have any room for me."

"I can make room. We'll figure it out."

Lauren shook her head. "No, Maria, you have your own problems to work out. You don't need to worry about me too. No matter what you decide about Hank, you will have a lot on your plate."

"Maybe I have a better idea," Avery said. Both of her sisters looked at her in surprise, almost as if they'd forgotten she was there. "I've been doing so much better since we all came here. It's been really good for me to be with both of you." Maria and Lauren nodded with interested, but puzzled expressions. "I don't live that far away from you, Lauren, and I have an extra bedroom that no one is using. We could share the rent. It would help us both. You wouldn't have to work so much, and I wouldn't have to be alone."

Lauren shook her head. "I know someday I'll have to say yes to some of this, and rely on both of you, but I don't want to do it any sooner than I have to." She looked down again, seeming almost ashamed, and Avery felt a stab of hurt because she knew she had helped that shame bloom. "I don't want to be a burden any sooner than I have to. When this week is over, and we get the money from the will, I'll be good for a while. I won't even have to work two jobs again right away."

"But that money won't last," Maria started, geared up to continue the fight.

"Lauren," Avery said in an even tone, "You would not be a burden. You would be helping me as much as I'd be helping you—maybe more in the beginning." She looked Lauren in the eye. "Do you know what I live like?" She paused a moment to see if Lauren would answer, but only silence filled the air. "I have three deadbolts on my door, and I still feel vulnerable. I barely ever leave my apartment, and I don't let anyone in." Avery choked back a sob as emotion rose up. She didn't want to go back to the life she was describing. "I can't even enjoy a good movie because I'm too busy checking all the windows, even though I'm on the third floor. When I look outside during the day, I am torn between desperately wanting to go out and an overwhelming fear of everyone and everything that is out there. Don't you see, Lauren, I need you."

Everyone was silent for a few seconds. Avery's heart pounded a drumbeat in her chest. Her sisters kind of knew all those things about her, and yet they may not have really grasped just how bad it was. Either way, it wasn't easy for her to say it out loud—*I'm afraid of the whole world*—but she had done it. Obviously, it wasn't easy. She had spent two years hiring escorts to take her to family events, largely so her family would not know the truth. She had done it, though, because this new idea that had bloomed in her head about having her sister (someone she could trust) live with her gave her so much hope that she couldn't let it go. This was the answer, she was sure of it. This was how she'd be able to move on.

"Avery, I'm so sorry. I guess I still don't know how to stop making everything all about me." Lauren smiled weakly. "Maybe we both would be better off together, but it won't be easy for either of us. I still get wrapped up in myself sometimes and forget the rest of the world exists."

"And I still want to run around like a crazy person and lock every door and window. I'm hoping we can both learn to do better." Avery looked at Maria, who was sitting quietly, watching them. "We'll need our big sister too. I hope you'll come by often."

"Are you kidding? If I do leave Hank, then I'm going to need some help myself, some good babysitters to start with. And I hope you will both come by and visit us from time to time. The kids need to spend time with their aunts."

Lauren and Avery reached out and linked hands with Maria and each other, forming a circle. "Of course we'll come to see you," Avery said. "Things are going to be different now."

Avery was sitting out by the lake, her feet dangling in the water. The coolness felt good as the sun beat down on her. She closed her eyes and tilted her face to the warmth of the sun. She wasn't afraid. She wasn't looking for danger. The ducks were surrounding her, quacking, but it almost seemed like they were talking to her. They were proud of her, happy for her. She could feel them telling her so.

Suddenly the sun began to drop, falling quickly and letting the darkness in. The ducks squawked, and scattered, leaving Avery alone. Her heart began to race. There was no light at all, not even one star shined in the sky. Fear wrapped around her like a suffocating blanket. She wanted to scream, but it got caught in her throat. She heard glass breaking and whipped her head around toward the sound. She wasn't on the dock any longer, she was in a room. She knew that because she could feel the smooth hardwood under her feet where the water had been only moments before. It was still too dark to see. She tried to move, but nothing worked. Her body would not obey her commands.

Avery began to sob as a hand grabbed her by the arm and pulled her across the floor. Shards of glass dug into the skin on her back, shooting pain through her. Then she could see, but only what was right in front of her. It was him, the monster; he was on top of her. His face split in two, then three. Avery screamed.

"Avery, it's ok. It was just a dream." Maria was sitting next to her on the bed. Avery tried to focus on Maria's face as tears burned her eyes. She shot up in the bed and threw her arms around her sister, burying her face in Maria's shoulder.

"It was him. I couldn't move," Avery sputtered.

"No, honey. He isn't here. It was just a dream."

Avery broke into sobs, letting it all out while Maria held her. "It's okay. You're okay," Maria murmured in Avery's ear.

She *would* be okay, Avery realized, now that she had her sisters' support.

Chapter 45

Lauren

The next day there were no notes from her father, no special requests. Lauren got out her paints and stared at her easel for hours trying to find an emotion inside her that was strong enough for her to visualize. The fury wasn't there, not the way it had been the day before. But after a while, she began to think about her parents, both gone now. She allowed the thoughts that she usually blocked out to fill her mind until the sense of loss was overwhelming. Then she closed her eyes and imagined the feelings as colors and shapes. She took a deep breath, picked up her brush, and began to fill her canvas with color, shades of blue mostly, with a bit of muted green and red in the background. When she was done, she stepped back and looked at the result. Tears escaped her eyes as she realized that she liked what she had painted. It was actually good, the best work she had done in a long time. It was possible. She *could* paint in a whole new way.

Looking at the painting, Lauren was suddenly filled with a sense of great joy. She moved the finished painting and put a new canvas on the easel. She closed her eyes and visualized the joy that filled her heart. She picked up her brush again and began to paint.

All day she painted, not stopping even when the trembling in her hand was at its worst. At dinner time, Maria came knocking on Lauren's door. "Lauren? You haven't been out of your room all day. You didn't have any lunch. Come out and have dinner with us. You've got to be hungry, and we've got pizza coming tonight."

"I'm almost done. I'll be out in a few minutes," Lauren called back. She finished the painting she was working on, then she looked around the room. She had completed four paintings in one day! And they were good.

She smiled as she looked at them. She hadn't felt this good in over a year. Even spending time with Blake could not compare, wonderful as it was.

Lauren cleaned up her paints and had dinner with her sisters. She told them that she had been painting, but she did not tell them how good the results were or offer to show them the work she'd done. She wanted Blake to be the first to see. He was the one that gave her this new direction.

The sun rose Tuesday morning behind wispy clouds, spreading pink across the lake water. It was truly beautiful, and Lauren still wished she could paint it, but she smiled because now she knew she could paint the way it made her feel. She sat down on the ground near the shoreline and waited for Blake, but he didn't come. Lauren was disappointed, but she figured Blake was either sleeping late or getting an early start on his work. She would take one of her paintings over to show him as soon as she finished breakfast with Maria and Avery. She was going to cook for them this morning. Cooking could be a difficult task for her, but she was pretty sure she could handle pancakes and eggs. It was important that she let her sisters know how much their support meant to her, and for that, she could certainly try.

Lauren got up from the ground and dusted herself off. When she got back to the house, it was still quiet inside. Maria and Avery were still asleep. Lauren smiled at the thought of surprising them as they woke to the smell of freshly brewed coffee and food cooking.

She pulled a box of pancake mix out of the cupboard and followed the directions to mix the batter. As she pulled a frying pan out, her left hand began to shake. She gave her hand a stern look, as if it were an invader rather than a part of her own body, and said, "Oh, no, you are not going to stop me today!"

Lauren sat the pan down as gingerly as she could, and hoped the clatter would not bring her sisters out before she'd had a chance to get things cooking. A couple of seconds passed and everything remained quiet, so she melted some butter in the pan and started the pancakes.

The pancakes were stacked in a warm oven, and the eggs were in the pan cooking when Maria stepped into the kitchen still wearing purple pajamas. Lauren smiled at her. "Good morning," she said.

"You're chipper this morning," Maria responded. "And you're cooking. I guess there's a first time for everything."

"Believe it or not, I have cooked before," Lauren said. "But I'll admit that it doesn't happen often."

"So what's the special occasion today?"

"Us. You, me, and Avery—acting like sisters again. I wanted to let you both know how much it means to me to have you *really* back in my life; to have your support."

Maria walked over and patted Lauren's back. "It means a lot to me too."

"Who's cooking?" Avery said, stumbling into the kitchen. She was also in pajamas with messy hair and a sleeping mask pushed up around her forehead.

"Lauren is," Maria said with a hint of amazement still evident in her voice. "If you can believe that. Maybe next you'll be cooking."

Avery arched a brow. "You'd probably rather I didn't. But if this tastes as good as it smells, maybe Lauren should do it more often." She dragged the sleeping mask off her forehead and went to the coffee pot, then sat down at the table, sipping her steaming brew.

Lauren smiled at Avery's words, then, scraping the eggs from the pan and into a large bowl, she said, "It's all ready."

As Lauren carried the bowl of eggs to the table, her left hand began to tremble badly, barely allowing her to get the bowl down on the table without a spill. She looked at Maria who was eyeing her with concern. “Hey, sis, could you get the pancakes out of the oven and bring them over?”

“Sure thing,” Maria said. Lauren could tell her sister was glad that she had been willing to ask for help.

Maria placed the plate of pancakes down on the table, then sat down. She reached a hand out to both sides of her. “How about we say a blessing?”

Lauren and Avery joined hands with her and bowed their heads.

“Dear Lord,” Maria began. “Thank you for this food before us. Thank you for the opportunity to be here together. And Thank you so much ...” Maria trailed off into a sniffle. Then she tried again. “Thank you so much for blessing us with a father who, not only worked tirelessly for years to raise us, but who also had the wisdom to know how much we needed each other, and the wisdom to know how to make us see it. In Jesus’ name, we pray. Amen.”

Lauren and Avery each squeezed one of Maria’s hands before letting go. They both had moist eyes as they looked at her. “Okay, enough mush, let’s eat now,” Maria said.

They all piled food on their plates and began to eat, but Lauren’s left hand was shaking too badly to use, and her right was trembling intermittently, causing her to drop food on occasion. “Damn it,” she muttered under her breath, trying to push back the anger that was rising up inside of her. She hated feeling like a child, dropping food all over the table. She found herself looking down to avoid the gaze of her sisters.

“It’s nothing to be ashamed of, Lauren,” Avery said. “It isn’t your fault.”

Lauren shook her head. “I know that. I still hate it though, losing control of simple body movements that a child can handle.”

"That's your right hand," Maria observed. "How long has that been happening?"

Lauren sighed. "A few days. It only happens once in a while."

"You know, I've heard about something new that might help you," Maria said. She looked up and met Lauren's gaze. "It's a spoon that will stay upright even when the hand holding it does not. Kind of like those gyro bowls they have for kid's snacks; it helps people with disorders like yours to eat without dropping food."

"Really? That would be amazing."

"I'll look into getting you one."

"Thanks, Maria." Lauren was surprised at how good it made her feel to have her sister offer something to help in this small way. Of course, it wasn't so small when you were the one affected.

Maria gestured to Avery. "That's what we're here for. We're all going to help each other now. That's what Dad wanted, and he was right. We need each other."

Chapter 46

Maria

It was late in the afternoon, and Maria had spent most of the day lounging on the dock, reading a romance novel. She hoped reading about someone getting the undivided attention of the man she loved would allow her to live vicariously. Three hours into it, when the story was getting really steamy, Maria realized how sad it was that she was trying to get what she needed through a fictional character's fictional romance. It was yet another reminder that she had stayed where she was for far too long.

When she looked at her watch and saw that it was three-thirty, she closed the book and went into the house. Avery was in the living room glued to a soap opera on television. Maria assumed Lauren must be in her room since she had not seen her sister leave the house. She went to Lauren's door and knocked, but there was no answer. She knocked again and listened close at the door. There was no answer and no sound coming from inside the room. Maria shrugged her shoulders and went into the kitchen for a snack.

Holding a small plate with cheese and crackers on it, Maria went into the living room and joined Avery in front of the TV. Maybe watching fictional characters would be more satisfying.

An hour later, Maria decided that watching was not more satisfying, and she was really starting to wonder about Lauren.

"Have you seen Lauren?" She asked Avery.

Avery glanced at her. "No. She's probably in her room. She's been painting a lot, I think."

"She's not in her room. I knocked twice an hour ago. Are you sure you haven't seen her?"

"I'm sure, but I've only been in here for about an hour and a half. I was in my room taking a nap before that. She could have left while I was in there."

Maria nodded. "I didn't see her go out the back door while I was out there, but she may have gone out the front."

"Probably went to see Blake."

"Probably, but I think I'm going to go look for her; see if she wants to help me make dinner tonight."

"If she's with Blake I doubt she'll be interested in coming back here to help with dinner." Avery turned from the TV and raised an eyebrow at Maria. "You just want to meet him don't you?"

"One of us should. We are looking out for each other now, right? You want to come?"

"Are you kidding? Patrick's about to propose to Elizabeth. I've been waiting five months for this."

Maria laughed, shaking her head. "Okay, I'll go alone."

She headed out the front door and walked through the trees toward Blake's house. She didn't see them outside as she approached the house, so she started up the steps to the front door. As she reached the top step, she looked up and saw Lauren sitting on the porch, slumped to the right of the door, clutching a canvas in both hands. She didn't seem to notice Maria's approach even though some of the steps had creaked. She looked zoned out.

"Lauren?" Maria said walking up to her sister. "Are you alright?"

Lauren looked up, a bewildered expression on her face. "He left. He went home."

"Blake? He isn't here?"

Lauren shook her head slowly. "I came to show him," she gestured to the canvas, "I wanted to show him first because he helped me figure out a new way to paint. But he isn't here. He went back home."

"Maybe he just went out. The store or something." Maria tried to reassure her sister.

"No, he went home. He didn't say goodbye, but he left a note." Lauren held out a neatly folded piece of paper. Maria took the paper, unfolded it, and began to read the hastily scrawled words.

Lauren,

I feel terrible writing this letter. I know I should tell you all this in person, but I can't bring myself to do that. You do things to me, things I can't explain and don't understand, and I know if I see you, I will lose my resolve. The way I have felt spending time with you over these last days—I haven't felt that way since I was a teenager. I find that I want to be with you all the time. But the other day, when you began to talk about a relationship that goes beyond our time here at the lake, I started to think about what that would mean. At first, I was just caught off guard. I don't really know why; we've been having such a good time together, and your desire to keep seeing each other makes perfect sense. For a short time, I even began to really like the idea of that. But then I started to think about Jerry, and what it was like for my mom when his condition got worse. I remember how hard it was on her, the pain she went through when he died.

I really like you, but I don't think I can go through all that again. I don't think I'm strong enough. I wish I were. I wish I could be the man you deserve, but I don't think I can. By the time you get this note, I will already be on my way back home. I'm sorry for leaving like this. I just don't know another way.

Blake

Still looking down, and avoiding her sister's eyes, Maria folded the paper back up. She searched her mind for the right words to soothe her sister's pain. She certainly knew what it was like to have the man you love (if, in fact, Lauren really did love Blake), leave you. Hank hadn't actually left her, not physically, but in every way that mattered, he had. Maria couldn't honestly think of any words that would help, so she eased herself down onto the porch next to Lauren and put an arm around her. "I'm sorry," Maria whispered. Lauren turned, and buried her face in Maria's shoulder, letting herself cry.

When Lauren's tears stopped, and she lifted her head, Maria motioned to the canvas her sister was still holding. "Can I take a look?"

Lauren looked down and evaluated the painting, then she nodded and passed the canvas to Maria. Taking it, Maria tilted it into view and took a look. She gasped. "Oh …, Lauren," Maria took in the swirls of color on the canvas, mostly shades of blue, and was overtaken by the deep sadness it clearly portrayed. She continued to gaze at it as she absorbed all the emotion it brought on. "This is amazing ... it's wonderful."

"You really think so?"

Maria looked over and met Lauren's eyes. "It's spectacular. It's better than any of the paintings I've seen from you in the past, and they were all great, but this—It makes me feel a heart-wrenching sadness, and I know that's exactly what you want me to feel."

Lauren smiled. "That makes my day a little better then."

Maria nodded. "This is something to be proud of. I knew you could do it."

"I'm glad you were sure. I know I wasn't."

"God made you to paint. So I knew there had to still be a way."

"For however long it lasts," Lauren said, her voice filled with sadness and bitterness all at once. She spread out her arms and frowned at her trembling left hand.

"Don't worry about tomorrow. Today you can do this," Maria pointed to the painting. "And it's because of your condition that you found a deeper level to your talent."

"Are you saying it was all meant to be?"

Maria shrugged. "I don't know about that. It's just that you're bound to see all the negatives to your situation, I'm pointing out one positive."

"Yeah, I guess you're right. Let's get out of here. I want to go back to the cabin now."

Chapter 47

Lauren

Upon returning to the cabin, Lauren went to her room after a brief conversation with her sisters. She got out as quick as she could. She was glad they were talking now, and that the problems in their past had been worked out, but her head hurt and her chest felt tight. She didn't really understand how she could be so upset about the end of a relationship that had started only days before. They barely knew each other. Still, she felt a loss.

Finding a man had never been high on Lauren's priority list. She was always so busy and focused on her art. Most men wanted a woman who had more time to give them, and Lauren hadn't cared enough about having a love life to give up any time in front of her easel. It really wasn't a problem for her—not having a man—until she met Blake.

Giving time to her art was still important to her—very, but now making time for a love life didn't look like an inconvenience to her. It was worth it, she knew that now. And besides, she would have more time now that she would be permanently working only one job when she became Avery's roommate. Also, Blake hadn't demanded anything from her. He understood how important her art was to her, and she was sure he would understand all the other things that took up her time as well. There was one thing, however, that he'd decided he couldn't deal with, and that was her Parkinson's.

"What a jerk!" Avery had said when Lauren showed her the note from Blake. "He's going to skip out on you because of a condition you can't help having?"

"He's not a jerk, Ave. He knows even better than I do what's coming. He's seen it. He has the right to decide not to go through that again. I'd run away from it too if I could."

Avery had shaken her head, and said softly, "No, if the roles were reversed, I don't think you would."

This got Lauren's attention. She had never been known as the dependable sister. She'd raised an eyebrow at Avery. "You don't? You think I, the oblivious sister, would not run away from this if I had the choice to?"

"Yeah, Lauren, sometimes you are oblivious because you're so focused on one thing, you can't see anything else. But Blake isn't oblivious. He's been spending time with you and getting to know you. And, if the roles were reversed, I don't think you would run away. Being oblivious of something isn't the same as running away from it."

It made Lauren feel good to hear that. She'd felt so guilty the last several days about the past and how much she'd been unaware of. She never meant to be a bad sister, but she hadn't really tried to be a good one either. She intended to change that, and it felt good to know that Avery had confidence in her ability to do just that.

Still, she couldn't agree with Avery about Blake. She knew the long, hard road she was in for as her disease progressed, and she knew what Blake had already been through with his step-father.

Lauren sucked in a deep breath and fell back on her bed. It was a good thing she had found a way to make painting work again because it was going to have to be her main focus going forward. She might have realized that having a love life was worth the time and trouble, but she also understood that it was unlikely she'd find a man who was willing to start a relationship with a woman who had Parkinson's.

Chapter 48

Maria

The next couple of days went by quietly. Maria and her sisters spent time together preparing and eating meals, and they went swimming together again. But most of the time, Lauren was in her room, trying to focus on painting instead of thinking about Blake. Avery spent a large chunk of every afternoon watching her soaps (it was a hard habit for her to break since the characters on those shows had been the only company she'd allowed herself to have for the last few years). This left Maria lots of time to read, take walks around the lake, and think about her family and her situation. She missed her children terribly, but she was finding it easier to let herself enjoy the time alone.

On the last day before they were supposed to go home, another delivery arrived just after lunchtime. Maria answered the door and smiled at Evan. "It's nice to see you one more time," she said. "But I didn't think there would be any more grocery deliveries. We're leaving tomorrow."

Evan shrugged. "There isn't much here. I think it's mostly about the letter I was told to slip into the bag."

"Oh, I see. Just a second." Maria left the door briefly to dig in her purse. She returned and handed Evan a ten dollar bill.

"Thanks! This is kind of a big tip for such a small delivery," he said handing her the one bag he was holding.

"You still had to drive out here for this small delivery. Put it towards your school funds."

"I'll do that. Have a good last day!"

"We will. Thanks, Evan." Maria closed the door and took the bag into the kitchen. Inside the bag was a small container of ice cream, a jar of hot fudge sauce, and sprinkles. There was also a letter.

"Lauren! Avery! We got a note from Dad!" Maria called out.

When her sisters joined her in the kitchen, Maria opened the letter and began to read it out loud.

My beautiful girls,

You might be wondering why you haven't heard from me in a few days. I guess you can say I ran out of tactics. I figured after all the other things I asked you to do, either you started repairing the rift between you, or you didn't. I hope the former is true. I hope you are talking again and getting to know each other for who you all truly are. I hope you've all put past grudges to rest, and started to make a new relationship. If so, you have fulfilled my greatest hope for you, and you can be sure your mother and I are both smiling down on you. If you haven't, there is nothing more I can do. But, I spent months before setting all this up, asking for God's help, and I know he is able, even if I never was.

Now, there is one last order of business to be handled. Tonight, I want you to take the bikes and ride back to the restaurant I sent you to that first night. Mr. Fisher will meet you there at six o'clock. I sent the ice cream for you to have sundaes for dessert when you get back. Perhaps you'll want to celebrate.

Girls, I wish you the very best throughout the rest of your lives. The three of you and your mother were the great loves of my life. Nothing was ever more important.

All my love,

Dad

Maria swiped a tear from her cheek as she finished reading. *We did it, Dad!* She Thought. *We mended the rift, and we have you to thank for our new relationship.* She looked at her sisters and smiled. "I wonder what this last order of business could be," she said.

"You don't think there's more money, do you?" Lauren asked.

"I can't even figure out how he managed to save six hundred thousand." Lauren and Avery nodded. It was a mystery they were not likely to ever figure out.

The rest of the afternoon dragged by as the anticipation gnawed at Maria. What else could there be to find out? Her father apparently thought it would make them want to celebrate, whatever it was. Maria tried to pass her time reading on the deck, but she couldn't stay focused, so she took a long walk around the lake. Then she decided that she'd better take a break so she'd have the energy for the bike ride. Aside from gaining a new, and far better than ever before, relationship with her sisters, she'd probably lost a little weight from all the walking she'd done in the last two weeks. She smiled at that thought, then mentally slapped herself when she instantly wondered if Hank would notice.

Finally, the time came for the bike ride to the restaurant. Maria and her sisters went out to the shed and retrieved the bikes. They hopped on and started down the road. Halfway there Maria noticed that it was a little easier this time. Her legs didn't feel like jelly yet. Maybe she needed to find more time to exercise in her normal day to day life—but when? She hardly had the time to do the things she had to get done as it was; work, make dinner, do the laundry, and help Jon with his homework. If she were ever to have any extra time on her hands, she would feel obligated to spend it with Melanie. *If Hank would help*, she thought, then shoved that thought away. There was no sense wishing for that. She might as well wish for a unicorn.

Maria looked around at her sisters. Lauren was still taking the front. Maria knew now this was because riding the bike was easier for her than walking. It made her feel free, and that was understandable. Avery, however, was not obsessively keeping her bike in between Maria's and Lauren's, as she had before. She was riding to the left of Maria and slightly behind. She was staying close, and Maria could tell she was still nervous, but this was a huge step for her, a stride forward that made Maria smile. She was amazed at how much could happen in two weeks.

When they arrived at the restaurant, Maria was winded but exhilarated at the same time. They parked the bikes and went inside. Mr. Fisher had not arrived yet, so they selected a booth near the back, and ordered three glasses of sweet tea.

Ten minutes later, Mr. Fisher arrived and joined them. "Good evening, ladies." They returned his greeting and made room for him in the seat next to Lauren. "Well, you made it through the two weeks. Perhaps you'd like some wine to celebrate," he suggested.

"In a while, maybe," Maria said. "I think we're all just curious right now. What's this we hear about another order of business?"

Mr. Fisher nodded. "We'll get to that. How did it go—the two weeks together?"

Avery looked skeptical, narrowing her eyes at the man sitting across from her. "Is that important?"

Mr. Fisher smiled half-heartedly and cleared his throat. "Not as far as the will goes. Your father didn't want to punish you. It was only important to him that you tried . . . but we all know what his hopes were—and that makes it matter to me."

"Why?" Avery said slowly, making it sound more like an accusation than a question.

Maria jumped in saying, "I think what my sister means is, wasn't our father just a client?"

"He was a client, but he wasn't *just* a client." Mr. Fisher looked at all the curious eyes watching him. "Years ago, my son attended the high school where your father was principal." He shook his head. "Jesse had been in and out of trouble since elementary school. His mother and I tried to set him straight, but nothing ever seemed to have much effect.

"When he came to your father's school, it was because he had been expelled from another school. Arthur met with us at the beginning and told us he would do anything he could to help Jesse—and us. We had heard that before, so it didn't mean much, not then. But when Jesse got into a fight with another boy, Arthur sat down with all of us and asked a lot of questions. He said that Jesse seemed to have trouble with impulse control and needed help. He got Jesse into an anger management class. That made some difference, but it wasn't a cure-all."

Mr. Fisher took a deep breath. "Then, later that year, the thing we had been worried about happened. Jesse got into trouble outside of school. He was picked up by the police for stealing money from a charity. This guy was outside of a store collecting money for the poor. When he stepped away from his bucket for a moment to help an old lady with her walker, Jesse grabbed his bucket and ran." Mr. Fisher's face was filled with shame as he remembered what his son had done.

"Jesse got a slap on the wrist, basically, from the court system since it was his first offense, and since the money had been recovered and returned. They didn't know everything else in his history, everything that had led up to him getting arrested. When Arthur found out about it, he asked my wife and me if it would be okay for him to help us with Jesse. We immediately accepted his offer, hoping he could make a difference before it was too late.

"He spent a Saturday and took Jesse to work in a soup kitchen." Mr. Fisher looked meaningfully at Maria and both her sisters. "Jesse was never the same again after that day. It was a while before he would really talk to us about that day, or what it had done to him. He spent several days just wandering around, hardly saying a word. When he did tell us about it, he said he couldn't believe he'd stolen money that was meant to help people like the ones he saw in that soup kitchen. He was horrified by his behavior and saddened by the suffering he'd seen on that Saturday with Arthur. He kept going back to that soup kitchen, and everything about him changed. He didn't get into fights anymore, and he didn't steal, or cause any other trouble."

Mr. Fisher grinned. "Jesse runs that soup kitchen now and does all kinds of good things for others. The man he's become is someone his mother and I would never have imagined when he was a kid. We have your father to thank for that." He paused and looked at all of them with sincerity. "So you can certainly say that Arthur was more to me than *just* a client. Every time I look at my Jesse, I thank him."

"Wow!" Lauren said. "That's quite a story."

"And I'm not the only one with a story like that. There are many lives that were affected by your father." Mr. Fisher's eyebrows drew together. "That's why I was so shocked when Arthur came to me a year ago and told me how his daughters had refused to see each other. I couldn't imagine *his* children as anything but perfect. He knew just what to do to help my son, how could he have had any problems in his own family?" He shrugged. "Well he asked for my help, and of course I agreed." His face darkened. "I didn't think I'd be doing this so soon though ... his death was so unexpected."

"Yes," Maria said, "it was."

"So, that's why it's important to me to know how the two weeks went. It was so important to Arthur."

Lauren reached a hand out from under the table and took Mr. Fisher's hand. "It went well," she said. "Dad knew what to do for us too, and you helped him see it through."

Mr. Fisher looked down at Lauren's hand on his, taking note, Maria was sure, of the way that it trembled, but after only a split second of hesitation, he reached up with his other hand and clasped it around Lauren's. He was grinning, obviously thrilled to have been a help to the daughters of the man who helped his son. "Your father would be so happy right now."

"I know he is happy," Maria said. "But we're still curious, what is this last order of business?"

Mr. Fisher cleared his throat. "Oh, yes, let's talk about that. You three will, of course, now get all of your father's estate divided among you, along with the one item apiece he selected for you. But there is one other thing he left behind for you as well."

"Something else?" Avery asked. "How did he save so much? I know he was thrifty, but I still don't understand."

"Well, this is merely speculation, but one of the young people Arthur mentored was the son of an investment banker. Perhaps he helped your father make good investments. I really don't know for sure. I do know that I never charged him a cent for my services. How could I?

"But on to the other item ... you know the house you've been staying in the last two weeks?" All three of them nodded. "It's yours."

"Ours?" Maria shook her head. "What do you mean?"

Mr. Fisher smiled at her surprise. "Your father bought that house last year."

"He bought a house at the lake? Why? Surely not just for this." Avery said.

"Partially for this, but not just for this. Arthur said that the times he spent with you girls, and your mother when she was alive, at the lake were some of the best times he could remember. He thought there would be a lot of good memories there for all of you as well. He had the money, as you now know, to buy the house, and he wanted to leave the three of you a place to go where you could spend time with those memories, and make new ones—maybe together. It's yours now, to do with what you like. If you don't want to keep it, you can sell it and divide the proceeds."

Maria looked at both her sisters, and they all smiled. "I think we might want to keep it," she said.

"Good. Wonderful! Arthur would be thrilled to hear that. Now," he said, clapping his hands and rubbing them together, "the business is done, let's order dinner."

The sun was setting when Maria walked out onto the deck. The sky was filled with color, but the actual setting of the sun was happening on the other side of the house, out of view. Lauren was standing by the railing, looking out at the lake, when Maria walked up behind her. Lauren tilted her head in the direction of Blake's house. "I figured I'd probably never see him again. Now it seems I might," she said.

Maria rubbed Lauren's back but didn't say anything.

"I bet he'll be surprised the first time that happens."

"And what about you?"

Lauren sucked in a deep breath. "I don't know. I can't place my feelings about that. It just makes it all seem less finished."

"Could be a good thing," Maria suggested.

Lauren shrugged. "Maybe. It might just make it all harder." She turned and looked at Maria. "Did you see this coming?"

"Are you kidding? Dad's been throwing us one curve ball after another. I never would have imagined that he'd bought another house—and the money—where did that come from?"

Lauren nodded with a smile. "Yeah, when he was alive he always seemed so predictable, who would have guessed he had such big secrets." Lauren looked down, her expression pained. "I wish I had listened to him more ... when he was still here."

"Me too. We could have had this relationship sooner. But I don't think he'd want us to dwell on that or beat ourselves up over it. He'd want us to be glad for what we have now, and forget what was in the past."

"That's tough, but you're right. Two weeks ago I thought I was facing a difficult future alone, without the joy of being able to paint." She looked into Maria's eyes. "Without my sisters to help me. Now I have you and Avery to support me. I'll soon have a roommate so I don't have to work all the time. And the extra time that will give me will be all the better now that I have a new way to paint."

Lauren's eyes shined with tears as she continued. "The most important thing is that I'll have both of you when my condition gets worse. I thought I would be facing it alone, and I was too damn full of pride to come to you and Avery and tell you what I was facing. I can't believe I was more willing to confront the future alone than I was to talk to my sisters. I was so stupid. I was so sure you'd see me as a burden that I wasn't willing to consider any other possibility."

Maria wrapped her arms around Lauren, squeezed her tightly, then let go. "You weren't the only one. I've needed you and Avery so much, but I couldn't seem to admit the truth to you. I didn't want to tell anyone that my husband . . . no longer loves me. I didn't want anyone to see how much I was hurting. But letting you both in has been the best gift. Dad knew it would be—for all of us."

Chapter 49

Avery

Avery was all packed up and ready to go home. She looked around the room she'd been staying in, wondering why this still felt so final when she knew she'd be back again. She could come back anytime. Still, there was a weight on her heart at the thought of returning home to her apartment. She didn't want to go back to life as she'd known it before the last two weeks when she'd stayed closed up in her home virtually all the time. She wanted to be with people again like she was here with her sisters, and heaven help her, she wanted to move past the fear inside that stopped her from letting Mike into her life. She wanted a real friendship with him—maybe more than that. But she'd have to allow their meetings to venture past the hallway if that was going to happen. Could she do that?

She wanted all these things, but it wasn't that easy. When she thought of all the people outside her apartment, all the possible danger, she couldn't help the fight or flight instinct that took over. She wasn't as bad about it as she had been, but it was still a very big, very real problem. It would get easier once Lauren moved in with her, she thought, easing her mind a little, but that wasn't going to happen for a couple of months. They had to wait until Lauren's lease was up. She didn't want to go back to the way she'd been for two months, but she couldn't imagine having the strength to combat the fear without her sisters by her side.

With a sigh, she glanced around one last time, picked up her suitcase, and headed out to the living room. Lauren and Maria were waiting for her.

"You'll be okay," Lauren said almost as soon as Avery looked up at her. She must be wearing her feelings more than she thought. Either that or Lauren was getting far more intuitive. Avery nodded.

"We're only a phone call away," Maria chimed in. "And I'll bring the kids by to see you next weekend."

Avery forced a smile. "I'll be glad to see them."

Lauren put down the suitcase she was holding and stepped close to Avery, putting an arm around her. "Ave, you can do this. You're strong enough now."

Avery dropped her own suitcase to the floor with a thump, and wrapped her arms around Lauren, as tears began to fall from her eyes. "Only because of my sisters. And I still need you."

"We're here," Lauren and Maria said in unison.

Avery stepped back from Lauren and dried her face with the back of her hand. Just then they heard a honk outside. "Taxi's here," Avery said.

They all walked outside and loaded their luggage into the trunk of the taxi, then they got into the car and gave the driver instructions to take Lauren home first, then Avery, and last, Maria.

When Avery got home, she tried not to revert back to the way she was before the trip. She forced herself to carry her suitcase to the bedroom before returning to lock the front door. Then she tried to lock only one of the deadbolts, but fear began to rise inside her, and she found herself flipping every lock in an automatic action that seemed almost out of her control.

Stepping back from the door, she realized Rocket was meowing at her and rubbing against her leg, begging her to pay attention to him. She looked down at the gray cat, his intense yellow eyes staring up at her. "I'm sorry, buddy. Mommy is too busy freaking out to even notice your needs, right?" She squatted down and rubbed the cat's head, smiling when he began to purr. "You missed me, huh? I missed you too."

She picked Rocket up, held him against her chest, and walked to the window. "It's not so bad," she said, looking out at the people and cars below. She put the cat down on the floor and slid the window open. The sounds of traffic rose up and filled her ears. She tried hard to ignore the tightness growing in her chest, but it overwhelmed her. She snapped the window shut, and locked it. Stepping back from the window, she waited for her heart to slow back down. She thought about Maria and Lauren. *I can do this! My sisters are there if I need them.*

Avery jumped when the doorbell chimed. Her heart racing again, she walked to the door and looked through the peephole. Mike was standing in the hall, waiting for her to open the door. She slowly turned each of the deadbolts and opened the door to Mike's smiling face.

"Bringing your key back," he said, handing it to her.

"Oh, thanks."

"Rocket was a real good boy. I think he likes me."

"I'm sure he does." *How could he not?* "He knows a nice person when he meets them." There was no way Avery could know if that was true. Other than Mike, Rocket had never met anyone but her and the people at the vet's office.

"Mind if I come in for a minute and say hi to him?"

Mike stepped forward, and Avery's heart started galloping. "No!" It came out in such a sharp, sudden way that it almost sounded like a shout.

Mike looked up at her, startled by her abrupt response. He looked so good, his dark hair falling against his forehead, and ice blue eyes staring at her. She wanted to let him in, but the thought caused intense panic.

She willed her heart and breathing to slow. *Mike is not a threat. You can handle this calmly.* "It's just not a very good time. I need to unpack." She forced a smile.

"I won't get in your way. I'll just spend a few minutes with Rocket, and then be out of your way."

Avery took a steadying breath. Making excuses to not let him come in was getting harder all the time, and now that he had been coming in at will for the last two weeks to care for Rocket, how could she explain banishing him? "Not right now, Mike. I'm sorry. I'm just really tired."

He nodded slowly as his face changed from a friendly expression to one that fell between confusion and hurt. "Do you not like me, Avery?"

"Of course I like you. Why would you ask that?"

"Because I can't figure you out. You seem to like me sometimes. I mean you wanted me there when your dad passed away, and you asked me to look after your cat, but you won't let me in when you're actually here, and you won't come into my apartment either. You keep refusing to go out with me." He looked down, then glanced back up, and met her eyes. "Sometimes it seems like you only want me around when it helps you out."

Oh, God! He thought she was using him. And why wouldn't he? It did look that way when you saw it from his side. She squeezed her eyes shut for a moment, then looked back at Mike's questioning face. "I do like you, Mike, very much. I promise someday I'll explain my crazy behavior to you." Tears sprung up in her eyes. She wanted to tell him, but something inside wouldn't let her speak the words. "I just can't right now. I'm sorry." She stepped back from him, wrapping her right hand around the doorknob. She watched his face change from confusion to concern as she pushed the door closed, leaving him in the hall.

She flipped all the deadbolts and backed away from the door. Falling into her sofa, she tried to stop herself from crying. She hated feeling this way. After the last two weeks, she never wanted to go back to this. But real life had to resume, and her sisters couldn't be with her every hour of every day. She had to figure out how to do this, and she hoped it would all be easier once Lauren moved in. At least then she'd have support sometimes.

Chapter 50

Maria

When the cab pulled up in front of her house, Maria stepped out, retrieved her suitcase from the trunk, and handed the cab driver some money. After the taxi had driven away, she set her suitcase down on the driveway and stared at the house. She had missed her children terribly and couldn't wait to see them, but she dreaded the conversation she needed to have with Hank. A part of her was screaming, "Just wait until tomorrow!" But that was what she had been doing for the past three years—waiting. She had waited, always hoping the old Hank would resurface, but that hadn't happened, and now it was time to be brave and do what she knew she needed to do.

After standing for a few moments outside the house, Maria realized how odd it was that she was still standing there alone. She'd expected the kids to run out and meet her, but there was no sign of them. For a split second, her mind tried to explore the reasons why that might be. Were there any circumstances in which this could be a good thing? She couldn't think of any, and that sent a little shiver of panic up her spine.

She bent down to pick up her suitcase, and, just as she was standing back up straight, the front door of the house opened and Sadie came running toward her. She let the suitcase drop again so she would be able to handle the very excited, very wiggly golden retriever. She stooped down, and let the dog lick her face while she ruffled her fur. "It's good to see you too, girl. Where are the kids?"

She looked up from the dog and saw Hank standing on the front porch—alone. Grabbing her suitcase again, she walked up the steps to where he was. "Where are the kids?"

A look of mild hurt flashed across his face for only an instant before he answered, but it was enough for Maria to realize he'd hoped for a warmer greeting. "Jonathan is at Allan's house, and Melanie is down the street helping Mrs. Crump with her garden."

Maria couldn't help feeling irritated, a little angry even. Surely he would know how much she'd missed them, and that she would want to see them now. She felt the urge to yell at him, but she bit her tongue. The conversation they needed to have would be hard enough without making it worse by screaming at him now. She let out a sigh instead and carried her suitcase into the house.

Hank followed her down the hall toward the bedroom. "I thought it would be easier to talk if we had a little time alone first," he said.

Maria glanced at him curiously. Hank *wanted* to talk? Was this the part where he was going to ask about the money from the will? Would he expect to tell her what they should do with it? "Talk about what?" she asked, keeping her tone light.

He took the suitcase from her hand and set it on the bedroom floor, then he walked to the bed, and sat down on the edge, patting the spot next to him. Maria sat down and waited for him to start the conversation. "First of all, I want to say that I hope you had a good two weeks with your sisters. I know you weren't really sure about spending the time with them."

This was an interesting start, not what she'd expected. She nodded. "It went well."

"Good. The next thing I wanted to say is—thank you."

Maria raised one eyebrow at him.

"I know you were worried about leaving the kids with me all this time, and you had every reason to be, but thank you for giving me the chance. I had a really good time with them."

She studied his face, and he looked sincere, but she couldn't believe what he was saying. Was this the man she'd left behind two weeks ago—the one who barely acknowledged his kids? "You did?"

Hank looked down. "I've been a terrible father the last few years, I know that. I don't know what was wrong with me. Those are great kids we've got." He looked back up at her, his green eyes meeting hers. "Jonathan is so tough, and he's smarter than he thinks. I took him to his baseball games—and this time I watched him play. He's really talented. We're working on his fastball.

"And Melanie is the sweetest kid. Do you know why she likes to help Mrs. Crump with her garden?"

Maria shook her head, and Hank continued. "Because she thinks it's important to help old people and learn from them. She likes to hear Mrs. Crump's stories. She's also a pretty good little dancer. I'm looking forward to her next recital."

"Really?" It was all Maria could manage to say. *Who was this man?* He certainly was not the Hank she knew, gushing about his children's positive attributes. In the last three years, he'd barely been willing to look up at them. Honestly, this entire conversation was a bit surreal. She wasn't even sure if she could remember the last time he'd been willing to have a conversation with her that exceeded ten words. Now he was talking to her—and he was looking forward to a dance recital? He sounded a lot more like the old Hank, the one she'd been missing for such a long time, but could she really believe he'd changed so much in two weeks? *Why not? You and your sisters did.*

A pained look came over Hank's face, and he said, "I did have a good time with them, but that's not all we need to talk about. This next part is harder though." He paused for a moment and looked like he was trying to find the words to say what was on his mind. Maria waited patiently. "Maria, I ... I've been ... cheating on you."

As soon as the words were out of his mouth, his head dropped, and he stared at the floor, waiting for her to respond. "I know that," she said, and his head snapped up.

"You do?"

"With Carina. If you wanted to keep it a secret, you should have washed her perfume off before you came home."

His mouth dropped open. "I guess I'm no good at sneaking around."

"Were you really trying to sneak around? Honestly, I thought you wanted me to know. It seemed that way."

He looked terribly ashamed, and for a split second, Maria felt a little sorry for him. "I'm so sorry I hurt you like that." He didn't deny that it might have been on purpose. Perhaps he really didn't realize that it was. He looked her straight in the eyes. "But that brings me to what I wanted to tell you next ... You ... you should leave me."

Maria was flabbergasted. She had planned on telling Hank that she wanted a divorce, but she wasn't expecting him to do that for her. She stared at him.

"I'll start looking for an apartment on Monday. Until I find one, I'll sleep on the couch." He paused, then continued. "But—there's just one other thing."

There was more? What more could there be? Maria wasn't sure she wanted to hear what was next. Was he going to tell her that Carina was only one of the other women he was sleeping with? She sighed and nodded for him to continue.

"After I move out, would it be okay if I still come by every day in the afternoon when the kids get home from school? You'll need someone to stay with them until you get off work, and I'd like it if it could be me. I've been working with Jon on his reading and math, and he's really making progress. I want to keep helping him. And I can make sure Melanie gets to her dance lessons."

Were her ears deceiving her? He wanted to spend time with the kids every day? She was so stunned that she couldn't seem to make any words come out of her mouth, so she just nodded. His answer was a broad smile that lit up his face, reminding her how handsome he still was. Then he stood up, kissed the top of her head, and said, "Thank you."

Chapter 51

Lauren

At six o'clock on the day she had arrived home, Lauren was clocking in for a shift at the pub. When she'd put in for the time off to go on the lake trip, she'd thought it was a good idea to go straight back to work when the trip was over. She hadn't wanted to lose any more income than she absolutely had to. Now she questioned the wisdom in that choice. She was dragging, and her shift had just begun. She wasn't used to this anymore. At the lake house, she was going to bed at a reasonable time every night, and waking up very, very early. The idea of working until midnight sat in her mind like a lead weight.

Part of her decision to rush back to this job had to do with the fact that her job at the store was gone, not that she cared anymore. It was all different now. Her sisters were there for her, they would help her when she needed. And she wouldn't even need financial help anymore once she moved in with Avery. Her living expenses would be nearly cut in half, and with the money from the will, she'd be able to pay off all her medical debt and have some left over. Her days of working every waking minute were over.

Now Lauren was excited to explore her life as an artist again. She had already unpacked the paintings she'd done at the lake, and she could hardly believe they were hers, that she was able to create something beautiful again. Learning this new concept for her art was having an effect on everything she did. Every emotion she had now flashed in her mind in vivid color, and she couldn't wait to paint them all. She wasn't just painting in a new way; she was seeing life, every part of it, in a new way.

She looked up as a tall lanky waiter named Lucas handed her a drink order to fill. Smiling at him, she pulled out a glass and filled the order, careful to hold tightly to every bottle she picked up. Luckily, today her right hand was steady.

She yawned as she handed Lucas the glass.

"Tired already?" he asked.

"Not much going on yet," she said. "It's easy to get sleepy when you don't have a lot to do. Besides that, I was up early this morning." She hoped there was truth to all she'd said. Maybe working this shift would get a little easier once business picked up. Then she wouldn't have time to notice how tired she was. She'd be far too busy filling orders and trying not to drop anything.

At ten o'clock, when it was time for Lauren's break, she went into the back room and called Avery.

"Hello?" Avery's voice still sounded wide awake.

"It's me," Lauren responded. "I just wanted to see how you're doing."

"I'm fine."

Lauren couldn't be sure, but there was a slight shakiness in Avery's voice that made her believe that her sister wasn't fine. She decided to go with that instinct. "No, you're not."

Avery let out a loud breath. "Well, I'm trying to be, and that's the best I can do right now. Let's talk about something else. How are *you* doing?"

"Oh, I'm alright—tired, but alright. I'm at the pub for another four hours, then I plan to fall into bed and sleep as long as my screwed-up brain will let me."

"I thought we talked about you not working so much," Avery chided as if she were talking to a child, or perhaps an ailing parent.

Lauren leaned back in her chair and put her feet up on another one. She wasn't' going to let Avery's tone be a source of hurt or anger—she knew her sister was only trying to help. "Sure, but this shift was already scheduled before the trip. I have tomorrow off, so I can rest then."

"You're off tomorrow? Want to come over for a while? I can show you the empty room, and maybe you could help me start cleaning it out so it'll be ready for you."

"I want to get some painting in, but I'm sure I could make it over there for a little bit. I'd really like to meet the infamous Mike."

Avery snorted. "I doubt *that's* going to happen."

"Why not, what's going on?"

"Oh, you know, he thinks I'm using him."

Avery had said the words in a flippant way, but Lauren could tell she was upset about it. Whether she wanted to admit it or not, Avery really liked this Mike fellow. "Why does he think that?"

"Because I asked him to take care of my cat for two weeks, and then I wouldn't let him through the door when I got home." Avery sighed. "Or maybe it was because I refused to go out with him for over a year, but asked him to go with me to my father's funeral. It's hard not to see his point."

"Yeah, but I didn't use to understand you either, Ave. And you didn't use to understand me. If we learned anything the last two weeks, it ought to be that communication is key."

"I should tell him my terrible secret, is that what you're saying?" Avery sounded unconvinced.

"Don't you think it's best to tell him? Then he would know why you've acted the way you have. He'd be able to understand."

"He'd understand that I'm damaged." Avery's voice held sadness and defiance at the same time.

Lauren thought about how to respond. She considered how she'd felt when she'd thought about telling Blake she had Parkinson's before he figured it out. Then she thought about the relief she'd felt when it was all out on the table. Of course, her condition was the reason he'd left, but no relationship would have been possible without him finding out. And it was partly his own past that had made him unable to consider a future with her. "You know, I think we're all a little damaged in our own way. Maybe he'll be able to accept what happened to you and help you through it, maybe he won't, but you won't get anywhere by not telling him. You'll just stand still."

Avery was silent for several seconds, and Lauren could only hear the sound of a cat meowing. "Maybe you're right—but I don't know how to tell him about that," Avery said, her voice wavering. She sounded close to tears.

"When you're ready, I'll be happy to be there with you and help you through it."

They talked a few more minutes after that, then Lauren said goodbye, and returned to work.

Chapter 52

Maria

Maria sat on the couch with Sadie watching a movie on *Lifetime*. The kids were in bed, and Hank had left to give her some time alone with them hours ago. He'd be back soon, she was sure, and she would give him the couch to sleep on for the night. For now, though, she was alone, so she stretched out while Sadie sat next to her, laying her furry head on Maria's chest.

"I missed you too, girl," Maria said, patting the golden head. "You would have loved the lake. I thought about you every time I saw a squirrel. And now that the house is partly mine, I guess you can go with me next time." Sadie wagged her tail in response.

Maria tried to watch the movie, but her emotions were getting in the way, and she couldn't seem to focus. Her reunion with the kids had been happy and full of hugs, and yet, there was something else about it that disturbed her. It wasn't anything with the kids. They were thrilled to have her back, and they had been well cared for while she was gone. That last part, though, was the problem. As much as she'd worried about them, and Hank's ability, or rather his willingness, to care for them properly in her absence, she now found herself bothered by the fact that he had done a great job. She'd listened all evening to the kids gush about their father and how great it had been spending time with him. She'd heard about what a great math tutor he'd been for Jon, and then she'd been given extensive details about the tea parties he'd had with Melanie (tea parties? Hank?). All the while, this strange feeling gnawed at her. In the last few years, as Hank had changed and grown more distant, she'd always felt that the worst part was the way he'd pulled away from the kids. So, she should be happy now—and yet, she wasn't.

All she could seem to think was, why now? But it shouldn't matter, should it? There was no expiration date on a father's chance to love his children. She should be happy that her kids had their father back. Of course, there was a part of her that wondered if this new Hank (that was much like the old Hank—the one she married in the first place) was going to last, or if his interest in the kids would wane, hurting them yet again. But even that wasn't the biggest reason why she wasn't happy like she should be. No, if she was going to be honest, the real reason was jealousy.

It was insane! She was actually jealous of her own kids. Maria didn't want to feel that way, but every time she heard about how great Hank had been while she was gone, all she could think was, why couldn't he have woken up sooner—before it was too late for their marriage. It was never too late for him to turn things around as a dad. He could change his ways, and be available to them now. Someday, the kids might not even remember that there was a time when their dad hadn't been interested in them, a time when he didn't care that his son was failing in school, or that his daughter was attention deprived. But none of his changes would erase his affair.

Maria supposed if she could find it within herself, she could forgive him for cheating on her. She knew there were couples who were able to stay together and move on after affairs, but she didn't know if she could ever reach that level of forgiveness. Maybe she just wasn't that good of a person. And even if she could, there was no indication that Hank wanted their marriage to continue. He'd said he was sorry for how he'd treated her, but that didn't mean he still wanted to be married to her. He was, after all, the one who initiated the separation. Maybe that's what he wanted all along—to end their marriage. After all, it had been a long time since he'd acted as though he was attracted to her in any way at all ...

but he hadn't seemed insincere when he'd apologized. He'd actually looked close to tears.

Maria shook her head. No matter how sincere he was about being sorry for his behavior, she knew he wasn't attracted to her anymore. That much had been obvious for years. So the kids would get their father back, and she was going to be happy about that, by God, but she would not get her husband back. It was too late for that.

Chapter 53

Two months later—August

Lauren

It was sweltering the day Lauren moved in with Avery. She wiped sweat from her brow as she carried a box into her new room. It was a large room, which was good since she needed the space for her work, and they had already painted it pale yellow. She smiled looking at the color. She had chosen it to remind her of happiness even on her bad days when it was easy to let fear and anger get the best of her. When those days came, she would look at the yellow and remember her mother's strength through hard times, and she would remember how fortunate she was to have had a father who loved her enough to orchestrate the healing of her relationship with her sisters from beyond the grave. Her sisters would help her through all that was to come.

Lauren stepped back out of the room and headed back down to the U-Haul trailer that was hooked up to Hank's truck. She still couldn't believe that Hank was here helping when he and Maria weren't even living together anymore. But Hank was a new man it seemed—at least that was what Maria kept saying. She wasn't sure if she could put full faith in this turnaround, and she knew her sister didn't have full faith in it either but, so far, Hank was standing by everything he'd told Maria. He spent more time with the kids than he had when he'd lived with them. It was funny, Lauren hadn't really noticed the way Hank had changed over the years to become the disinterested husband and father that he was until recently, hadn't even realized he had changed so much—but now, with this new turn around, she realized she was once again seeing the man who had slowly faded away before.

And, thank God, he was here today because they needed his help with all the heavy stuff.

She walked over to the trailer, and started to pick up another box, then stopped when she heard Hank talking to Maria. "I can't carry the mattress up the stairs by myself," Hank said.

"I'll help you," Maria answered.

"Maria, it's a queen-size mattress. You're not going to make it all the way up."

"I'm glad you have so much faith in me. I can hold one end of a mattress."

"It's two flights of stairs. Do you really think you'll make it? Because I remember the summer we moved that dresser up from the guest room to Jon's room and you only made it halfway. It's easier to get help before you start moving the thing."

Maria sighed and nodded. "Fine."

"I can help, Dad," Jonathan chimed in.

Hank ruffled his hair. "I appreciate it, big guy, but you're not quite big enough yet. I need another man for this job."

Lauren stepped forward, intending to insist that she and Maria could hold one end together—never mind the fact that she would likely offer little help to her sister, and would run the risk of tripping and falling down the stairs—but before she could say a word, someone else piped up.

"You need some help?" asked a tall, handsome man with dark hair, and stunning blue eyes.

"Actually, yes, if you don't mind," Hank said with relief evident in his voice.

"I'm happy to help," the man said extending a hand to Hank. "I'm Mike. I live just upstairs myself."

With a smile, Lauren stepped forward and interjected. "Mike," she said thrusting a hand toward him, "it's great to meet you. I'm Lauren, and I'm moving in with my sister, Avery. You might know her."

"Yeah, sure, I live right across the hall from her."

So this is the guy her sister was always talking about. Lauren had hoped so as soon as she'd heard his name. Now she had the perfect opportunity to help Avery past one of her stumbling blocks. Her sister was upstairs with Melanie, getting the girl a snack, and Lauren was going to make sure Mike made it past the apartment's threshold while Avery was inside.

"Oh, that's wonderful! We're going to be neighbors then. It's so good to meet you. You must be the one that cat sits for Avery."

"That's me," Mike said. Maria—who was now standing to Mike's left and slightly behind him since he had turned to talk to Lauren—tipped her head in Mike's direction and mouthed the words, "*The* Mike?" Lauren answered with an almost imperceptible nod, and Maria smiled, knowing what Lauren was up to.

Mike gave Lauren a smile and dimples flashed in his cheeks. No wonder Avery is interested in him, Lauren thought. He looked a little like Clark Kent without the glasses. Then he picked up one end of the mattress while Hank grabbed the other, and they started into the building. Lauren snatched a box from the trailer and hurried toward the elevator so she could beat them upstairs, and open the door for them. Maria and Jonathan slipped into the elevator with her, each carrying something.

"So ... you have a plan?" Maria said. Jonathan looked at his mother in confusion.

"Right now the only plan is to get Mr. hot dimples through Avery's front door while she's inside."

Jonathan looked up, eyes wide, and Maria raised her eyebrows in Lauren's direction. "Remember the company you're in."

"Oh, right," Lauren responded.

"Are you trying to set Aunt Avery up?" Jonathan asked.

Lauren looked at her nephew. "It's complicated."

"Oh, brother," Jon rolled his eyes. "Adults always think everything is *so* complicated." He shook his head, then his face brightened as he glanced up at Lauren again. "I can help! I'll go in first, and make sure Aunt Avery stays in the kitchen until Dad and the man get inside."

Lauren considered this and nodded. "Good plan, kid."

Jonathan winked at her, clearly enjoying this mission. "I got you covered."

Just then the elevator door dinged, and the three of them stepped out, Jonathan darting ahead to get the door and complete his mission. "Aunt Avery, can you make me a snack too?" he called as he entered the apartment.

Lauren smiled as she walked through the door, and set the box she was holding down. "That's one cool kid."

"Yup, always ready for a covert op," Maria said.

Just then, they heard the two men coming down the hallway from the stairwell. "Go to your left ... No, your other left ... I mean my left. That would be your right. Sorry!" Hank called out directions for Mike, who was walking backward.

Maria rolled her eyes in Lauren's direction. "Now you know why we were always getting lost on the way to our vacation destinations."

Lauren stifled a laugh as the men started through the doorway.

"Now which way?" Mike asked.

Hank looked up past Mike and thought about his response. "To your left. I mean that this time ... yeah, that's good. Keep going straight ahead for a few more steps ... okay, now move left again. Careful, you're going through the bedroom door. Step back, step back. Great! Now, put your end down for a second, and we can line it up with the bed frame."

The two men lifted the mattress again and laid it down on top of the bed frame. "There it is! Thanks for your help, man," Hank said, shaking Mike's hand.

"Sure. Is there anything else you need help getting up here?"

"I don't think so. There's a chair, but it isn't that big. I think we can get it up on the elevator," Hank said.

"Okay, then." Mike started toward the front door of the apartment. "I guess I'll see you around, Lauren."

"Wait—Mike!" Maria called. "I was just going to get everyone some lemonade. Why don't you stay a few minutes and have a glass."

Mike smiled, flashing his dimples. "Sure, I wouldn't mind a glass. It is awfully hot today."

"Great," Lauren said, stepping forward. "Why don't you sit down while Maria and I get that."

Mike nodded and stepped toward the couch, while Hank eyed Maria and Lauren suspiciously.

In the kitchen, Avery was sitting at the table with the kids. She didn't seem to realize Mike was right outside the door. Jon must have kept her so busy listening to him that she didn't hear Mike's voice in the other room.

"Hey, Avery, we're all about to sit down and have a glass of lemonade. Why don't you come on out and join us?" Maria said.

"I want some lemonade!" Melanie said.

Jonathan looked around at the women and decided to help out once again. "Sure, Mel, let's have some in here, though. We were going to play go fish, remember?"

"Okay. I'll win, though, Jon. I always win at go fish."

"Not *always*," Jon said defensively as he winked at Lauren. She smiled at him and ruffled his hair. What an awesome kid he was! Realizing this, she wished she'd spent more time with him over the years.

Lauren turned from the table and helped Maria fill glasses with lemonade. She put two on the table in front of the children, and then picked up two more. Maria handed one glass to Avery and grabbed two in her own hands, and they started into the living room.

"Wait," Avery said, "don't we have one glass too many?"

Maria shrugged and kept walking. Lauren decided to follow suit and let Avery see for herself why they had an extra glass.

As they stepped into the living room, Maria handed the two glasses she had to the men on the couch and then stepped back and took one of the glasses Lauren was holding for herself.

Avery stopped dead still as she saw who was sitting on her couch. Even in this setting, with so many people there to help her, Avery was still overcome by fear because this man was in her home.

Lauren set her glass down, and went to Avery's side, taking hold of her right arm. "Mike was kind enough to help Hank get my mattress upstairs," she said. Avery still didn't move or say a word, and she was trembling.

Maria came over and stood on Avery's left side, taking her other arm. "We really needed his help," she explained. "And it's so hot today; I thought we should thank him with a cold drink."

Avery glanced at Maria, then over at Lauren. She inhaled deeply, and in a shaky voice said, "Yeah, that's a good idea. Thanks for helping, Mike."

Chapter 54

Maria

Maria sighed as Hank pulled his truck up in her driveway. It had been a long, hot, sweaty, and tiring day. Maria felt good about all that they had accomplished, not the least of which was getting Avery to take a huge step forward in her emotional healing, but her body was suffering some consequences.

She looked over at Hank and smiled. “Thanks for helping today. I don’t know how we would have done it without you.”

Hank nodded. “I’m glad I could help.”

Maria reached to open her door. “I better get going. Maybe I can muster up the energy to do a load of laundry before Jonathan gets home tonight.” They had dropped both of the children off already at the homes of friends. Melanie was attending a sleepover birthday party, and Jonathan was going out to a late movie with another boy from his baseball team.

“Wait,” Hank said, stopping her with a hand on her arm. She looked at him and waited for him to explain what she was waiting for. “Aren’t you hungry?”

She furrowed her brow at him, wondering why he was asking. “I guess. I’ll probably just make a sandwich or something—why, do you want one?”

“Actually, I was thinking of going out for a bite.”

“Oh, well, I hope you enjoy it.” Maria was confused by him even starting this conversation.

“I was thinking maybe you’d like to go with me.” His voice told her he was a little nervous, though she didn’t really know why, and she had no idea why he was so interested in taking her out to dinner.

"How would Carina feel about that?" As soon as the words were out of her mouth she could tell by the look on his face that they had stung him, and she regretted saying them.

He glanced down into his lap. "I guess I deserve that, but I stopped seeing her right after you got home from the lake. I'm not *seeing* anyone anymore."

Maria felt bad for hurting him, though she wasn't sure why she should. Didn't he deserve it? Hadn't he spent the last few years hurting her? Still, she didn't feel right about the spiteful words she'd just let slip. She breathed out another sigh. "I'm sorry, Hank. That was an uncalled for jab. I mean, we're separated, and on our way to divorce. I don't have any right to judge your personal life now."

Hank looked back up at her. "It's okay. I did far worse to you ... So, what do you say? Can I take you for a bite to eat?"

She thought about it, looking at the house that was waiting for her empty, except for the dog. She loved Sadie, but it still seemed lonely and depressing. She looked back at his face, a hopeful, anticipating look on it. "I need to go in and let Sadie out. And I'd like to clean up a little first."

He smiled. "Sure, of course. Mind if I come in? It would be nice if I could wash up a little myself."

She nodded. "You can use the kid's bathroom."

Maria walked into her house with Hank just behind her. Sadie jumped up and danced with glee, running over to greet her. After lavishing Maria with kisses, Sadie ran to Hank for some more attention. That was something the dog would not have bothered to do just a few months ago, as she knew at that time to expect nothing from him. But now, he had time for everyone, it seemed, the dog included.

Maria let Sadie out and then turned to Hank. "She'll be out there for a little while. I'm just going to go take a quick shower."

He nodded and she headed into the master bedroom. Stripping off her sweaty clothes, she went into the bathroom and stepped into the shower. She let the water run over her face and body and felt invigorated as it washed the dirt and sweat of the day away. When she was finished in the shower, she put on clean clothes and dried her hair. She didn't use the hairdryer much because it fluffed her curls up into a style that made her look like she was returning to the eighties, but she didn't want to go to a restaurant with dripping hair, so tonight the fluff was going to have to do.

When she walked back into the living room, Hank was there with his wavy, blond hair damp. He didn't have any clean clothes here to change into, but it appeared he'd decided to shower. He had let Sadie back in and was playing with her. Maria smiled as she watched. She was seeing a version of Hank that had been gone for a very long time, and she was still amazed by the return.

Hank tossed the toy he had been using to play tug-of-war with Sadie, and stood up, smoothing his pants out. "Ready to go?"

"Sure." She grabbed her purse and threw the strap over her shoulder as they headed out the door.

When they reached the truck, Hank opened her door for her, then proceeded to the other side to let himself in. "I think the last time you opened the car door for me was sometime during our first year of marriage," Maria commented.

"I'm pretty sure I remembered to do it both times you were in labor."

"I stand corrected. Some of that time is a bit of a blur for me."

Hank glanced at her, then turned his eyes to the job of backing the truck out of the driveway. "I want to treat you right—make up for some of the wrongs I've done."

Maria didn't think he could ever open enough doors to make up for three years of emotional absence, occasional hurtful comments, and sleeping with another woman, but Hank was trying so hard lately, and she didn't want to say anything to ruin it. "That's nice," she said instead. After all, it was nice to see *this* Hank again; it was nice to have him treating her kindly and to have him present in their children's lives again.

They rode in silence until Hank pulled up in front of *Johnny's Pizza.* They walked inside and found a booth. After a quick look at the menu, they agreed to order a Medium pizza with the works on one side and just meat on the other.

Maria sipped her soda and regarded Hank sitting across from her. His now half dry hair was falling over his forehead on one side. He lifted his hand and pushed it back. When his green eyes met hers she felt her stomach flutter as if she was a school girl with a crush, and it irritated her. She didn't want to feel anything about this man any longer. It was time to let him go. "So," she said, "you wanna tell me why we're here?"

He shrugged. "Pizza seemed like a simple and easy option. I wasn't sure either of us was up to any place fancy, or a place where we had to make many decisions about the menu choices."

"No, Hank, I mean why are *we* here—together?"

His face showed complete innocence at the question, and the exasperation in her voice. "Why shouldn't we be? I know we're separated, and we've filed for divorce, but that doesn't mean we can't be friends."

"You want us to be friends?"

"Yes. Don't you think we should try to be? We are still raising two kids together. It would be better for them if we can be friends."

She searched his eyes for a moment. "So, it's all for the kids?"

A tiny smile tilted the corners of his mouth, and he leaned forward as if he were sharing a secret with her. "It isn't *all* for them." He reached his hands across the table and wrapped her hands up in his. A shiver shot up her spine at the contact, and she wasn't sure whether she wanted to pull away or allow him to continue holding onto her hands. She sure didn't want him to know that his touch still had an effect on her, so she decided to play it cool—at least that was how she hoped it would appear. "I know I've messed it up for us as a couple, but I want us to have a good relationship now. I want us to be friends—at least that."

At least that? What was he saying? It sounded like he was telling her that he wished they could fix their marriage, but he'd made it clear over the last few years that he wasn't attracted to her anymore. So, what was he doing here—messing with her?

She pulled her hands out from under his and looked down to avoid his gaze, as it always made her weak. "I'm sure we can be friends, Hank. That would be nice."

A moment later their pizza arrived, and they talked about the children while they ate. They were both looking forward to Jon's baseball tournament, and seeing the garden Melanie had planted with Mrs. Crump.

When Maria got home, she snuggled up with Sadie and fell asleep on the couch watching a sappy romance movie.

Chapter 55

Avery

Avery walked into her room, reeling from a barrage of conflicting emotions. She looked down at her hands that were still trembling, but a glance in the mirror revealed a tentative smile. Fear was still coursing through her, making her want to check every lock—yet, she was also feeling excitement. She was proud of herself for getting through the half hour Mike had spent in her apartment without flipping out, but she wasn't sure she liked her sisters' sneaky method of getting him through her front door. On the other hand, she had to admit that there was likely no other way it would have happened, and they couldn't have been any more "there for her." They both lent their support, and their hearts were most definitely in the right place. Still, it made her wonder what else they might do to push her forward.

Trust them, she heard the words in her head, *they only want to help you.* The voice in her head was speaking in her father's voice, and she knew she needed to listen to it.

She picked up the framed picture of her mother that now sat out in the open on her dresser. Tracing the outline of Eve's face, she said, "I'm doing so much better, Mom, and it's because of Maria and Lauren. I know you and Dad would both be pleased about that."

Avery set the picture back down and went to her bed. She laid down on top of the comforter, and closed her eyes, letting her mind drift back to earlier that day when Mike had been sitting in her home, talking to her family. That felt good—like it was right. She imagined for a moment the possibility that she and Mike could someday be a couple, and a smile broadened across her face as her heart fluttered in her chest. She tried to picture herself kissing him, but in this vision, Maria and Lauren were still in the room. No—that was just wrong! But she still couldn't quite imagine herself completely alone with him in a place other than the hallway of their building. To do so was still a little too scary. She wondered if she would ever get to a place where she could overcome that fear, and she wondered if Mike could really handle knowing the truth about her. She felt so dirty and undesirable when she thought about what had happened that night two and a half years ago. How would he feel when he knew about it? Would he look at her differently? Would he even still want her? And the best question yet—could she ever reach a point where that would matter? She didn't know if she would ever be able to let a man touch her again, regardless of how much one part of her wanted Mike to do just that, because this other part panicked at the very thought.

Avery's thoughts were interrupted by a knock on her bedroom door. She jumped at the sound, then, placing a hand over her racing heart said, "Come in."

"Ave, are you okay?" Lauren stepped in hesitantly. "Was it too much? If you're upset, be mad at me. It was my idea. I just wanted to help you get past a barrier."

Avery sat up and smiled at Lauren. "I'm alright. I'm not mad at you. I know your heart was in the right place. It was scary though, and I don't know how I'm going to make it to the next step, and then the next one. You can't push me through every door that scares me. Some things I'll have to do on my own."

"That's true. But I'll always be here to support you, and give a little nudge when I can." She shrugged. "Just take it one step at a time, and don't try to think about it too far ahead. That will just be overwhelming. Remember, you have Maria and me when you need us, and we'll try to be gentle when we push you."

"You're right—it is overwhelming to think ahead about it. I was just doing that."

Lauren walked over to the bed, sat down next to Avery, and hugged her tight. "You took a step today. Don't worry about tomorrow's steps."

Avery nodded. “You’re right. Let’s go have some ice cream to celebrate.”

“Sure, sounds good to me. Who needs dinner?”

Chapter 56

Lauren

Lauren stopped painting and put her brush down when she heard the doorbell. Stepping out of her room, she started toward the front door. She had been living in this apartment with Avery for two weeks now and, with Avery's blessing, had added splashes of herself to the décor. Besides adding a few knick-knacks around the living space, she had also hung some of her paintings—a couple of the older ones, from before Parkinson's had become a part of her life, as well as a couple of the newer ones. On the wall over the sofa, she had paired a forested landscape with an abstract depiction of sorrow. On the opposing wall, she had paired a tropical landscape with an abstract representing love.

She got to the door, only tripping once, and opened it to see Mike on the other side. "Hi, Mike. Avery's not here if you're looking for her."

"Actually I was hoping to talk to you a little." He rocked on his feet and seemed to struggle with moving the conversation forward.

"Okay, you want to come in?"

He glanced around at the interior of the apartment behind Lauren as if to make sure Avery wasn't there. "If you're sure it's alright. I don't think Avery likes for me to come in."

"She won't be back for at least another hour. She's babysitting our niece and nephew."

"Okay," he said, cautiously stepping inside.

"Wow! This is amazing!" Lauren turned from the door to see Mike examining one of her paintings.

"You think so?" she asked.

"Yeah, I've never seen anything like it." He pointed to the painting depicting sorrow and studied it closely as if trying to increase his understanding of its meaning. "It's so deeply emotional. Where did you get this?"

"I painted it."

Mike turned and regarded her as if seeing her for the first time. "*You* did this?"

Lauren nodded, her cheeks reddening with the attention.

"You're very talented," Mike continued. "Are you showing them or selling them?"

"Only to the people who come here and see them—so, that would be a no."

He considered the painting again, with its dark, compelling colors. "These should be seen. I know someone whose cousin owns a gallery downtown. I could talk to him and see if his cousin might like to take a look at your work."

"Wow! Really?" A rush of excitement filled Lauren's chest. She had assumed her work would always be mostly for her own fulfillment. She tried to restrain her elation. After all, there was no guarantee that Mike's friend's cousin would even want to see her work. But it was a chance, and she was grateful for it.

"I'll ask him. I've been to his cousin's gallery, and I think your work would be of interest to her."

Lauren nodded, smiling at him. "Thanks, Mike, that's really nice of you. I can see why Avery likes you."

Mike turned to her with his eyebrows lifted. "Does she?" he asked.

At that moment, Rocket sauntered out from behind the couch and began rubbing up against Mike's leg, as if to agree that he was likable. Mike reached down, and picked up the cat, holding him gently, and rubbing his furry head. He looked back at Lauren and continued, "Because that's what I came to talk to you about. I can't figure her out. One minute she seems to like me, and the next she's pushing me away again, or making an excuse to not go out with me. I mean, why would she continually refuse dates with me, and then beg me to go to her father's funeral with her? Why won't she let me through the door when she's home, but give me a key so I can take care of her cat when she's away? Why won't she set foot in my apartment? She acts like the floor is going to turn into quicksand the moment her foot touches it."

Lauren sighed. "I wish I could explain all that to you, I really do, but it would be a breach of Avery's trust if I did. I can tell you that there is a reason, and she does like you. I've been encouraging her to talk to you about it herself, but she will have to decide when she's ready to do that."

Mike's face showed curiosity, relief, and disappointment all at once, but he nodded slowly. He set the cat back down on the floor. "I understand. I guess I can wait till she's ready to tell me. At least you cleared one thing up for me. I thought I might go crazy wondering what she really thought of me. I was beginning to think it was time to just move on."

Lauren put a hand on his arm, not worried about him seeing it tremble. He was a nice man, and Lauren hoped Avery would be able to let him into her life someday as more than just a neighbor. "I really do see why Avery likes you, Mike, so I'm going to tell you this—when and if she does talk to you about her behavior, you will need to keep patience in mind. You'll need an extra share of it if you want to have a relationship with her."

Mike looked a bit perplexed but shook it away quickly. "I've been trying to get her to go out with me for quite a long time. Most guys would have given up after the first few fails. I think I have the patience if that's what is needed."

Lauren smiled as they walked back toward the front door. "I'm glad to hear that," she said.

After she let Mike out of the apartment, Lauren turned around, glanced at her paintings on the wall, and wondered if it was possible that they might someday hang in a gallery. She thought back a few months to remember when her life had seemed to only get bleaker with each passing day, a time when she didn't think she would ever paint anything worthwhile again and spent most of her time worrying about medical bills and how she'd get by when her symptoms got worse and she couldn't work anymore. She was amazed by the way things had changed since those two weeks at the lake, and she was grateful for every bit of it.

Chapter 57

Maria

Maria jumped up from her seat and cheered wildly as she watched her son round first base, and slide into second. Hank was by her side, cheering just as loudly. A year ago, only she and Melanie, and occasionally her father, had been there to cheer for Jonathan. Now he had both his aunts and his father at every game. *What a difference a year or even just a couple weeks can make*, Maria thought as she dropped her hands back to her sides. Her fingers brushed against Hank's, and her heart fluttered in response. Try as she might, she couldn't seem to make herself stop responding to his touch, even one as minor as this. She took her seat once more and did her best to focus on the game again as the next batter took his position and waited on the pitcher. He missed the first two pitches, but on the third, the bat cracked against the ball and sent it soaring into the outfield. The batter ran for first base, and Jonathan took off as well. He hit third and decided to keep going, barely making it into home. The umpire yelled, "Safe!" and the entire family erupted in cheers again. When the rest of them had taken their seats, Melanie continued to shout, "That's my brother!" as if Jonathan had scored the winning run. In reality, there was still one more inning to go, and his team was a run behind.

"Hey, Mel," Hank said. "Maybe you should be the team's cheerleader."

Melanie wrinkled her nose. "No way! I want to be the mascot."

Hank raised his eyebrows. "That would certainly be interesting. I'd like to see that costume," he said. Jonathan's team had chosen their name by allowing all the players to write their choice down and put it in a drawing. The winner had chosen to call the team *The Flying Fish.*

When the game was over, Hank insisted on taking everyone out for ice cream. Jonathan shrugged, saying, "But we didn't win, and I struck out in the last inning."

Hank took Jon's shoulders and looked him in the eye. "Did you work hard in practice?"

Jonathan nodded.

"Did you try your best today?"

"Yeah, but it wasn't good enough."

Hank nodded. "Are you going to work even harder to win the next game?"

"Yes."

"Son, I'm glad you want to do better, and you want your team to win, but as long as you did your best, and plan to keep working hard, then I think you deserve ice cream. Now, if you had been slacking off and not trying, it would be different." Jonathan smiled, and Hank put an arm around him. Maria followed behind them to the car, feeling so happy that she could watch her son with his father like this again.

Maria stood in the backyard, in her hiding spot between the fence and the large bush, and took a puff from the cigarette between her fingers. Sadie ran around the yard chasing squirrels as the sun began to go down. "Hey there," came a voice from behind, nearly causing Maria to choke on the smoke she was exhaling.

"Hank! I thought you were with the kids inside." She said turning to face him, feeling silly for hiding behind a bush like a misbehaving child.

"I was—but both of them are sound asleep now, and I wanted to find you, and say goodbye before I went home."

Maria looked at her watch and saw that it was only ten after eight. "They're both asleep already?"

"I guess the game wore them out."

"Or it could be a sugar crash from all the ice cream they ate." Maria took another puff.

"I thought you quit smoking a long time ago," Hank said, leaning against the wooden fence.

Maria shrugged. "I started again—also a long time ago."

"My fault then," Hank said sadly.

Maria took another puff, about to agree with him that it was indeed his fault, then suddenly, she heard her father's voice in her head. *Who are you really trying to hide it from, Maria? Them or yourself?* The memory of his admonishment made the smoke go acrid in her mouth, and she couldn't spit it out fast enough. She looked at the cigarette slowly burning, and, for the first time in a long time—maybe ever—she was disgusted by it.

"No, Hank, it's not your fault. I made the choice to start up again all by myself. I'm going to quit again though." She said it with conviction as she bent down and crushed out the cigarette on the ground. "Unfortunately I'll probably gain ten pounds doing it."

"So what?" Hank said. "You'll still be beautiful—and healthier too."

A little bubble of anger rose up inside Maria at his words and most of all at the sincerity with which he said them. "I don't understand you, Hank. What are you trying to do—mess with me?"

"Mess with you? No, I'm just trying to be supportive."

"Hank!" She nearly shouted it and then forced herself to calm down. She didn't want to wake the kids. Sadie came running over at the sharp sound of her voice, looking to protect her. Maria patted the dog's head absently and, holding back her fury as best she could, her voice came out in a low rumble. "For three years you were barely willing to look at me. You made plenty of comments about my weight, and would only make love to me in the dark." Her voice broke on the last word, and tears spilled from her eyes. She swiped at them angrily, hating the fact that her emotion was so transparent. "Now, suddenly, you're acting like the Hank I married again. And I'm thrilled for the kids to have you spending time with them now, but the rest of this ... you saying we should be friends—*at least that*, and now you're telling me I'm beautiful. What do you want from me, Hank?"

He looked down, and his face was full of shame. *Was it real, though?* Maria didn't know what to believe. "I'm so sorry I did this to you," he said. "It was never really about you. It was always about me. I was unhappy with myself, and I projected it onto you." He looked up at her. "I guess it's what they call a mid-life crisis—I don't know. I just looked in the mirror one day and … this old man was looking back at me. Lines around my eyes and mouth, grey hair in my eyebrows, and all this luggage under my eyes—not to mention the belly that extends over my belt. I hardly recognized myself, and it scared me. I was feeling unattractive, so I put that on you."

Hank's face scrunched up, and he cast his eyes downward again, crossing his arms over his chest. If this wasn't real emotion, he was a better actor than she'd thought. "Then one day at the office Carina gave me a compliment. It wasn't anything big, but it was the first time I'd felt good about myself in a long time. I started fishing for more compliments—you know, asking her if my shirt looked good—that sort of thing, and before I knew it she was taking it a step further and flirting with me. I knew I should stop it right there, but I was weak. It felt so good to have that kind of attention." He looked at her with sad eyes, and his voice was little more than a whisper. "You know the rest."

For a long moment, Maria just stared at him. He had just been telling her how he'd come to cheat on her, yet strangely she felt like she needed to console him. *What was that about?* "You've always been handsome, Hank. I never stopped thinking so."

He patted his belly, and looked at her, silently asking if he was still handsome even with that. She shrugged and patted her own.

He nodded as tears slipped from his eyes. “I should have counted on you to bring me back from that darkness, not Carina. I wish you could know how sorry I am for that.”

Maria looked down for a moment. There was still one more important thing she needed to know. She glanced back up and looked him in the eye. “Hank, what about the kids? Why did you pull away from them back then?”

He shook his head. “I was ashamed. I was cheating on their mother. I knew I was ruining our family, and when they looked at me, I felt that shame burn through me. I didn’t want to feel that, so I pulled back from them, from anything and anyone that made me face the truth. I spent as much time away from home as I could. At home all I ever felt was shame.”

More tears were running down Hank’s face, and Maria didn’t think she’d ever seen him this emotional before. She didn’t know what to say to him.

He put his hands on her shoulders and looked her in the eye. “Just know, Maria, that it was all me. You *are* beautiful. You always were.”

Without thinking, she reached up and touched his face, wiped the tears from his cheeks. He took her hand in one of his and brought it to his lips, kissing her fingers. Butterflies exploded in her stomach as her heart jumped into high speed. Then his mouth was on hers, softly kissing her—and, God help her, she didn’t want him to stop.

He pulled back, looking into her eyes. “I guess I should go now.”

She didn’t say a word as he let go of her hand and turned away, walking toward his truck. *Was this really happening? And did she really want it to happen?* She contemplated that as she walked back into her house with Sadie at her heals. Was it possible for something so broken to be restored? Her father would say that it was.

She went into her bedroom and got ready for bed. Then she found herself getting down on her knees in front of the bed, and folding her hands the way she did as a child. "Dear God, It's been a long time since I prayed, so I'm not sure how to do this. I guess I'll start by saying thank you for helping Lauren, Avery, and me to restore our relationship." She felt a tear running down her cheek, though she hadn't been aware that she was crying until then. "Lord, I thought my marriage was too broken to be restored, but now I'm not so sure. I guess what I'm asking is—if Hank and I are meant to be a couple again, then, Lord, show me the way, and help my heart to forgive him for everything that happened in the past." She looked up at the ceiling, trying to see past that, trying to see right through to heaven. She was wishing for a sign, some assurance that God could hear her, and then, in the back of her mind, she could see her mother's face. She smiled as a warm feeling flooded through her. "You're there, Lord, aren't you? You're really there. Well, since I'm here talking to you, I want to pray for my sisters too. Lord, help Lauren to have as much good time as she can before her condition gets worse and send her all the love she needs to see her through the challenges to come. And, Lord, please help Avery to heal, and move on from the terrible thing that happened to her two years ago. Help her to let herself live again." Maria paused, considering whether or not she had anything else to add. When nothing else came to mind, she finished her prayer by saying, "In Jesus' name I pray. Amen."

Avery

Avery stood in the hall in front of Mike's apartment, her hand hovered in front of the door, but she couldn't quite bring herself to knock. Her stomach was flip-flopping, her hands were sweating, and her heart was galloping. She felt light-headed and thought she might just pass out.

She dropped her hand and stepped back. She couldn't do it. She could knock on his door to borrow some sugar, or to ask him to cat sit, but she couldn't do it with the intention of asking him over to her place for dinner. This was too much like a date, and Avery hadn't been able to ask for or accept a date since that terrible night over two years ago. She wanted to give Mike a chance, believe that he was different, but a protection instinct deep inside her kept begging her to run.

She turned and reached for the doorknob of her own apartment, resigned to giving up, but then she thought about her father and her sisters—the way they had encouraged her to step out of her fear. They would tell her that she could do this—that she needed to, and she knew that was true. She had to push herself forward if she ever hoped to move on and have a life again.

Closing her eyes, she gathered her courage, then she opened her eyes again and stepped back toward Mike's door. Reaching up, she rapped on the door before she had time to think about it and chicken out again. She waited several seconds for his footsteps to come toward the door. Her heart was pounding so hard that the sound of it filled her ears in a deafening drumbeat, and she thought again about running away.

No, she told herself, *I'm going to do this!*

A tiny gasp escaped her throat when the door swung open. Mike stood looking at her with a furrowed brow. "Avery? Are you okay?"

"Yes," she spat out, trying to regain her lost composure. She took a slow breath and continued in an even tone. "I'm fine, Mike. I, uh, wanted to see if you—well, if you wanted to come over and have dinner—with Lauren and me."

A smile spread across Mike's face, revealing the dimples in his cheeks. Avery was torn between the conflicting emotions of melting in the presence of his amazing smile and the incredible fear that was lashing up through her body, making her struggle to keep her feet in place.

"I'd love to. I thought you'd never ask," Mike said.

Avery wasn't sure how to respond to that, and she was sure she was going to lose her cool any moment. "Great. Come over around six-thirty," she said, then spun around, and went back to her apartment without waiting for any further response.

As soon as the door was closed behind her, Avery secured every lock, then turned, and pressed her back up against it. She let the anxiety drain out of her as she stood there for several seconds with her eyes closed. When she opened them, Lauren was just coming out of her room. She looked at Avery, trying to read her expression.

"Did you do it? Did you ask him?" Lauren asked hope etched all over her face.

Avery nodded, and Lauren clapped in response. "You did it! You took the next step. I'm proud of you, sis!"

Avery felt a little silly having her sister congratulate her on asking someone over for dinner, but at the same time, she couldn't help but smile. She was proud of herself too. Now she only hoped she would be able to take the next step and tell Mike about her darkest moment.

"How does this look?" Avery asked striding into the kitchen.

Lauren, who was attempting to put some of the simplest cooking lessons she'd learned from Maria to good use, turned and looked at her. "It looks fine," she said with the shrug of one shoulder.

"Fine?" Avery's voice was filled with self-consciousness and doubt. "Maybe my burgundy top would be better. It brings out my eyes."

"Whatever you think, but you look good in the one you have on, and he already likes you." Lauren turned back to the stove and stirred a pot of pasta.

"I need to do better than fine. After all, if I get up the nerve to tell him—well, you know—then he might not be so interested anymore."

Lauren glanced over her shoulder at Avery. "I think you're worrying too much. Mike's a nice guy. If you tell him, he'll be understanding."

"I hope you're right, but I'm still going to change." She looked at Lauren stirring the pot on the stove carefully. "You want some help with that?"

Lauren waved her off. "You already chopped all the vegetables for the salad. I can do the rest."

"I don't want you to burn yourself. Let me go change and then I'll help."

"And risk getting a stain on your burgundy top?" Lauren mocked, then she held both her hands out for Avery to see. "I'm doing good right now. Even the left one is pretty steady. And I promise I'll let you know if I really need you." She shooed Avery away. "Now go get ready for your date."

Avery felt her cheeks heat up at the word date. She tried to smile, though hearing that word made her feel a little queasy. "It's not a date," she insisted, wanting to push that word out of the conversation and out of her own head. "But if you're sure you don't need me, I'll go put the other shirt on."

"I'm sure."

Avery turned and left the kitchen, walking to her room with deliberate steps. She glanced at the clock and saw that it was almost six. Her heart started to beat a little faster at the thought of Mike's impending arrival. Lauren was going to answer the door and let him inside. They had planned that in advance to rule out any possibility of Avery freaking out and refusing to let him in.

She went to the closet and pulled out her burgundy top. It was soft and had a ruffled collar that was cut a little low, but not too low. She peeled off the blue shirt she was wearing and replaced it with the burgundy one, then evaluated herself in the mirror. Just as she had told her sister, it brought out her caramel colored eyes. She tried a smile and decided that this was the right outfit.

After putting on her make-up, she went back into the kitchen and attempted to help Lauren finish the dinner preparations. She hoped Mike would like it, but without Maria's help, it felt a little like the blind leading the blind. Neither she nor Lauren had spent much time learning to cook.

"Do you think this is going to turn out okay?" Avery asked skeptically.

Lauren rolled her eyes. "Stop worrying, sis. The sauce came from a jar, and I think we can manage boiling noodles, and putting the salad together."

Avery nodded. Lauren was right; she was worried about the wrong thing. The food would be fine, and her outfit was great. The real worry was conversation. What would they talk about? Mike had lived across the hall from her for three years, but she had been willing to talk to him so little that she really didn't know much about him, and he knew little about her. They had established that they both liked cats. That had happened when Rocket escaped from her apartment just shortly after Mike moved into the building.

Mike was the one who found her cat wandering around, and brought him home. It was the first time she'd ever talked to him, something she probably would not have done if he hadn't been rescuing Rocket. If things worked out, she supposed she'd have to thank that cat for getting it all started.

Tonight, though, they needed to talk about something other than the cat, and Avery had no idea what that would be. She also had no idea how she was going to bring the conversation to the point of telling him why she behaved the way she did. It seemed crazy to even consider telling him that when they knew so little about each other—almost like telling a stranger. But he wasn't a stranger, and their relationship could not even start until he was able to understand her and understand what he would be getting into. She would have to tell him soon—somehow.

She looked up at Lauren, who noticed the angst etched on her face, and smiled encouragingly. Her sister's blue eyes seemed to reach out to her, letting her know she had support. Avery marveled at the comfort she felt from that simple look. It was hard to believe that this person who was helping her through such a big emotional step in her life was the same sister she'd once thought of as someone who couldn't be depended upon. Lauren used to be the one who hardly noticed anyone or anything outside the bubble of her own world—a world that revolved around art. She was the one who was always looking for the help of others without ever thinking that they might need help from her. She wasn't that person anymore. Now Lauren was present and aware, a confidant and friend. Maybe she would help Avery get the conversation where it needed to go tonight.

Chapter 59

Lauren

When the doorbell rang, Avery looked up from the pot of sauce she was stirring in alarm, panic marking every feature of her face. Lauren put a hand on her shoulder. "Relax and stay here for a minute. I'll go get the door," she said.

Avery nodded, relief mixing with her angst.

Lauren went to the front door and opened it. Mike was standing in the hallway with a small bunch of wildflowers. His hair was neatly combed, and he was wearing a button up shirt and sport coat. Lauren wondered if this was his work apparel, or if he was trying as hard as Avery to look his best.

She opened the door wide and gestured for him to come inside. He lifted the bouquet of flowers and said, "I didn't know what kind Avery likes, so I brought a variety."

Lauren smiled. "They're lovely. I'm sure she'll like them." In all honesty, she didn't know what Avery's favorite flower was either. They were still building their relationship, and that hadn't come up. For a fleeting moment she thought about Blake, and the game they'd played telling each other their favorite things. Flowers had never come up, and now she wished she could tell him her favorite was daffodils. She felt a stab to her heart at the thought of Blake. Tonight was about helping Avery with her love life, but Lauren's heart still ached for the relationship she had wanted to have with Blake, and for a moment she couldn't help wonder where he was and what he was doing. Most of all, she wondered if he ever thought about her.

"Lauren?"

She shook away the thoughts of Blake and looked up at Mike. "Yeah?"

"It seemed like I lost you there for a second. Everything okay?"

She forced a smile and nodded. "Of course. Avery should be out in just a second," she said, hoping her sister would hear and make her entrance. The next one to come through the kitchen door, however, was not Avery, but Rocket, who ran directly to Mike and began to rub against his leg. "He really likes you. He only comes to me like that when I have a treat for him."

Mike shrugged. "I'm a cat person. The thing with cats is that they don't just love you because you are there like most dogs do. You have to be willing to let them know you care about them first."

"I see. So I need to work a little harder at it, then?"

"And give it time."

"Looks like Rocket wants to steal the show tonight," Avery said as she entered the room.

Mike looked up at Avery, his face lighting up as he took in the sight of her. "No chance of that. You look beautiful." He walked toward Avery, ignoring the panic that filled her face at his approach, and handed her the flowers.

"Thank you," she said, taking a step back. "I'll go find a vase for them. Why don't you and Lauren come on in the kitchen and sit down? I'll get the food on the table as soon as I get these flowers in some water."

Lauren watched as Avery nervously fumbled with the vase and flowers. "Want me to come help you with the food?" she asked.

"No, no, I've got it," Avery responded. She got the flowers arranged and then began placing food on the table. Lauren wondered if Avery was hoping Mike would think she had cooked it all herself, or if she was just having a hard time sitting down at the table with a man. Finally, she sat down and gave Mike a nervous smile. "Let's eat!" she said.

"Oh, do you mind if I say a blessing first?"

"Absolutely not," Lauren said with a grin. She liked Mike more and more every time she talked to him, and she had hope that he would be the kind, patient man that Avery was going to need if ever she was to move beyond the pain and fear of what had happened to her that one terrible night.

They all folded their hands and bowed their heads. Mike said a short, simple blessing thanking God for the food, and the time they were all spending together. When he was done, they all began to eat, and Lauren wished she knew a good way to get a conversation going. She had never been good at taking the lead, but Maria wasn't here, and Avery was still struggling with the mere presence of a man. Lauren's mind fumbled for a topic to bring up. The weather was too trivial, and getting right to the point with Avery's issues was a recipe for disaster.

Just as she was about to ask Mike about sports, something she knew nothing about, he saved her by starting the conversation himself. "So, Lauren, I'm going to see my friend tomorrow—the one whose cousin owns a gallery—and I was wondering if you could give me some pictures of your work. It would be much easier and quicker if I have something to give him instead of just asking if his cousin is interested with no visual."

"Oh, I've never thought of taking pictures of them. I could take some with my phone and send them to you."

"Maybe it would be better if I take them with my phone while I'm here. But I want to get a good variety for him to show his cousin. It won't be anywhere near as good as seeing them in person, but it will be a good way for her to decide if she's interested in seeing more."

Lauren nodded. "I can show you all the ones that are hanging around the apartment and the ones stashed in my closet."

"In a closet? That's terrible! We need to get them out of there where they can be seen."

Lauren smiled, feeling elated by his compliments. Then Avery chimed in. "She's good, isn't she?" Avery sounded so proud, and it made Lauren's heart swell.

"She is, and it's a shame no one else is seeing it. But maybe that will be remedied soon."

"She's been painting since she was six. I wish I had a talent like hers," Avery said.

"Oh, I'm sure you have your own talents, but we've really talked so little, I don't even know what it is you do."

"I'm a web designer. My company puts pages together for other businesses, and I'm one of the chief designers."

Mike gave her an appreciative look. "So you're an artist too."

Avery's cheeks flushed. "I guess so. I never thought about it like that before. I just thought of it as IT work."

"I'd love to see some of your work. Maybe after we eat, you could show me."

"You've probably already seen some of it," Lauren said. "She's done pages for a lot of local businesses—the store right down the street included."

"Hobby Village?" He looked at Avery, amazement in his eyes. "I shop there all the time, and I've seen their page. It's great and very creative. You did that?"

Avery's cheeks grew redder as she nodded. She looked at Lauren and smiled. It was probably the first time she realized that Lauren ever paid any real attention to her work.

"It is creative. Avery is very good at what she does." Lauren paused a moment, not wanting to move on too quickly and take away from Mike's recognition of Avery's work. After a few moments, she spoke up again. "So what is it you do, Mike?"

"Me? I'm just a simple teacher."

"A teacher?" Avery said, a little surprised by this. Lauren wasn't that shocked. It seemed to fit and explained his high level of patience. "What grade?"

"This year I'm teaching fifth grade, but I'm hoping to move to third next year."

"That's interesting. Not a lot of men teach elementary school," Lauren said.

"That's true, but I enjoy the younger kids. They give me a good laugh once in a while with the things they say and they can be so sweet. I'm hoping to move to the younger grade again because I love the way they all seem to be able to be friends when they're that age. The older they get, the more things get in the way of that. The compassion I see in the young kids gives me a lot of hope, and who doesn't need that in this world?"

Avery nodded, then a devilish smile crossed her face. "I wonder how many of those little girls are harboring a crush on their handsome teacher."

Mike's face turned crimson, and his eyes dropped to the table. "I wouldn't know."

Avery didn't let his embarrassment faze her. At the moment she was her brash, bold self, and it was hard to imagine she was afraid of anything, but Lauren knew the truth. "I sure had a crush on my first male teacher. You remember that Lauren, the year I had Mr. Frank?"

"Oh," Lauren started with surprise. "I don't know ... Mr. Frank ... I had him one year, too." Lauren felt embarrassed by the fact that she did not remember. The bubble she used to live in seemed to never stop haunting her. "Some of my friends had crushes on him."

"Some of her friends, but not her," Avery said looking at Mike, who was still blushing a little. "It takes quite a man to get Lauren's attention away from the easel."

Lauren wasn't sure if Avery was trying to bring up Blake, but the comment certainly made her think of him. "I guess that's true," she said dismissively, not wanting to delve any further into this subject that made her heart ache for something she had lost. "Art has always been my first love."

"I can respect that," Mike said, the color in his cheeks normal again. "I've lost a couple of girlfriends over my dedication to work ... and with your talent ..."

"Thank you. It's nice to have someone appreciate my work." Lauren looked up and smiled.

"It looks like we're done here," Avery said. "Why don't we go take a look at Lauren's work now, so you can get those pictures? Lauren and I can take care of the dishes later."

They all got up and walked around the apartment looking at Lauren's paintings.

"This one's my favorite," Avery said, lifting a canvas that depicted flowering trees overhanging a body of water. It was an old painting; one Lauren had done a few years earlier, before the Parkinson's.

"You like this one that much?" Lauren asked.

"I do. It reminds me of our time at the lake."

There was no need to say more. Lauren hadn't thought about it before, but she knew what Avery was saying. It wasn't about the painting itself, or how aesthetically pleasing it was. It was about the memory it brought to mind, of the two weeks that meant the world to both of them now.

"You should have it then," Lauren said.

Avery's smile lit her face. "I'll hang it in my room where I can see it every day when I wake up."

"This is really something," Mike's voice interrupted. He was holding up one of Lauren's more recent paintings, the one that depicted peace. Waves of pale blue and purple filled the canvas in such a way as to make the on-looker feel like a baby being rocked to sleep.

Mike snapped a picture of it, then moved on to the next one. When he felt he had enough to show his friend, the three of them went into the living room. Avery insisted that Mike and Lauren sit down while she brought in dessert—a chocolate cake they had bought at the store.

For a few long moments, after the cake was brought out, they all ate in silence—no one seemed to know what to talk about. Lauren nervously decided to break the silence.

She cleared her throat, then said, "So, Mike, I suppose you must have a cat yourself since you seem to like them."

"I have two actually. Ariel and Eric."

Avery's eyebrows lifted. "I didn't know you were into Disney princesses."

Lauren could tell by the bemused smile on Avery's face that she was barely holding back a snort of laughter.

"My little niece, Ellie, named them," Mike said, meeting Avery's smile with one of his own, not fazed for a moment by her amusement. "She was four when I got them, and head over heels in love with *The Little Mermaid.* When she saw that I had gotten a female cat that is a red tabby and a male cat that is mostly black she felt Ariel and Eric were the obvious names to choose." Mike shrugged. "Who was I to argue? Ellie knows her cuteness always wins with me."

"So you have a niece. I never even thought to ask you if you have any siblings, but I guess the answer to that is yes," Avery said.

"I have one older sister. Along with that, I have a brother-in-law, and, of course, Ellie. I'm going to have another little niece or nephew in a few months. I'm hoping for a boy this time to even things up."

"Well, you've already met my family. Maybe someday I'll get to meet yours."

Lauren was impressed with Avery's willingness to talk about such future possibilities. It meant her mind was opening up to the idea of a bigger world with more people in it.

"Maybe you will," Mike said with a grin.

Lauren stood up and began to collect everyone's dessert plates. "I'll just take care of these," she said as a way to excuse herself from the room. When she got to the kitchen, she cleared the dishes off the table from dinner and began to scrub them and place them in the dishwasher. When everything was cleaned up, she quietly peeked into the living room to see how things were going. Mike and Avery were talking quietly. Lauren wished she could hear them so she would know if Avery needed her. She debated whether or not to go back into the room with them, but Avery didn't look distressed, so Lauren decided to leave them alone, and hope Avery could get where she needed to go on her own. She strolled back into the kitchen and picked up the phone. She'd call Maria, she decided, and see how things were going there.

Chapter 60

Maria

Maria was weary as she slipped into the seat of her car. She had just finished working an extra four hours to help cover for a staff shortage. It was almost eleven, and she was heading home at last. The kids would already be asleep, and she hadn't even seen them awake since it was a Saturday, and they had still been asleep when Hank had arrived to spend the day with them. Lucky for her, he was able to stay late and keep them while she worked.

Her fingers kept a steady drumbeat against the steering wheel. She desperately wanted a cigarette, but she was not going to let herself get off course when it came to quitting. Instead, she reached into her purse and pulled out the nicotine gum she'd bought to help her get through the first few weeks of being a non-smoker. She pushed a piece of it into her mouth with a grimace. She hated the stuff, but it was either this or she became the dragon lady who bit everyone's head off the moment they spoke to her. The gum calmed her nerves at least and allowed her to behave in a civil fashion.

Yawning, she pulled into her driveway and climbed out of the car, gathering her things from the other seat as she went. She turned around to see Hank coming out the door to meet her, the porch light glinting off his blond hair.

"The kids are asleep," he said hurrying to his truck.

"I hope so at this hour. What's your hurry? You got a hot date or something?" Maria watched him with curiosity as he rushed to leave. He usually found reasons to stick around a while.

Hank shrugged with a mischievous smile. "I guess we'll see."

Maria scowled at him. *What did that mean?* She wondered. At the same time, she felt a little stab of hurt at the idea that Hank might have a date. She shouldn't feel that way. He wasn't hers anymore—or at least, he wouldn't be much longer.

Hank was almost in the truck when he suddenly stopped, and, drumming his fingers on the roof of the car, he said, "Oh, I almost forgot, Lauren called a couple of hours ago. She wanted me to tell you that Avery and Clark Kent were getting along well." Raising one eyebrow Hank asked in a conspiratorial tone as if to safeguard a secret, "So, your sister is dating Superman now?"

Maria laughed at the question, remembering how much Mike resembled the everyday version of the superhero. "You might think so. He's the guy that helped you carry the mattress up the stairs when we moved Lauren."

Hank mulled that over for a few seconds. "Superman, huh? I don't see it."

"I guess it's something only us girls can see."

"Probably. Have a good night, Maria. The kids were great today."

"Thanks, Hank. You, too."

Hank drove off and Maria dragged herself up the front steps, and into the house. At this late hour, even Sadie didn't get up to greet her. Maria could hear the big dog snoring from where she was sleeping in the living room. She closed the door, locked it, and set her purse down on the foyer table. That was when she noticed the red rose sitting there with a note tucked under it. Curious, Maria picked up the rose and the small slip of paper that simply had her name on it. *Had Hank left it here? It couldn't have come from anyone else, could it?*

She tipped the rose toward her nose and breathed in its scent. Then she carried it into the kitchen to get a vase. When she got there, she saw a pink rose on the counter with another note. It read "you are." She frowned at it. Where was this going?

She opened a cupboard and retrieved a vase, then filled it with water, and dropped the two flowers in. Turning, she opened the refrigerator to look for something to eat. On the top shelf she found another red rose, and this time the note read "beautiful." Looking down at the next shelf of the fridge, she saw a box with her name on it. Inside she found a burger that Hank and the kids had saved for her to have when she got home. She was grateful to have something she could just heat up without thinking about it. She opened the microwave to put the burger in and found herself looking at another flower (pink again) and a note. "Oh, Hank, what are you up to?" she asked looking at the paper. She put the flower in the vase and the burger in the microwave, then went back to the fridge for something to drink.

She ate her burger hastily, without taking time to taste it much—she was too tired to care about taste. When she was done, she gathered the vase and the notes and headed into the bedroom. She stopped first at Jonathan's room to kiss him and found another rose and paper waiting for her there. Then when she went into Melanie's room, she found another set. She gathered them up without looking at the notes and went into her own room. At this point, Sadie bothered to get up and follow her into the bedroom, where she plopped back down on her big pillow in the corner.

Setting the vase, now with six roses in it, down on the dresser, Maria picked up the one he'd left for her there, and added it to the group. She looked at the bouquet—four red and three pink, then she lined up the slips of paper and read them.

Maria, you are beautiful. Will you go out with me, please?

She stared at the message. Was he really asking her out on a date? And what was she feeling? Fear? Yes, a little. Temptation? Definitely, though a voice inside told her she shouldn't. And what would she do about it?—that was the real question. But she couldn't think about that right now. It was late and she was exhausted, as well as grungy. She went into the bathroom and got in the shower, relishing the hot water that gushed over her, washing away the smell of disinfectant that always lingered on her skin after work. When she finished in the shower, she fell into bed and drifted blissfully to sleep. She would worry about Hank's question tomorrow.

"Mom! Are you up?" Jonathan called.

"Yeah, I'll be out in just a minute!" Maria hollered back from where she stood in front of her dresser looking at the lined up pieces of paper. She had slept well for a few hours during the night, but then the thought of these notes and the decision she'd have to make began to gnaw at her even in her sleep, waking her up.

She'd been standing there staring at the message for twenty minutes, her mind spinning in circles. It was like on TV when people had the angel on one shoulder talking to them and the devil on the other—only Maria couldn't define which voice was the angel and which was the devil. On the one hand, Hank seemed to once again be the man she'd fallen in love with all those years ago, and how could she not take the opportunity to make things work with him again? It was the one thing she wanted more than anything. Her heart swelled just thinking that it might be possible.

On the other hand, the thought of letting him back into the center of her life and her heart scared the hell out of her, and the voice on that side of things was screaming that she might have to go through all the pain again if she let him back into her life this way. He might start ignoring her—and the kids—again, he might even choose again to turn away from her and fall into the arms of another woman. It had happened before.

People change, trust what you see and feel. The thought ran through her head in a voice that sounded a lot like her father's. She considered the thought. Her relationship with her sisters was wonderful now, and she wouldn't have it if she hadn't been willing to open her heart and mind to the idea that they had both changed as people. Perhaps the same could be true for Hank. But, she thought, this was different, because she didn't think her heart could take it if she let him in only to lose him again.

She looked at the roses, touched one of them with the tip of a finger. She wanted it all to be real, she wanted to give him another chance. There was nothing she wanted more than that right now, except maybe to keep her heart in one piece.

You have to take chances to live, Maria! Again it sounded like her father's voice in her head, but she still wasn't sure she should listen, and now all the worrying about making this decision was causing her stomach to hurt.

"Mom! Are you coming?" Jonathan yelled again.

Maria pulled herself away from the roses and the notes and went out to the kitchen to help her kids get their breakfast. When she got there, she saw a box of chocolates on the table, and on top of it was an envelope with her name on it. "What's this?" she asked.

"It was on the front porch this morning," Melanie said absently, as she reached for a bowl in the cupboard.

"The front porch? Did you open the door for someone? You know you're not supposed to do that." Maria said with a sudden burst of panic.

"Relax, Mom," said Jonathan. "We didn't open the door for a stranger. The envelope was pushed under the front door. I picked it up and then looked out the window and saw the box of candy on the porch, so I brought it in. That's okay, isn't it?"

"I suppose," Maria said as she picked up the envelope. She gingerly opened the sealed top and pulled out a piece of paper, unfolded it, and read it.

Roses are red, violets are blue, Hank is a jerk, but he really loves you.

Please give me one more chance to show you how much I want you back in my life. I know you find it hard to believe me, and you have every reason to doubt, but I really have changed, and I want to be the husband you deserve. Will you please go out with me next weekend?

All my love,
Hank

Maria sighed, drawing the attention of both her children, who looked up from their cereal bowls to stare at her. "What is it, Mom?" Jonathan asked.

Maria looked up at her son. "Oh, nothing," she said. "Do you kids want some eggs to go with the cereal?"

They said, "Yes!" in unison, and Maria went to the stove and got out a pan. Today was her day with the kids. They were going to go to church with Lauren and Avery, and then spend a little time in a park near her sister's apartment. She would think about Hank's request tomorrow.

Chapter 61

Lauren

Lauren awoke Sunday morning at six o'clock, which seemed like sleeping in compared to her normal waking times. She sat at the kitchen table in her pajamas sipping her coffee and eating a bowl of oatmeal. She was looking forward to church with Maria and the kids, and she was pretty sure the night before had been a tremendous success for Avery and Mike. She had stayed in the kitchen for an hour before sneaking past them to go to her room. They were so deep in their conversation that they barely even looked up at her. It was a good bet that Avery told him about her past—the cause of her fear, or that she at least built a foundation that would soon lead to that discussion.

Another thing Lauren had to be happy about was the fact that her left hand was trembling only slightly, and her right hand was steady. Part of her wanted to hurry back to her room and paint while her body was functioning so well, but, no, she would not do that. Life was not just about her and her art anymore. She had her sisters, and her niece and nephew in her life now, and today was set aside for them, and for time with God. Sometimes, when she thought about her father planning to use his will to bring his three daughters back together, she had this image in her head of Arthur and God conspiring to make it all happen. She knew God was in it, and she needed to praise him for that because there was little else she'd ever felt more grateful for.

Lauren heard Avery humming before she walked into the kitchen. Looking up with a smile, she greeted her sister. "Good morning! You sound happy today."

Avery looked at her, trying to restrain the grin that was inching across her face. She was wearing pajama pants and a purple tank top, and her hair was pulled back in a ponytail. "It's a beautiful day."

"It sure is. ... Sooo, you talked to Mike last night?"

Avery went to the counter and poured herself a cup of coffee. "We talked."

"And?"

"And what?" Avery said with a dismissive shrug on her way to the pantry, where she picked out a box of cereal.

"You know what! Did you explain to him?"

"Explain my craziness, you mean? I didn't go into a lot of detail, but yes, I did."

Lauren turned as Avery sat down on the other side of her at the table, and began to eat her breakfast. "How did he react? Did he understand?"

Avery gave a small nod. "Yeah, I think he did. He said we could just be friends for a while, and get to know each other if that's easier for me, and I think it might be a good idea if we do that." She looked up at Lauren. "I know it isn't going to work if we move too fast. I told him that I don't know when I'll be ready to make him more than a friend, and I'd understand if he would rather find someone else."

"And what did he say?" Lauren blurted out the question when Avery paused for a few seconds.

"He said we'd just be friends, and we can both keep our options open for now, but he also said that he hasn't had eyes for anyone else but me since we first met, and he doesn't think that will change."

Lauren let out a squeal in reaction. "That is the sweetest thing. You are one lucky girl, Ave."

Avery's cheeks turned pink. "He is pretty amazing, isn't he? He's probably better than I deserve."

Lauren shook her head. "No, you deserve it. You deserve the best."

"You know what really surprised me?" Lauren shrugged, and Avery continued. "He didn't ask me if I pressed charges. He didn't ever make it about what I did afterward. Come to think about it, you and Maria didn't either."

Lauren furrowed her brow and glanced down at the table. "I did wonder about that. So, don't give me too much credit. I wanted to ask."

Avery got up from the table and took her bowl to the sink. As she rinsed it out, she said, "I know I should have gone straight to the hospital, and reported it." She shut off the water and turned to face Lauren. "It's easy to know the right thing to do before something like that happens, and after, but at the moment that it did happen the last thing I wanted was for anyone to know—for anyone to see me. I didn't want to tell them how stupid I was. I was so ashamed—of the idiotic choices I made, and of what happened as a result. I just wanted to clean every speck of those men off me, and forget it ever happened. I just didn't realize it would be so hard to forget."

"It wasn't your fault, you know. You may have made some bad choices, but that doesn't mean you deserved what those bastards did to you."

Avery sobbed. "I didn't even know the name of the man I went home with, or how to get back to his place. He dumped me off close to the bar where I met him when he and his friends were done with me."

Lauren jumped up and wrapped her arms around her sister, tears running down her own cheeks. "Oh, Avery, I'm so sorry. You don't have to explain anymore."

Lauren held Avery until her tears were gone and then, when Avery was ready, they got dressed for church.

Chapter 62

Avery

After church, Avery and her sisters went to a nearby sub shop to pick up lunch, then they took the food to the park for a picnic. When they were done eating, Jonathan and Melanie ran to the playground that was in sight of their picnic table, and joined a couple of other kids, leaving Avery and her sisters alone.

Avery's mind was not with the moment. The words she'd heard in the church service were bouncing around in her head, making her see things in a new way. As her mind drifted, everything around her seemed to make her senses explode—the sun on her cheeks, the warm breeze blowing against her skin, the sound of the leaves rustling up above her. Sitting there, for the first time in a long time, she didn't feel frightened or on alert, she was relaxed and able to take in all the beauty around her.

"I heard you had a good time with Mike," Maria said to Avery, jerking her mind back into focus.

"Huh?" Avery responded.

"Your date," Maria said, "I heard it went well."

Avery felt her mouth turn up at the thought of Mike. "Yeah, it did. He's a good guy."

"He certainly is," Lauren agreed. "But what's with you? You've been in your own world since we got here. Is it all this open space? Are you feeling scared?"

Avery met Lauren's concerned eyes and shook her head. "It's not that. In fact, I'm feeling really good out here. I was actually thinking about what the pastor was talking about today."

Lauren furrowed her brow. "About not judging people? Is there someone you've been judging?"

"No, I mean the story he read—about the woman who was about to get stoned for committing adultery. It's got me thinking about some things."

When Maria and Lauren both stared at her and waited for an explanation, Avery continued. "The part that struck me was when Jesus saved her, then he told her to go and sin no more." Maria and Lauren both nodded. "He didn't punish her or berate her. He didn't ask her to hold onto the guilt. He only asked her to change her ways, and choose a better path."

Avery looked at both her sisters, expecting a response at this point, but they both just nodded again. "Well, I've done that. Don't you see? I changed my ways. I don't go out and get drunk, and go home with strangers anymore. But I still continue to see myself as the same stupid, reckless person. I'm still judging *myself*, and that isn't what God wants from me. He wants me to forgive myself." She looked at her sisters meaningfully. "I think I can do that now."

"That's good, Avery. I think Dad would be thrilled that, not only are all three of us attending church again—*together* but that you were able to gain something really meaningful today."

Lauren agreed, and Maria spoke again. "So, tell me more about your date."

Heat rose to Avery's cheeks. "I don't think we should call it a date since Mike and I have agreed to take it slow and just be friends for now. But it was a nice evening. He wants Lauren and me to come for dinner at his place next week."

Maria didn't have to ask about Lauren's attendance at the planned dinner. She understood that Avery would need support for a while.

"That's great!" Maria said. "I had an interesting evening myself."

Lauren raised her eyebrows. "Really? At the hospital you mean?"

"No, when I got home."

Maria stopped for a moment, looking a little uncertain about continuing. "Go on," Lauren urged.

"When I got home—very late—Hank practically ran out the door to leave before I could even get in. He was acting really strange. I thought he was in a hurry to see someone—a replacement to Carina maybe, but when I got inside, I found roses and little slips of paper left all over the house for me."

"What did the notes say?" Lauren asked leaning in as if a big secret were about to be revealed.

"When I put them all together, they said, 'Maria, you are beautiful. Will you go out with me, please?'"

Avery sucked in a breath. "Whoa, that's big!"

"Yeah, and there's more. This morning he left a box of candy on the front porch with another note."

"What did that one say?" Lauren asked.

"There was a corny little poem where he admitted to being a jerk, then it said he had changed and really wanted to be the husband I deserve. That was followed by another request for a date."

"Are you going to do it?" Lauren blurted out.

Maria shrugged. "I don't know. Part of me wants nothing more than to say yes, but there's this other part that keeps warning me that he might not be sincere, that he might just hurt me again—and even worse, hurt the kids again. I don't know what to do."

Lauren reached out and touched Maria's arm. "You still love him, don't you?"

Maria nodded, a tear escaping one eye to roll down her cheek. "Yes, I don't think that will ever change."

Lauren looked at Avery, then back at Maria, and said, "I think you should do it. Go out with him. Give it a chance."

"You really think so?" Maria asked with her brow furrowed, glancing at Avery to see if she agreed.

Avery nodded. "Yes, you need to give it another chance. If you don't, you may always regret it."

"But what if—what if he changes again? I don't know if I could take that."

"How about if we help you think this through?" Avery asked putting on her best *I'm the logical one*, face. She knew logic would appeal to Maria right now because it was obvious that she was trying to make this decision entirely with her head while keeping her heart as far away from it as possible.

Maria nodded, and Avery continued, "You're having trouble trusting what he's telling you, but it seems to me he's done all the right things to make his case."

Maria's forehead wrinkled. "What do you mean?"

"When you got home from the lake, he admitted to all the things he did wrong—willingly, and he told you to leave him."

Maria still looked confused. "Yeah ..."

"That was the right thing to do because, for one thing, he deserved it, and it seems like he knew that. For another, it allowed him the opportunity to, not just tell you he'd changed, but to show you." Avery shrugged. "Hasn't he done that?"

Lauren chimed in saying, "I think Avery's got a point. Look at how he's acted since you two have been living apart."

"But it's only been two months," Maria argued.

"We were only at the lake for two weeks, but you trust that Lauren and I have really changed—and haven't you?" Avery said.

"Yeah, but this is different."

"It is, but then again it isn't really," Lauren said. "Any time you let someone into your life in a meaningful way, you have to take a risk. Let me ask you this, how long was Hank a good husband before he changed initially?"

Maria sighed. "Nine years."

"So then, how long would he need to be a good guy this time in order for you to believe he might continue to be that way?"

"I guess I don't really know."

"That's the point. You can't ever be sure that someone you let into your life and into your heart isn't ever going to change and hurt you. You have to take a leap and trust them—or not. The choice is yours, but I don't think it's really about more time."

"I agree with Lauren," Avery said. "I think you should ask yourself if you can really pass this chance up. You still love him, and it seems like he still loves you. Could you live with it if you didn't give it a chance, always wondering if it could have worked?"

Maria bit her lower lip and shook her head.

Avery and Lauren both reached out and took one of her hands. "Whatever happens, we'll be here for you," Lauren said. "Take the leap, and do what your heart tells you. People can change. We certainly know that now."

Maria looked at them with tears in her eyes and nodded. "Yeah, people can change, and I hope Hank really did. But I think I'll take a little advice from you and Mike, and take these next steps very slowly."

Chapter 63

Maria

Maria was half expecting another overture from Hank to be waiting for her when she got home, but there were no more notes, candy, or flowers. Sadie was turning circles by the back door, so Maria let her out in the yard before ordering a pizza. Once the dog was back in, and the pizza had arrived, she and the kids, exhausted from their day at the park, settled down in the living room to watch a movie. The kids picked out *Cheaper by the Dozen*, and Maria popped it into the DVD player before curling up on the sofa with Melanie leaning against her chest.

As the kids watched the movie and laughed, Maria found her mind wandering to other things. She couldn't help but think about how good the moment felt. With Hank spending more time with the kids and helping Jonathan with his school work, her load felt so much lighter. Jon was doing better with his math and reading, and even though school had only just begun for the year, Maria could already tell that she wasn't going to have to worry so much about his success. She also wasn't so worried about Melanie getting the time and attention that she deserved. Hank was having tea parties with her, planting flowers with her, and on some days, taking her to her dance lessons. And with Jonathan doing better in school, and getting more help from his father, Maria was able to pay Melanie more attention as well.

She let out a sigh, as she realized how nice it felt to have some of the weight off her shoulders. She wondered what would change if she started seeing Hank again. At least at first, she imagined it would mean he'd spend even more time around the house. But she wondered if that would last. Would he get comfortable with them being a couple again and then start going back to his old ways? She wanted to believe him when he said he had really changed. She wanted to believe that he had found something great in the company of his children and that he wouldn't give that up—but was it true?

Maria felt her heart racing at the decision she had to make, with all the uncertainties. She remembered her sisters' advice to follow her heart and realized she was letting her head do all the work, and her heart was on a roller coaster ride trying to keep up. Of course, using her head was important, but the answers to her questions could only be found by taking the chance. Spending a lot of time fretting over it would only make her head hurt.

When Maria was little, and she had a problem that was upsetting her, her father had always told her to give it to God. She realized now that in the years of her youth, she had gotten a lot of relief from following that advice, but it had been a long time since she'd tried it. Maria closed her eyes and decided to do something she hadn't done in a long while. As her kids watched the movie on the TV screen, oblivious to what was going on inside her mind, she said a short prayer, and asked God to take away this burden, and help her come to the right decision about Hank.

When she opened her eyes again, Maria felt the worry drain out of her. She looked at her children, their smiles bright, and silently thanked her father for his good advice.

A few days went by uneventfully, and it seemed to Maria that Hank might have forgotten about his request for a date. For three days, she worked her shift and came home to find Hank getting the kids ready for bed. He didn't say one word about the notes he'd left. Then, on Thursday, when Maria had a day off, her phone rang just after she got home from dropping the kids off at school. Hank's chipper voice greeted her when she answered. He made small talk for a few minutes, asking about Jon's next baseball game, and discussing the costume that had been chosen for Melanie's dance recital. Then, he moved on from the small talk saying, "Maria, I wanted to give you a few days to think before I brought this up, but, what do you say? Will you go out with me?"

The question flowed straight to Maria's heart, and without even thinking about it for a second, she found herself saying yes. She didn't feel any trepidation with the answer she gave, or worry about whether or not it was the right choice. Instead, she felt completely at ease, and she knew her prayer had been answered.

She talked to Hank for a few more minutes and agreed to a date the following night since it was another one of her days off. Then, she called Avery to see if she and Lauren would be able to come over and watch the kids. As she talked to her sister, she felt her heart warming to the idea of giving Hank this second chance, and she realized that, not only was she not worried, she was beginning to get excited.

Chapter 64

Lauren

Lauren stood at her easel and tilted her head as she considered the work she had done on the canvas in front of her. She smiled at the splashes of yellow interspersed with swirls of blue and purple, hoping the proper emotion was being expressed. She'd had a dream the night before about her mother. In it, she was a child again, but only in form; her mind was that of her adult self. Her mother didn't speak to her, but words seemed unnecessary. Everything was conveyed through her mother's touch as they held hands. Eve missed all her girls deeply, but she was happy. She was with Lauren's father, and she was with God.

Eve squeezed Lauren's hand, and the words, "We'll be together again one day," flowed into her mind. Then, Eve kissed Lauren, turned into pure light, and faded away.

Lauren woke up with a mix of emotions—joy, sadness, and so many others seemed wrapped up together, and that was what her current painting was meant to express.

She picked up her brush again, and studied the pallet of colors in front of her, looking for the right one to add. When Avery's phone began to chime in the next room, Lauren waited until the sound stopped before continuing her search for the appropriate color. She was poised with her brush about to dip into a darker shade of yellow when a knock came on her door.

Sighing, she called, "Come on in, Avery."

Avery stepped into the room. "Mike's on the phone."

"Okay?" Lauren said with a hint of aggravation. *Was it necessary to come and announce her personal calls?*

"He wants to talk to you," Avery matched her tone and held her phone out toward Lauren. "But he didn't have your number."

"Oh." Lauren put her brush down and took the phone from her sister. "Hello?"

Rolling her eyes, Avery left the room.

"Hey, Lauren. I hope I'm not calling at a bad time," Mike said.

"Oh, it's fine. I was just working on a new painting, but I can take a break. What's up?"

"I'm glad you're working on a new painting. I think you might need it soon."

Lauren furrowed her brow. What an odd thing to say. She didn't respond but waited for him to speak again.

"Remember my friend's cousin—the one who owns a gallery?"

"Yeah."

"I got a call from her yesterday, and she wants to meet you and see some of your work in person. She really liked the pictures, and she said that if she likes them as well in person—and I'm sure she will—then she wants to include some of your work next month when she does an event featuring new, local talent."

Lauren stood there speechless. *Was this really happening? Her work could be on display at a gallery?* She had hoped for this, but somehow never really thought it could happen.

"Lauren? Are you still there?"

"Uh, yes, I'm here, Mike. I'm just shocked, that's all."

"In a good way, I hope."

She could hear the smile in Mike's voice, and it made her smile too. "Yes, in a good way. I just can't believe it. I guess I never really thought it would happen."

"I'm not surprised. Your work is amazing. You deserve this, Lauren."

"Well, I'm not there yet. I have to impress her in person now."

"Which I have no doubt you will."

Her cheeks grew hot at the compliment. “Thanks, Mike. You are a great guy! If Avery doesn’t end up marrying you, then she’s crazy.”

Mike cleared his throat, and when he spoke again, Lauren thought it sounded like he was blushing a little himself. “Slow down. We’re not even officially dating yet, remember?”

“I remember.” Lauren smiled, marveling at Mike’s patience. “So, when and where do I meet your cousin’s friend?”

“My friend’s cousin,” Mike corrected. “Her name is Gloria Birch, and she said you should come to the gallery—with a few of your paintings—sometime this week after six in the evening. I’ll text you the address if you give me your number.”

Lauren rattled off her number, thanked Mike again for all he had done, then said goodbye to him.

Lauren knocked on Avery’s bedroom door and waited a beat. When the door opened, Avery met her with an annoyed expression. “Can I help you?”

Lauren shook her head, trying to hide her excitement, and held the phone out like a peace offering. “I’m sorry I was short with you. Forgive me?”

Avery gave her a “what’s in it for me” look, and snatched the phone from her hand. “Only if you tell me what that was all about. Why did he want to talk to you?”

Lauren tried to hold in her emotions, but a smile was breaking through at the corners of her mouth. “He just wanted to tell me that the gallery owner he sort of knows wants to meet me, and see some of my work in person.”

Avery’s eyes grew big a split second before she threw her arms around Lauren. A high pitched squeal rang out, and then she said, “Oh, wow! That’s amazing, sis!”

Avery let her go and grinned. “All is forgiven. Now we need to call Maria and arrange a celebration.”

“Whoa, easy there, Ave. I still have to impress this lady in person.”

"If she liked the pictures, then she'll love your work in person. You got this, Lauren."

Lauren smiled. "Thank you, Avery. We can call Maria, but no celebrating until it's for sure."

With Avery looking over her shoulder, Lauren dialed Maria's number.

"Oh, Lauren, thank God! I'm freaking out here. That's crazy, isn't it?"

"Um, I don't know," Lauren said, surprised by how this phone call was starting. "What are you freaking out about?"

"Hank and this date. ... That's crazy, isn't it?"

"Well ..."

"I mean I've tried on six different outfits—like a teenager would do."

Lauren was about to speak, but Maria started up again before she could get the first word out. "It's not like I own a single thing that he hasn't seen me in already. What is wrong with me? Why am I so worried about a date with my husband?"

"Well, he is your husband, but you have been separated for a while now, and I suppose you're freaking out because you want so badly for it to work out."

"Yeah, I guess you're right. What do I do about it?"

Lauren thought about that. "Pick an outfit that you are comfortable in. Don't worry so much about what he will like. Pick something that you like. If you're more comfortable, it might be easier to relax."

"Okay. I'll keep that in mind."

"You sound a little calmer already."

"Yeah," Maria said, sounding a little surprised by the truth of it. "I guess talking to you is helping."

"Would you like Avery and me to come over early?" Lauren offered, glancing at Avery, who was looking at her curiously.

"Oh, Lauren, that would be wonderful! Thank you!"

"No problem. We'll be there in twenty minutes."

"Great!—Oh, Lauren, what did you want to tell me?"

"Oh, well, I have some good news. You remember that gallery owner that Mike knows?"

"Yes."

"Well, Mike called, and the lady wants to see some of my work in person. If she likes it, then she'll feature some of my paintings at an event for new, local talent."

"Oh, Lauren, I knew you'd make it!" Lauren beamed. Maria didn't squeal as Avery had, yet somehow her unfailing confidence was even more satisfying.

Chapter 65

Maria

By the time Lauren and Avery showed up, Maria had stopped trying to pick an outfit. She answered the door in her bathrobe and ushered her sisters inside.

"Maybe I shouldn't do this." The words tumbled out of her mouth as soon as the other two women walked through the door. "If it was right, I wouldn't be this nervous, would I?"

She waited a beat and then continued. "I should just call Hank and tell him it's off. We could have a girl's night—after the kids go to bed."

"Where are the kids?" Avery asked.

"They're playing a video game in Jon's room."

"Alright, that's good. Now, calm down," Avery said, as she and Lauren each took one of Maria's arms. They led her into her bedroom, where a chaotic array of clothing was scattered over the bed. "You're not going to do any such thing. This is just a case of the nerves, and you know it."

"That's right," Lauren chimed in. "You are not going to throw this chance away because you're nervous."

"We all know you still love Hank, and you want this chance," Avery said. "You didn't let me lose my chance with Mike because I was too afraid to try. You and Lauren pushed me right on through that—well, mostly—and now Lauren and I are going to give you the push you need."

"Absolutely," Lauren agreed.

Maria stood staring at them. She didn't know how to fight their combined force, and she was also oddly proud of how they were working so well together, even if it was in an effort to push her around. Besides, they were right. She did still love Hank, and she did want this chance to make their marriage work again.

Sighing, she pointed to the mess on her bed. “Then help me.”

Lauren and Avery began to examine the clothing lying about. “This one is nice,” Lauren said, holding up a blue dress.

Avery shook her head. “She’s too nervous for heals tonight. We want her comfortable while still looking hot, remember? Besides, blue is your color, not so much hers. We want to bring out her eyes.”

Lauren nodded and went back to the choices. “Maybe you should handle this, Ave. I don’t think I’m too great with fashion.”

“You’re an artist. This shouldn’t be so hard for you,” Avery said.

“You wouldn’t think so, but I’ve never really been good with clothes and make-up. It’s a different kind of art. Remember what Mike said—you’re a kind of artist yourself, and I think this is more up your artistic alley.”

Avery shrugged, and a few minutes later, she held up a beige, short-sleeved sweater. She walked over to Maria and held it up in front of her body. “This might work with a pair of black pants. You could wear flats and stay comfortable, and the beige will go nicely with your eyes, hair, and skin tone.”

“I don’t know, Ave, I’ve put on a little weight since I quit smoking. That top might be a little tight.”

“Perfect!”

“Avery!”

“What? You don’t think Hank will like it?”

“I’m sure he’ll probably like it, but ...”

“But what? Try it on.” Avery shoved the top into Maria’s hands.

Maria looked at Lauren for support, but it was clear that she was on Avery’s side. Maria huffed out a breath. “Fine. I’ll try it on.”

“You wanted our help, remember?” Avery called behind her as she went into the bathroom.

She pulled the top on and looked in the mirror. It was snug, but not as tight as she had thought it would be. She turned a couple of times, looking at it from all angles before showing it to her sisters.

When she walked back out of the bathroom, Lauren was the first to speak. "Avery was right. That top looks great on you! That's the one."

Avery agreed with a nod. "Now we need some black pants to go with it."

Thirty minutes later, Maria was dressed, had her make-up done, and was ready to go. Jonathan and Melanie had come out of Jon's room and were in the living room when Maria and her sisters came out.

"You look great, Mom!" Jonathan said. "Dad will think so too."

"Why can't we go?" Melanie whined.

"It's a date, Mel. You don't take other people with you on a date. Not even your kids."

Melanie glared at her brother. "But it's just Daddy, and he likes us too."

"Of course he does," Maria assured her. "He's going to spend time with just you and Jon tomorrow afternoon, but tonight it's just the two of us. We need a little time together. And you guys will have a fun night with your aunts."

Melanie poked her lower lip out in a pouty expression but didn't continue the complaints.

Maria went to the mirror that hung in the foyer over a small table and checked her hair and make-up one more time. When the doorbell rang, she jumped at the sound. Lauren came up behind her. "Breathe. You look fantastic. He'd be a fool not to think so."

When Maria nodded tentatively, Lauren turned and opened the door. "Hi, Hank." As she moved aside and allowed him to enter the house, he looked at Maria and whistled.

Maria smiled as her cheeks turned pink.

"Well, you two have fun tonight," Lauren said, walking back into the living room, and leaving Maria and Hank alone.

Maria gathered her purse, kissed the kids who had come into the foyer, and headed out the door with her husband.

Maria was expecting Hank to take her to the steakhouse that had always been their favorite, but instead, he drove her downtown to a restaurant that seemed too fancy for his budget. She glanced at him as they parked. "This is where we're eating?"

He nodded and looked at his watch. "I have reservations for seven 'o clock." He looked back at her perplexed face, then said, "This is a very special occasion, and it deserves better than the usual."

"Special occasion?"

He nodded. "It isn't every day that a man is given a second chance with his wife after he has made catastrophic mistakes."

Maria felt her throat constrict, and she wondered what Hank's expectations were exactly. "Hank . . . I don't know that this will lead to putting our marriage back together."

He patted her arm. "I know. That's why I called it a chance. I know how much I've done wrong. I don't even deserve a chance at all." He paused, then looked her in the eye and said, "Regardless of what happens down the road, I want you to know how grateful I am to be given this chance.

It means more to me than you know. I screwed up—and I know that word doesn't even do justice to my behavior—but I still love you. I realized that when you were gone. It didn't take long to see how stupid I'd been. I took everything good I had in this world for granted, but I don't intend to let that happen again."

Sucking in a breath, Maria nodded. This was the Hank she'd fallen in love with so many years ago. More and more, she believed that he really had become his old self again—the loving Hank she used to know.

Chapter 66

Lauren

Lauren's hands shook badly as she fumbled with her canvases, trying to pick out the best ones to show Gloria Birch at the gallery. She knew it wasn't just her Parkinson's that was causing the dramatic trembling. She was nervous. This was, after all, a chance that she didn't think she'd ever get. She had always known she was a good artist, but she hadn't ever believed she was good enough to make it as an artist. Or maybe she just hadn't let herself believe that. *Get a hold of yourself, Lauren! You haven't made it yet, and even getting into this showing doesn't guarantee that anyone will want to buy your work.*

She stopped, took a breath, and stared again at her hands. What about her Parkinson's? Would her condition matter to Gloria Birch? After all, there was no telling how much longer she would even be able to paint. *Should I tell her?* Lauren wondered. She thought about that and decided it would be best to be forthright about it. It was getting hard to hide, especially when she was nervous. She would tell Ms. Birch and let the chips fall where they may. But maybe she could get a little help.

Lauren looked up, visualizing past the popcorn ceiling. "Lord, I thought my time as an artist was over when I was diagnosed, but you showed me it didn't have to be. You, along with—maybe through—my sisters, showed me there was another way that I could still use my talent. If it is your will, Lord, help me today with this opportunity that has been laid before me. Amen."

Lauren wasn't well practiced when it came to praying. She had only started to since her time at the lake, but as soon as she finished the prayer she felt more relaxed, and her hands were a little better. She looked at the canvases again, carefully considered them, and chose four that showed as vast an array of emotions as four paintings could. She packed them up in a large carrying case that would protect them from damage and headed out.

Lauren was not familiar with downtown—at least not familiar enough that she wanted to drive herself there on a day when she was already nervous, so she'd called a cab. The driver had arrived at her building promptly and had expertly driven her to the address. She wasn't sure how long she would be inside, so she paid the cabbie, and told her that she would call another one when she was ready to leave.

When she was out of the cab with her case of paintings, she looked up at the gallery in awe. Could her work really hang here—be sold here? She looked up past the building to the blue sky above, and prayed silently, "Be with me, Lord."

Sucking in a deep, steadying breath, she pushed open the door and walked inside. Her heart was banging a drumbeat against her chest, making her feel a little lightheaded, and even more off balance than usual. She stumbled, almost falling into a statue. Catching herself, she stopped, took a couple more long breaths, and willed herself to take careful, deliberate steps. She planned to tell Ms. Birch about her condition, but she certainly didn't want to give her a demonstration.

She found an employee of the gallery and told him that she was there by invitation to see Gloria Birch, and the young man led her to an office where Ms. Birch was working at the desk. The woman looked up, and she appeared to Lauren like a librarian—the type men hoped to meet—sexy meets studious. She was probably in her mid-forties but wore it very well. She had dark hair arranged in a loosely held bun, with some strands falling free in the front, green eyes under long lashes, and a slender, delicate face with black-rimmed glasses that fell to the tip of her nose when she glanced up.

"Ms. Birch, I'm Lauren Anderson. I was told that you'd like to see some of my paintings in person."

"Yes, the friend of my cousin's friend. The pictures of your work looked promising, but I don't make any decisions without seeing the work in person first."

"I can certainly understand that. I brought some samples of my work." Lauren lifted the case slightly.

Gloria waved her into the office. "Come in and let's see ... oh, and call me Gloria."

She got right to the business at hand, Lauren thought, as she walked in and set her case down on a chair. She opened it and took out the first painting. Gloria pointed to an easel to Lauren's right, and she set the canvas on it.

Standing up from her desk chair, Gloria walked to the painting and examined it closely. "This is beautiful. I can't help but feel a sense of joy when I look at it."

Lauren smiled. "Turn it over," she said.

Gloria gave her a perplexed look but complied. "Joy," she said, reading the title of the painting from the back. She turned her eyes on Lauren and smiled.

Lauren pulled the next painting from her case and put it on the easel in place of the first. Gloria looked it over. "This time I feel like I'm looking at a representation of how I felt when my first boyfriend dumped me."

Eyeing Lauren, Gloria reached for the canvas and turned it over. "Heartbreak," she read.

Excitement rose inside Lauren as she removed that canvas and replaced it with another. "This one is dramatic in a way the others weren't," Gloria said. "I felt this way when I saw the Grand Canyon." She flipped the canvas, and read the single word title, "Awe." She beamed at Lauren as the last painting was placed on the easel.

Gloria looked at the dark, ominous colors on the canvas before her. "I feel a deep sense of hurt." She looked at Lauren again earnestly. "This is the way I felt last month when my beloved dog, Oscar died."

"Turn it," Lauren said.

Gloria did, and read the word, "Loss." She shook her head. "This is amazing. You have a real gift for putting feelings into a visual form."

"It's a gift I only recently discovered. I used to paint landscapes."

"Yes, my cousin showed me a few of those in the pictures. They were good, but not like these. These stand out. I'm glad you discovered that gift. I definitely want to put some of your work into my show."

Lauren couldn't hold back the grin that spread across her face. "Thank you, Ms. Birch. I really appreciate the opportunity."

"Gloria, please," she said. "So, tell me, what made you start painting this way after doing landscapes?"

"I'm glad you asked. It's something I wanted to talk to you about anyway." That perked up Gloria's attention, and she kept her gaze on Lauren, waiting for the story.

Lauren took a deep breath and continued. "About two years ago I was diagnosed with Parkinson's disease. One of the main symptoms I had was trembling in my left hand—I'm left-handed—and as time went on after my diagnosis, It became harder and harder to paint. I simply couldn't achieve the detail that was required for painting landscapes. I had never painted anything else, so I thought my painting career was over. I stopped for a while, but recently my sisters—along with one other person—convinced me to try painting another way." She gestured to the canvas that was still on the easel. "This is the result of that."

Gloria looked at her for a long moment, as if taking an appraisal. "Your work surprised me even after I'd seen pictures of it, and now I'm surprised again."

Lauren nodded. "Because I could have easily given some other reason for the change in my work, and not told you about a condition that will eventually make it impossible for me to continue painting."

"Yes ... most people, when given an opportunity such as this, are afraid to say anything that might hurt their chance."

Lauren shrugged. "You would have found out eventually."

"Well, maybe ... maybe not. I'm offering you a chance to show your work here. If it does well, then I'll likely make arrangements to continue showing it. You could have easily waited to tell me this *if* the arrangement works out."

Suddenly Lauren felt a burst of confidence that was unlike anything she'd ever experienced before. She didn't know where it was coming from. Maybe God was answering her prayer. "*When* it works out," she said, lifting her chin.

Gloria smiled wryly. "So you may as well just tell me now?" Lauren nodded, and Gloria spoke again, "I like your confidence." She glanced at the easel again. "I share it."

"Then my condition won't change your mind?"

"Why should it? Anything can happen to anyone at any time. No artist can ever promise to keep supplying me with their work for any particular amount of time. They may think they can, but tomorrow something unexpected may happen." She looked Lauren in the eye. "Today you can paint—boy can you paint—but no one knows what tomorrow will hold. I'm only worried about what you can do today ... And the day of the show, of course."

Lauren grinned and reached out to shake hands on the arrangement. "Thank you, Ms.—Gloria."

Gloria shook her hand. "Keep painting, Lauren, for as long as you possibly can."

Chapter 67

Late September

Maria

Maria hopped down from the passenger seat of Hank's truck. Hank and the kids, along with Sadie, followed. "So this is it," Hank said.

Maria nodded, looking at the front of the small house where everything had changed. "This is it." She glanced at Blake's house next door, wondering if he was there. Before this day was over, she had one important task to complete, but he didn't need to be home for that. She didn't really want to have a face to face with him anyway.

"Mom, can we take Sadie down to the lake?" Jonathan asked.

"Sure, but keep her on the leash. There's no fence here."

"We will. Come on, Mel!"

The kids and dog ran around the house toward the lake beyond, laughing all the way. It was a beautiful Saturday, nothing but blue sky, and they were going to spend the day here. They wouldn't be spending the night. She and Hank were still "dating," but hadn't moved beyond that yet. He still went to his apartment every night. They were both determined to take this slow. It meant far too much to both of them to rush it.

"Are we going inside?" Hank asked.

Maria shook her head. "Let's go down to the lake first. The kids are having fun. We should go enjoy that first."

"Sounds good to me."

They walked down to the lake and joined the kids. They took off their shoes and waded in the water. It was a little chilly for swimming, but that didn't stop Sadie. She went as far as her eight-foot leash would allow and loved every second. Maria smiled at her family having fun here together feeling glad this place could still be a part of their lives.

"Hank, why don't you go get the kid's bikes from the truck. We can put Sadie in the house and take a ride before lunch."

"Mind if we take a look in the house before we go?"

"We can do that. But let's get the bikes down and ready first. I'll go to the shed and get two for us."

He nodded and hurried off toward the car.

Maria put her shoes back on and went to the shed to pull out two of the adult bikes. By the time she came out, Hank was finishing up with the kid's bikes. Maria called the kids and headed for the back door with her key in hand.

They went inside the house and Hank and the kids looked around. "It's not a bad little house," Hank said. "Hard to believe your dad had this place and all that money and no one knew."

"I know. He sure threw us all a curve ball," Maria said thinking of the surprise she'd felt when she found out about her father's estate. She used her share of the money to set up a savings account for the kids.

"Yeah, the best curveball ever." Hank smiled. "Changed everything."

Maria smiled as Jonathan came running into the kitchen where she and Hank were talking. "Sadie's ready to take a nap. Let's go on the bikes now!"

"Sure, buddy," Hank said. "Tell your sister."

They strolled out the door and walked the bikes up to the road. Maria turned to Hank and asked, "Could you go ahead with the kids? I'll catch up. There's just one thing I need to do first."

"No problem. Come on guys," Hank said, leading the kids down the road.

Maria walked her bike a few steps until she was standing in front of Blake's house. She hadn't seen him and suspected he wasn't at the lake this weekend. She went to his mailbox, opened it, and laid a small piece of paper inside. She didn't know if he would get it, or if it would be in time if he did, but she felt the need to make this small effort all the same. The rest was out of her hands.

She took one last look at the house, and then set off on her bike to catch up with her family.

Chapter 68

Lauren

Lauren wanted to pace, but she knew that wouldn't be a good idea. Not only would it look unprofessional, but it would likely lead to an embarrassing fall, potentially with injuries. She wrung her hands instead, which helped alleviate some of her nervousness, and also made it harder for people to see the trembling in her left hand. After all, she couldn't hold them behind her back for the entire night.

She looked around at the other artists getting ready for the gallery to open for their special showing. Some of them were still arranging their work. Others were walking around greeting each other. Lauren wondered if they were as nervous as she was. They didn't really look it—except for one very young man who had produced some rather interesting sculptures. He was fiddling with a piece of paper, and his eyes were darting around as if he were searching for an escape route. She could understand how he felt. Though she'd been hoping for this chance for most of her life, it was scary and overwhelming now that the day had come. She wondered what people would think of her work, and what kind of criticism she might get. She also worried that people might notice her Parkinson's, and she wanted this night to be about her art alone. She didn't want anyone to pity her, or think she had been given this chance for any reason other than her artistic ability.

One of the other artists, a man that was just a little older than Lauren, wandered over and inspected her work. He was short for a man and had thinning brown hair and glasses. He pointed to one of Lauren's paintings. "These are interesting abstracts—very emotional." He looked Lauren in the eyes. "I bet you'll get a lot of attention tonight."

Lauren shrugged. "I guess we'll see. Where are you set up?"

He pointed to the left corner of the room where some lovely photographic portraits were set up. "That's my work over there. I use a camera rather than a brush."

Lauren looked from one of his pictures to another. "They're very good. You really capture the feelings of your subjects."

He smiled. "Thanks! I've been looking around this room at all the wonderful paintings and sculptures, and I'm not so sure I measure up as an artist. The camera does most of the work."

"That's not true," Lauren argued. "Sure, anyone can snap a picture, but it takes a real artist to capture a moment with so much depth. Not to mention knowing how to get the right lighting."

He nodded. "I guess you're right. Thanks for the boost."

"You're welcome—and same to you."

Her friendly visitor left and she realized she was feeling a little less nervous. She glanced at the glass door and saw that a line of people was waiting to get in.

Just then Gloria walked out of her office. "It's time to open the door! Is everyone ready?" All of the artists answered yes, and Gloria walked to the door and unlocked it. She pushed the door open and greeted all of the people as they began to stream in.

Lauren stood beside her paintings. Two of them were on the wall, and the other two were set up on easels. She also had a few more in a case. If anyone showed interest in purchasing some of her work and wanted to see more, they would be available.

A few browsers came by, glancing at each piece, and talking amongst themselves, but showing no more interest in her work than anyone else's.

“Lauren, this is amazing!” Avery said as she walked up with Mike at her side. Hank and Maria were just behind them.

“Thanks! I’m glad you guys are here. I’m so nervous.”

“Don’t worry. You’ll do fine. You made it this far,” Maria said. Something about her tone was reassuring and gave Lauren a sense of peace.

She nodded and told them to go and look around at all the other artwork on display.

An hour later, Lauren was beginning to feel her feet protesting about standing in one place for so long, but she was still afraid to move around. The last thing she wanted was to fall in front of this crowd. She endured the pain, trying to smile and not grimace. Several people had shown interest in her work, and she’d had mostly good comments, but so far no one was buying. That wasn’t the end of the world. As long as her work was attracting a reasonable amount of interest, Gloria would keep at least one or two of her paintings on display at the gallery after this showing. If she could sell some of them, then Gloria would probably give her a larger display going forward.

As Lauren carefully took a couple of steps, trying to ease the pain in her feet, she noticed a man walk up to her display. She couldn’t see his face right away, but he caught her attention. There was something familiar about him and the way he carried himself. When he turned toward her, she caught her breath. It was Blake!

Lauren’s eyes widened. *Blake was here? How had he known about this?* There had been an announcement in the local paper, but unless you were looking for events in the arts section, it was easy to miss. *Had he been looking?*

Lauren tried to smile and not look shocked, but her heart was racing and her knees felt a little weak. *Did he really have this much power over her?*

“Hey, Lauren,” Blake said.

Lauren squeaked out a, "Hi," but seemed unable to find any other words.

"I got the notice you left in my mailbox."

She squinted at him. "Notice? What notice? I didn't put anything in your mailbox. I haven't even been back to the lake." That was when it dawned on her that Maria had been to the lake the previous weekend.

"Well, someone left it in there."

"Maria. She was at the lake last weekend. She must have done it." She looked at him earnestly. "I didn't know she did that." Lauren was torn between feeling embarrassed and a little angry with Maria. Of course, she knew her sister meant well, and she supposed it was similar to what she had done to Avery with Mike on her moving day. But the difference was that Blake had already rejected her while Mike was very interested in a relationship with Avery. *Though, if Blake really didn't want to be with her, then why had he come tonight?* Perhaps it was just to see her work. He'd had a part in helping her get here after all. She decided to go forward on that assumption. "I guess you're here to see the paintings. You helped me learn how to paint like this after all." She looked down, averting her eyes from him. "I tried to show you ... back at the lake, but you were already gone."

Hesitantly, she glanced back up at him. He scratched his chin, and said, "Yeah, I shouldn't have left like that. I should have come to you and explained in person."

"It's okay. Your note explained it all." It still didn't feel okay, but what else could she say? There was no point in getting into a further debate about it, especially not here and now.

He spoke again in a voice that was barely above a whisper. "I was a coward, but I knew I'd never be able to do it face to face. It was too hard."

Lauren looked him in the eye, but she didn't really know how to react to what he was telling her.

"I really need to talk to you, but this isn't the time or place. Do you think we could talk after you're done here?"

"Well, it'll be late." She was so surprised by his request that she almost stammered.

"I don't mind."

"Oh ... okay. I guess that will work."

He looked back at Lauren's paintings and examined them. "You really did something spectacular here."

She felt her cheeks heat up, and a slight smile spread across her face. "Thanks. You helped."

"I encouraged, but this is all your talent. I had no idea you were this good."

Suddenly she remembered something her father used to say when she had shown him her paintings as a child. She looked back at Blake and said, "God gives good gifts. I'm only making use of the one he gave me."

"You certainly are." He held her eyes for several seconds until an interested browser walked up, hoping to talk to the artist. "I'll just go look around for a while. See ya later, Lauren."

When the showing ended at eleven that evening, Lauren was tired, but not sleepy. Her adrenaline was running too high to fall asleep any time soon. That wouldn't be an issue since Blake was waiting for her. He was the only one left who was. She'd told Avery and Maria to go on home a couple of hours ago. They'd seen all there was to see, and it appeared she was going to be busy for a while longer anyway.

As she started to pack up her paintings in the carrying case she had with her, Gloria approached her. "How did it go for you tonight?"

Lauren offered her a weary but genuine smile. "Good, I think. I sold one painting, and there were several who voiced a possible interest."

"Wonderful! That's a good start. I want to keep two of your paintings up in the gallery going forward. I want you to pick two that are depicting very different emotions. When one sells, I will let you know, and you can replace it with another. If interest picks up, we'll see about giving you more space than that."

"That would be amazing. Thank you, Gloria."

"With any luck, I'll be the one thanking you soon for making me money."

"I hope so."

Gloria walked away, and Lauren continued to pack up. She could see Blake standing outside, and she wondered what he wanted to talk about.

Gathering her things, Lauren congratulated the other artists on her way out. Everyone was tired, so the conversations were short. When she pushed through the door, Blake was waiting for her. "Can I help you with your case?" He asked.

She slid it off her shoulder and allowed him to carry it to her car. "Just let me lock these in the car, and then we can find a place to talk."

"Sure. Are you hungry? I think there's an all-night diner up the street."

Lauren hadn't thought about being hungry, but it had been a while since she'd eaten. She nodded. "A little something to eat might be a good idea."

She walked with him to the diner, and they took a seat in a booth near the back. The diner was set up fifties style, with a checkered black and white tile floor and red and white vinyl seats. Lauren ordered a burger and fries, and Blake ordered a turkey club.

"So," Lauren said as they waited for their food, "what do you want to talk about?" She did her best to sound nonchalant. It might be childish, but now that he was here in front of her, she didn't want him to know how much his sudden departure from the lake had affected her.

He looked down and fiddled with the packet of silverware in front of him. "I've missed you, Lauren." He looked back up, his eyes hopeful, but Lauren was not ready to give him the satisfaction of a reaction. She kept an impassive expression. "I told you that it was too hard to tell you I was leaving face to face ... but I thought I'd be okay once I left." He sighed. "I haven't been. I think about you all the time."

He stopped and looked at her expectantly. She wasn't ready to respond yet and remained quiet. He picked up a packet of sugar and flipped it between his fingers. "I was with my mother a couple of weeks ago, and I started talking about you. She stopped me and told me that I brought you up every time I was with her. She wanted to know why I had ended the relationship when it was obvious to her that I still cared for you."

"So you told her about my condition," Lauren spoke up without even thinking about it.

"Yes. And I told her that after what we went through with Jerry—what I saw her go through—I just couldn't continue the relationship." He looked Lauren in the eye again. "She said I was being an idiot."

"I understand your reasons, Blake, even if your mother doesn't."

Blake looked almost hurt by her statement—or maybe he was just feeling the pain of making the decision all over again. But if that was the case, then why was he here revisiting the whole thing?

"She told me that if she had it to do over again, knowing what she knows now, she absolutely would. She said that every moment she had with Jerry was precious and worth whatever price she paid. She reminded me that the time we both had with him in our lives was the best our lives ever were. Then she told me that I was letting my memory get clouded by the pain." His brow furrowed as if he was fighting back emotion. "I spent some time thinking about what she said. I imagined what it would have been like growing up with Jerry never being a part of my life or my mother's life. It wasn't a pretty picture. My mother was right. I wouldn't want to take Jerry out of our lives even knowing about the painful part."

Blake looked at Lauren earnestly. "What I'm trying to tell you is that I was wrong to end our relationship. I don't know if we're meant to be together, or if it could even work out long-term, but I care for you. I want to give it another try ... if you'll give me the chance."

Lauren just stared at him for a moment. She wasn't really sure what to think or feel. She had been hurt by his sudden departure from the lake, and the way he'd done it, but as she sat there looking into his blue eyes, she couldn't deny that she still had feelings for him as well. She tried to think about what she should say and do, and then she realized that she was making a choice that was very similar to the one Maria had made. It wasn't exactly the same. After all, Blake was not her husband. They had only been seeing each other for a short time. And while he had hurt her, he hadn't done anything like what Hank had done to Maria. Yet, when Maria had to make the choice of whether or not to give Hank a second chance, Lauren had told her that she should do it. She had told her sister that if she still loved her husband, then the risk was worth taking. Maria had a lot more on the line, especially with the kids involved. So, if she could take a leap and give Hank another chance, shouldn't Lauren take a chance on Blake?

"I understood why my condition made our relationship a problem," Lauren said. "I didn't blame you for making the choice you did, but it did hurt me. I don't want to start this up again only for you to realize that you really don't want to deal with it all. I'll get worse and I know you know how hard it will be—maybe better than I do. Are you sure you're ready for that?"

He reached across the table tentatively and clasped her hand. His hand was warm and wrapped around hers so comfortably. “I didn’t come here tonight without thinking it through. I can’t promise things will work out between us, but I can promise that if it doesn’t, it won’t be because of your Parkinson’s.”

Lauren squeezed his hand. “Fair enough,” she said, smiling. “I’m free this weekend.”

Chapter 69

June

Avery

Avery pulled her car up to the lake house and parked. She looked over at Lauren in the passenger seat. "Here we are."

"Looks like we beat Maria here."

Avery smiled at the little, rustic house before her, feeling none of the trepidation that she'd felt the year before. "Well, let's take our bags in. We can draw straws for the master bedroom when she gets here."

They got out of the car and took their bags from the trunk. When they got inside and put the bags down, Lauren said, "Let's go wait for Maria on the deck. It's a beautiful day."

"I think I remember you saying that last year when you arrived," Avery said as they went out the back door and sat down at the table. The sun shone hot overhead and a light breeze—rare this time of year—blew, cooling them just a little. Avery gestured toward the house next door. "Won't be quite the same without Blake next door."

Lauren smiled. "No, but this is our time. He understands that. Actually, he said he rented the house this week. He thought it might be nostalgic if we met someone new next door."

Avery laughed, pushing her blond hair back as the breeze blew it. "Well, last year when we met someone new next door, you ended up falling for him. So I have to wonder how nostalgic he wants it to be."

"Not that nostalgic. But he knows my heart belongs to him. Also, I'm pretty sure the renter is a woman."

"Well, that gives him a pretty good safety net," Avery said, giggling. She glanced at the ring on Lauren's left hand, sparkling in the sunlight. "Have you guys set a date for the wedding yet?"

Smiling, Lauren played with the ring. "No, but we're keeping it really small and simple. I don't think we'll need a long planning period. Blake wants to make sure it's going to work out with the house he's trying to buy for us in Maria's neighborhood. He wants me to still have the support of family close by."

"I understand, but remember, even when you move out, I'm only a phone call away."

"You remember that too."

"I will, but I think I'm going to be okay. I'll miss having you right there, but I'm doing so much better."

"Yes, you are. And, of course, Mike is just across the hall."

Avery smiled as color rose in her cheeks. She and Mike were still taking it slow, but their relationship was definitely growing into something more than just friendship. She was no longer afraid to go into his apartment, nor was she afraid to allow him into hers. "Yes, he is."

They stayed on the deck, talking intermittently, for almost an hour before the back door opened and Maria walked outside.

"There you are," Lauren said.

"Sorry, I'm a little late getting here. I know we said four 'O clock. Melanie and Mrs. Crump wanted to present their flower garden. They just planted it together last week. We were going to do it earlier, but Mrs. Crump fell asleep and wasn't answering her door when we got there. Of course, the fact that she wasn't answering made Melanie worried that something bad had happened to her, and she insisted that we call for help."

"Did she?" Lauren asked.

"She sure did. After all Mrs. Crump is getting older, and she could have fallen." Maria shrugged. "It does happen, so we had to consider the possibility. The police came and pounded on the door. She woke up and came to the door just in time to keep them from breaking it down."

"Sounds exciting," Avery said.

"I think Mrs. Crump considered it embarrassing, but at least she's alright, and the flower garden was lovely. It's something that Mrs. Crump couldn't do without help. She just can't get down on the ground like that anymore."

"It's sweet that Melanie helps her. She's a great kid," said Lauren.

Maria smiled. "She is a great kid. Jonathan helps out with some other things—taking out the trash and stuff like that. They're both great kids."

"They sure are," Lauren said. "Are they looking forward to the week alone with Hank?"

"They have lots of plans. I guess father-kid alone time has suffered a little since Hank moved back in. They still get plenty of time with him when I'm working, but it isn't the same. It's more ordinary now, so it's good to have a week like this when they can make it special."

Avery watched Maria's face, happy and unencumbered. She remembered a year ago when her sister had been chewing her nails with worry over leaving her children alone with their father, but now they were a family again. "Maybe we need to send Hank off with Mike and Blake for a week so the kids can have mom-kid alone time. I'm sure Blake could bring them all to his house next door for a week."

Lauren giggled. "That would be interesting, but I'm not sure they're ready for that yet."

Laughing, Maria said, "I'm not sure *we're* ready for that yet. What do you think the three of them would do with a week alone together?"

"I'm picturing a lot of poker, pizza, and beer. It might be better if we don't know. But if things continue as they are, it might happen someday," Lauren said.

They talked for a while longer, enjoying the blue sky and the serenity of the lake. When the sun began to lower in the sky, Avery said, “Why don’t we go on inside and draw those straws. I’m feeling lucky this year.”

After they drew the straws and unpacked their things, they would take the bikes out of the shed and ride to the restaurant down the road for dinner, just as they had done last year. This was to be their new tradition. In honor of their father and his final gift to them, the three of them—and no one else—would spend one week out of every summer together here at the lake house.

Discussion Questions

1. In the first few chapters you see, not only the argument that sends the sisters off in their separate directions, but also a glimpse into each of their lives. What differences did you notice in the way they see each other verses what is really going on?

2. When you found out that Avery's date was an escort, what did you think her reason could be for taking a paid date to a family gathering? Did your thinking change when you saw her behavior after she arrived at home?

3. Chapter 3 gives you a first look into Lauren's life. Were you able to figure out what her medical issue was? If not, what possibilities did you think of?

4. What were your thoughts about what was going on in Maria's life?

5. When their father's will was read, Maria and Avery were both reluctant about going on the required trip. How would you react if you were asked to do something like that in order to receive your inheritance?

6. Arriving at the cabin, the sisters struggle to figure out how to treat one another. They all have misconceptions about each other that are rooted in the past and, in some cases, they revert back to childish ways of relating to each other as oldest, middle, and youngest. If you have siblings, do ever find it hard to relate to them as equal adults? Do events in the past ever cloud the way you see them or the way they see you?

7. When they watch the video left for them, the sisters see their father's reason for putting so much effort into bringing them back together, and they see their mother's heartache over the lost relationship with her own sister. This is also when Maria finds out how Avery feels about the loss of their mother and her lack of any memories. Which do you think would be worse, remembering the loss of a parent or losing a parent and having no memory of them at all?

8. The truth or booze game brings out a few bits of information about who each sister really is and what they are dealing with. Avery brings up her feelings of abandonment to both of her sisters. What did you think about the expectations she had for each of them? What did you think about their reasons for not fulfilling those expectations?

9. As the oldest, Maria was able to remember the most about their mother. Before her death, Eve asked Maria to help her father look after her sisters. Do you think Eve meant for Maria to take on the role of surrogate mother or do you think Maria turned the promise into something it was never meant to be? What do you think Eve did expect from her daughter?

10. As each sister's secrets and past frustrations come to light, they begin to talk and see each other in a different way. Often, disagreements are rooted in a lack of understanding or an inability to see the other person's side. Have you ever experienced this? Do you think relationships can truly be healed when both parties are open to seeing the other's point of view?

11. When Maria tells Lauren about Hank's affair, she is uncertain what she plans to do about it still. As a loving mother, she wants to do what is best for her children and has a hard time deciding just what really would be best. How do you feel about her concern that leaving her marriage might cause her children to lose their father entirely? Based on what you saw before the lake trip, do you think they had anything left to lose?

12. When Lauren got Blake's letter telling her that he was leaving, what did you think of his choice?

13. When the sisters met with Mr. Fisher the last time, they found out that their father had been a life-changing help to some of his students during his time as a principal. At the same time, he was unable to stop the problems developing with his own daughters. Besides being unable to deal with Avery when she was a troubled youth behaving recklessly, he also watched the relationship between them deteriorate and was not able to stop that either. What

do you think about this? Is it sometimes easier to see the truth about someone else's problems than your own?

14. When the lake trip is over, Maria is planning to go home and tell Hank she wants a divorce, but before she can do that, he tells her to do that very thing and admits everything he has done wrong. Were you surprised by his turn around? Do you believe that people can truly change? Did you like this turn of events or did you want the story to go a different direction?

15. Upon arriving home, Avery is greeted with Mike's developing belief that she is using him. He has been patient for a long time and it seems that patience is wearing thin. But when Mike finally finds out the truth about why Avery behaves the way she does, he decides he can be patient once again. What do you think about this? Would you be willing to wait so long for someone to be ready to date you?

16. Once Maria officially leaves Hank, he begins a campaign to woo her again. Do you think he deserves a second chance? Do you believe a marriage can be good again after one person has betrayed the other the way Hank did?

17. After believing she would never really be able to paint again, Lauren not only finds a new way to paint, but gets her work into an art show. What do you think about her transformation in this area? Have you ever had to learn a new way to do something? If so, what was that like?

18. What did you think when Blake showed up at the art show?

19. By the end of the book, each sister had grown and changed. Who do you think grew the most? Who do you think had the biggest obstacles to overcome?

About The Author

Rebecca L. Marsh is an author of women's fiction and member of the Paulding County Writer's Guild. She grew up in the mountains of Western North Carolina, and now lives in Dallas, Georgia, with her husband and daughter.

When she isn't writing or taking care of her family (cats and dog included), she occasionally likes to make home-made candy and work on her scrapbooks (she is woefully behind).

Visit her website at rebeccalmarsh.com

Or follow her on Facebook at

Author: Rebecca L. Marsh

ACKNOWLEDGMENTS

A special thanks to those who took the time to help me in any way—all my beta readers. Thank you to Sally-Anne Wherry, a nurse who specializes in working with Parkinson's patients. She was kind enough to give me information and answer my many questions. Also to another nurse and friend, Angie Young, who is always willing to help me with the medical questions that crop up along the way. Thank you to the Paulding County Writer's Guild who are both friends and support group for me, and especially Heather Trim who did such a nice job designing the cover for this book. Most of all, I want to thank my family—all of them, but I do want to give a special shout out to my mother as she provided the inspiration for this novel. I also want to give a very special thanks to Joe and Maegan for being my support all along the way.

NOTE FROM THE AUTHOR

Thank you for reading *The Rift Between Us*. I value all my readers, and hope you have enjoyed it. Independent authors really depend on reader's support for their work. If you'd like to leave a review on Amazon or Goodreads, I would greatly appreciate it. You can also follow me on Facebook@ Author: Rebecca L. Marsh.

Thanks for your support!

Made in the USA
Middletown, DE
28 September 2021

49272271R00179